THE SURGEON

A DETECTIVE VIC GONNELLA THRILLER

BY

LOUIS ROMANO
WITH
PAUL YOUNGELSON

Vecchia Publishing

ISBN: 978-1-944906-48-1

"Brothers and sisters, I implore you to look down upon your children right now. Go ahead, look at them right now. Look at their innocent faces and know that if things continue to go forward as we are seeing, these innocent babies have no chance for salvation. NONE!!!!"

-Reverend Christian Stewart -

Also available in this series:

INTERCESSION

JUSTIFIED

YOU THINK I'M DEAD

THE BUTCHER OF PUNTA CANA

THE PIPELINE

SHANDA

CHAPTER 1

Paul Vogelbach sits toward the rear of the Unified Free Church of Truth, taking in the hundreds of congregants as they all sit in the light brown oak pews in rapt anticipation of their esteem pastor Christian Stewart's entrance. The modest two-story red brick church with a six-foot cross resting on a sphere that symbolized the earth, built by mostly middle-class congregation in 1990. Christian Stewart is beloved by his flock since he is the church's first pastor.

On this particular Sunday, not one seat remains empty. Rather than speaking with the other parishioners, Vogelbach is instead focuses on the large gold cross behind the lectern. Some of the members are chatting in their quietest church voices, catching up with friends and discussing the latest political confusion and nonsense coming out of Washington, D.C. Earlier in the week Reverend Stewart had implored that children be encouraged to attend this special service.

The children are well behaved, all sitting still, the little girls dressed in long flowery dresses with ribbons in their hair, the boys all in button-down white shirts and clip-on ties under close-cropped haircuts. They all wear highly polished shoes instead of their normal sneakers and Crocs.

The adult men wear suits in varieties of blue, gray, and black and a dotting of tans and browns. All of them wear neckties. A few chose to wear bowties. The ladies, moms, grandmoms, aunts, and sisters, are all dressed in long summer dresses barely showing their ankles. Some wear lace headcovers, while others opt for plain bonnets.

The sun is not yet high in the sky for the early service, its warm beams of light coming through the floor to ceiling windows peeking through the heavy lavender draperies. The congregation looks more like a Norman Rockwell print than a 2023 artificial intelligence poster.

Every member of the church is white.

Vogelbach, a renown general surgeon at nearby Milwaukee General Hospital, has practiced in the community for 22 years. Top of his class at Case Western Reserve in Cleveland, Ohio, he has completed his residency at MGH and decided to stay. A quiet creature of habit, Vogelbach never misses church, always eats his meals at home, and dresses in conservatively fitted suits with a sincere plaid checkered tie. As a confirmed bachelor, Paul Vogelbach is always shy around women, he even spent his prom night at the library of his small-time Ohio high school. At six feet, three inches tall, with an athletic build, he wears his 250 pounds well. Paul works out nearly every day, his strong physique attesting to his workout discipline. He wears his hair conservatively short and wears black tortoise shell glasses. Most women find him strikingly handsome, due in part to his erect stature, sharp jaw line, and piercing light blue eyes. Paul often gets flirted with by nurses and, at times, his patients. He seems immune to any seduction.

A few of the congregants recognize Dr. Vogelbach and nod politely, getting a half-smile in return, but with little eye contact from the physician.

Reverend Stewart enters the church from the rear vestibule, walking straight down the center aisle. He is 15 minutes late to the service, which is done intentionally to build anticipation. Stewart keeps his focus straight ahead, making no eye contact with the worshipers. He carries his tattered black bible.

Stewart is a thin, wispy man and at five feet, seven inches does not pose a commanding presence, at least not until he uses his practice gift of oratory. To hide his receding hairline, the reverend combed over his auburn dyed hair. He wears contact lenses rather than glasses to help him read, but he never even has glanced at his bible, quoting chapter and verse from the book by memory. He wears a black suit over a white shirt and basic black tie.

The congregation quickly goes quiet, with some rustling in their seats. An occasional cough is heard.

Stewart slowly walks to the light oak lectern, two lights shining down upon him from the recessed ceiling receptacles. A cup of water is the only thing on the lectern aside from his prop bible.

Stewart has studied the speeches of Adolf Hitler to learn how the Nazi leader had mesmerized millions. He stands with his arms folded, gazing out at the flock until there is absolute silence. Even one cough will delay Stewart's opening. The revered starts in an almost shy, nervous manner, capturing the imagination of the gathering. Many of the congregation felt anxiety for the reverend.

Finally, when there is virtually no sound from the assembly, Stewart coughs and begins his sermon.

"Last night I went to bed angry. Angry about the state of our national demise from the radical homosexual agenda that has engulfed us in the past few years. Then it dawned on me that the Lord doesn't make mistakes. Everything the Lord does is for a reason. Part of his grand plan for us. A calming peace came over me, and I slept well. Those among us who are lost must be found, and their behavior must be changed in the name of our King and Savior. We are the vessels of the Lord, who must make the changes back from the destruction of the bedrock of our society by any means necessary. Gay men and lesbian women and the new misled transgenderites have redeveloped the modern-day Sodom and Gomorrah, and the Bible clearly tells us how God's rath dealt with that debauchery so many centuries ago."

Reverend Stewart's voice begins to rise, and he uses his arms to emphasize his displeasure, raising them above his head, and crashing his hands down upon the lectern.

"Those among us, in our beloved country where our forefathers spilled their blood for our very freedom from tyranny, who support this radical homosexual agenda and will not rest until the sacred sacrament of marriage is devalued into nothingness, should be punished by evaporating into a lake of fire," he says.

"Let me be clear," the reverend continues. "Children will suffer the most from this homosexual and transexual debauchery, and our future generations will be destroyed by our enemies in Russia and China. Their Marxist teachings and their predictions of the fall of our once great county are now upon us. Children...the Lord made you in his own image. He made you a boy, or he made you a girl, and that is what you are. Anyone who tells you to think differently...and I mean anyone...these folks are doomed to hell for their transgressions against the Lord." Stewart is almost screaming in a fevered pitch now. Spit flies from his mouth, seemingly as dragon fire from the corners of his mouth. A white spittle foam forms like a rabid dog.

"What these degenerate lawmakers have approved with same-sex marriage and interracial marriage and turning our youth into thinking it is righteous to change their gender is simply diabolical," Stewart continues. "Having trans bathrooms in public places such as schools and movie theatres is clearly Satan's work and must be stopped now before our culture, the culture we so much love for our families, is gone forever."

"Brothers and sisters, let me be blunt, at the risk of stepping over a delicate line. Homosexuals aren't happy with what perverted actions they take into their own lives, into their own bedrooms. They have now pushed their unholy actions into the classrooms, teaching our children they must accept abhorrent sexual behavior. I bring your attention to Genesis 1:27 which literally states. *'So, God created mankind in His own image, in the image of God He created them; male and female he created them'*."

Stewart picks up his bible, raises it above his head, and continues.

"Furthermore, in this, our holy of holy book, it clearly states in Leviticus Chapter 18, Verse 22. '*You shall not lie with a male as with a woman; it is an abomination.*' And here is the most telling verse, the most instructional verse I know of with respect to this devilish alternative lifestyle. Again, Leviticus Chapter 20, Verse 13... '*If a man lies with a man as with a woman, both of them have committed an abomination; they shall surely be put to death; their blood is upon them*'." The Reverend smashes the bible down on the podium, a sound so loud that many in the congregation jump in their seats.

"Did you hear what it said?" Stewart hollers, "They should surely be put to death!"

The reverend takes a sip from his water cup and stood staring out at the silent and awe-struck congregation. Sweat is pouring down his face, his arms folded across his heaving chest. Stewart raises his chin looking out at the assembly. Again, he waits for absolute silence. No one dares even cough.

"Now, I am not saying that we should all run out and shoot the first limp-wristed faggot we see. Or stab the first transexual or bisexual we encounter, even though I believe in my heart of hearts our Lord will welcome you with his open arms in paradise for doing so. What I am advocating is not electing these soulless politicians who will see the devil's work be done. Not shopping in stores that promote homosexual and transgender lifestyles. Never go to a movie or a theme park that will no longer call our children boys and girls instead referring to them as believers or friends. Never buy an insurance policy from a company which promotes the mixing of races or homosexuals holding hands and kissing in their television commercials. Vote with your money. You have a choice, brothers and sisters, to boycott these politicians and corporations that are pushing this sickness upon us and our children. These homosexuals are coming for our children. They are, in effect, telling our boys and girls that sodomy is an acceptable lifestyle."

Reverend Steward slams his right hand on the lectern.

"This whole mess about pronouns, the he-she-them-it and I am now identifying as a cat, or a ferret, is spitting in the face of our creator. They have become a plague, a cancer on our mortal souls. If your school is teaching this sickness to your kids, take them out of that school tomorrow morning. Home teach them, if need be but immediately take your loved ones out of the den of inequity that we are slowly becoming."

"I am here to tell you, my brothers, and sisters, about a preacher who said Jesus Christ didn't condemn homosexuals in the New Testament, therefore he would not be against their behavior. That Jesus loved everyone equally. Another moron preacher spewed the nonsense that God loves everyone. That he hates the sin but loves the sinner. I submit that even Jesus himself would not imagine the depth of depravity that men and women are capable of. He surely would have cast these despicable people into the depths of hell where they all belong. That is not the Lord's love, which is the Lords rath."

"Brothers and sisters, I implore you to look down upon your children right now. Go ahead, look at them right now. Look at their innocent faces and know that if things continue to go forward as we are seeing, these innocent babies have no chance for salvation. *NONE!!!!* They are condemned by our not rising and stopping this insanity while we still have the chance."

Stewart steps back from the lectern, wipes his forehead with his handkerchief and bowed his head.

The assembly rises as one in a thunderous applause.

All but one. Paul Vogelbach sits in his pew, tears running down his face. His face begins twitching uncontrollably in anger, his fists tightened rock hard, and his jaw clenched so hard he could feel his teeth almost about to crack and shatter. Vogelbach's fury at Stewart's words has made his entire body as ridged as a block of granite.

Vogelbach gathers himself, raises from his seat, and applauds louder than anyone in the congregation.

CHAPTER 2

Vic Gonnella and Raquel Ruiz are on a vacation in Florence, Italy. They wanted to get away by themselves for a while. They have been to Florence before on business, but this was a much-needed romantic holiday, to take in the sights and relax. Their daughter, Gabriella, and Raquel's mom, Olga, stayed at the townhouse in New York City under the watchful eye of their driver, an ex-NYPD detective named Pando, and others from their rapidly growing security company.

Vic and Raquel had been on a major city tour promoting their best-selling book, *'Catch Us if You Can'*, which saw eighty-two weeks on the top ten New York Times Bestseller list. The book has forty thousand likes on Amazon. Television appearances, book signings at Barnes and Noble stores, countless podcast interviews and commencement speeches at John Jay College of Criminal Justice, and other schools, had exhausted the globally known power couple.

Raquel was getting on Vic's nerves, and vice versa. Talking about their chasing down serial killers every day for six weeks is enough to fray anyone's nerves. The John Deegan case is the most popular among readers and the case that vaulted the couple into international stardom.

Their last case, which has garnered tremendous attention, is of the shooter who targeted Hasidic Jews in Rockland County, New York, which had an ending that the couple still lamented.

Florence, a walking city full of history, architecture, music, and art is where Raquel wanted to spend as much time as possible. She loves history and the arts, so she decided to take the nine-hour flight despite her phobic disdain for flying. Valium helps. Vic wants a few winery tours and to sample the food from the north of the motherland, although it is very different from the Neapolitan food his mother served when he was a boy.

They have taken an executive suite at the Four Seasons Hotel, sparing no expense. After all, business is great, and the book is a smashing hit. The hotel is a Renaissance-era former convent, with a fifteenth-century palazzo advertised as a 'destination unto itself'.

"Not bad for an Italian kid and a Puerto Rican gal from the Bronx," Vic blurts. He and Raquel are sitting under a white marble statue in the della Gherandesca lobby at the hotel. The marble friezes around the perimeter of the second floor of the lobby, with green and pink hand paintings, looking more like a museum than a hotel lobby.

"I could never have imagined a place like this baby. It's more like a dream than reality," Raquel replies. She raises her red Aperol Spritz to click the glass of Vic's Macallan's 15 Scotch.

"Hey, we worked hard for this," Vic remarks. "I guess some would say this is white privilege, except Italians weren't considered white until 1940."

"And Puerto Ricans are still not considered white," Raquel laughs.

Vic loves her exotic look and sexy voice. He smiles as he looks into her big brown eyes. Raquel is wearing a tailored white linen jumpsuit that shows every luscious curve. Her Gucci shoes are white, and her outfit is finished by a string of black pearls Vic had surprised her with on the flight from JFK to Florence. Vic's beige linen pants and red and black Nat Nast shirt are being finished with a sockless pair of maroon Ferragamo loafers. They look more like European aristocracy than two former NYPD cops out of the South Bronx.

"It's only five o'clock," Vic says. "The Italians don't start eating dinner until eight, so I think a nice walk around town would build our appetites."

"Let's go. I can use a nice expresso or a cappuccino in one of those cafés along the way."

"Honey, it's espresso. I'm going to have to correct you as we go. And just for your information, no one in Italy has cappuccino after eleven in the morning." Vic smiles.

"Look buster, it's my vacation and I'm American, so if I want a cappuccino that's what I'm having," Raquel replies.

"Suit yourself, but I'll do the espresso and a nice biscotti."

"I think it's a biscotto, but who am I to correct the Italian Stallion."

Vic roars with laughter. He knows she is right.

They walk for the longest time, looking at the throngs of tourists, and window shop in the stylish stores along the way.

They find themselves on the stone pavement at the Piazza della Repubblica in the middle of town. The square is filled with artists, street vendors, and selfie takers. A violin player and a singer have drawn a small crowd of onlookers. Raquel opens her purse and takes out a five euro note, which she tosses into the violinist's case under his feet.

"Vic, I remember reading that this is the exact place where the Romans started the City of Florence. Actually, by Julius Caesar. I can't even imagine what it looked like back then. How this place came to be what it is now is an amazing tribute to man's imagination."

"There was probably horse shit everywhere," Vic jokes.

"VIC! Can't you ever see just the sheer beauty in things?"

"Sure, every time I see you in bed," Vic replies.

"Jesus!"

"Let's go to that big restaurant over there. I'm getting hungry and my paws hurt," Vic utters.

"Caffe Paszkowski? It sounds Polish and looks like a tourist trap. I was thinking about a small, intimate spot where the natives eat."

"C'mon...they have live music and it's not pretty crowded already," Vic insists.

The maître 'd greets them with the romantic sounding "Buona Sera signora e signore" and finds them a table near the music. Vic has slipped him a twenty Euro note. Raquel turns more than a few heads as the gumshoe couple walk through the white linen-covered tables. Vic is proud that Raquel was such a gorgeous woman and on his arm.

Everyone in the crowd of diners are well dressed. Mostly Europeans, Americans, and Japanese are being served cocktails before their dinners. This isn't a t-shirt and jeans place. It reeks of elegance.

"Really not what I expected, baby. This place is very nice," Raquel offers.

"Fancy, schmancy, if I say so myself. I'll order us drinks, and then I must find the men's room," Vic says.

"The restrooms are downstairs inside the café," a voice from a table behind them offers.

"Thank you," Vic replies without turning his head. Raquel glances at the table and smiles politely.

"Vic don't turn around now. The guy behind us is wearing a New York Mets shirt and a Mets hat. And he has these weird looking eyeglasses. I guess he didn't get the memo. He looks so out of place with all these well-dressed people. I feel sorry for people like that."

"It's Florence. Probably a tourist from Queens," Vic chucks.

A waitress comes to the table. She offers menus and asks if they want to start with a cocktail. She speaks Spanish after seeing Raquel.

"Sure," Raquel responds, "I'll have a chilled Prosecco, and he will have a McCallan's 15. And a large bottle of sparking water, please?"

"Oh, forgive me, I didn't realize you were American," the waitress blurts.

"Is the price higher now?" Vic jokes.

"No...no. It's just the lady looks Spanish and the way you are both dressed...is not...not typically...."

"He's only joking. But he tips well," Raquel says.

Vic find the men's room and returns to the sound of a musical trio playing an upbeat Bossa Nova. Vic bops to the table on the downbeat. He glances at the guy in the Mets regalia and almost laughs aloud before sitting down.

"Jesus, this Met fan is a riot. All the old guy needs are a Daily News and a cowbell."

"Vic, use your inside voice. I think he heard you! You can be so embarrassing at times."

"Let me ask him how Verlander is doing? It's been a while."

"Vic, you will not."

"Team sucks. They are in next to last place. I'm going back to the Yankees where I belong," the voice replies.

Vic turns a bit red and embarrassingly and slowly turns his head around. Raquel looks at the bubbles in her drink.

"Hey, I'm a New Yorker. We have big mouths. I apologize sir."

"No need. I'm a New York boy myself. My wife is always on me about my voice carrying. Yankee fan?"

"Only my whole life. I'm a Bronx boy myself," Vic offers.

"Me, too. Say you two look familiar. How do I know you? Television or something."

Raquel looks up and smiled. Then her face goes as pale as a Boricua with her olive skin tone would allow.

Vic has turned back around for a pull on his scotch.

"I know! You guys chased me half-way around the world," the man says.

Vic has a look on his face that brings the moment all together. He looks up at Raquel. "Can't be," he mutters.

"Oh, yes it can," Raquel responds.

***

"Come on over and join us, John," Vic says without turning his head. Raquel stands to embrace the Mets fan.

John Deegan laughs so loud the other diners look from across the large, covered space.

"How the hell did you find us this time? And that disguise? You look like you should be on the 6 train," Vic states.

"Elementary, my dear boy. Raquel's mom, my dear Abuela Olga, told me where you guys were going last week when I called to speak with my loving niece. Boy, your daughter sounds like she's all grown up. The rest was easy. I followed you from that fancy hotel. We decided to take the train down from Lugano. Four hours. Only 40 bucks per ticket on the fast train."

"We?" Raquel asks.

"I left Gjuliana at the hotel. She's bushed from the trip. I gotta get back. We have dinner for four at Buca Mario at eight tomorrow night. Best Florentine steak in town."

CHAPTER 3

ONE MONTH LATER

Layla Cole is Instagram famous. For the past year Layla has been posting short videos of herself honing her craft. At last count she has over 20 million Instagram followers and a fan base that is recognized by SONY Music, who signed her to a two-album record deal. Just for starters.

A jazz singer, Cole has taken songs from the 1980s and made them popular with her smooth, smokey voice and gorgeous looks. Layla is bi-racial. Her mother is white, her father is Afro-Caribbean. Her skin tone is like Alicia Keys, who is one of Layla's heroines, and the reason she studied piano and plays the instrument in her act.

At 5'8" with auburn, past-the-shoulder, curly hair, rounded, high cheekbones, a perfect gleaming white smile, and almond-shaped green eyes which she inherited from her dad, Layla is a total smoke show.

Layla also happens to be an unattached Lesbian who, for the moment, wants to play the field.

It's Thursday night and Layla Cole is appearing for the umpteenth time at 'Don't Tell Mama', in one of their famous cabaret showrooms on West 46th Street in restaurant row in Manhattan's theatre district. Sadly, for

Layla and her loyal New York City fans, this is to be Layla's last weekend at the storied night club. The singer is booked to be in the studio for a month, and then she is to take off on a promotional European and North American tour as part of her new contract. For a young singer, this is a dream come true.

'Don't Tell Mama' is where Layla had her first professional appearance and the place where she felt most at home. Tickets are sold out, the excitement building on Instagram and Facebook, and other social media platforms for months. Not even the scalpers can provide tickets unless the buyer is prepared to pay big money.

For Layla, the management of the joint has moved the piano from the piano bar to the showroom for the weekend, all to feature the singer's musical talent.

From her one-bedroom apartment in a four-story walk-up building on North Moore Street in Tribeca, Layla takes an Uber ride to the venue. She will arrive at six o'clock that afternoon for her 8 p.m. show. A second show will start at midnight, enough time for Layla to relax, have a nice, late dinner with friends and wind down with a few drinks before the 2:30 a.m. close. She likes to be early to feel the room. The red-topped bar stools, red billowing draperies over the bar, and the back lit pinkish hues of the stage curtain gave the spot a very speakeasy-like feel.

The earthy voiced singer started out her career performing old ballads — music by Cole Porter, Irving Berlin, and performances by Frank Sinatra from the 20's and 30's and 40's. Songs like 'Night and Day', 'I've Got You Under My Skin', and 'Always' were among the best in her repertoire.

Layla find that this timeless music, while great, has little appeal to a younger more woke crowd, so she started a brand-new genre. Layla took music from heavy metal bands of the eighties, who most people couldn't even hear nor understand the lyrics, and broke them down into sexy, jazz based, sophisticated ballads. Bands like Motörhead, with delicious lyrics like 'Everyone dies to break somebody's heart', and the band Pantera, whose song 'This Love', with the lyrics 'If ever words were spoken, painful, and untrue I said I love you, but I lied', was transformed into mesmerizing melodies. Layla hit paydirt with her revolutionary idea.

At 7:30, the enthusiastic audience is being seated by the staff as the excitement begins to build. Lots of gay and lesbian couples, all tatted up in artistic renderings of their imagination, some heavy metal fans, still with the seedy long hair and tattoo sleeves with skulls and bloody scenes which were their forever calling cards, are the Layla fans on hand. A dotting of music executives makes up the intimate venue. One lone patron, at the packed bar wearing a waist-length black leather jacket with a hoody under it, long jet-black hair and wraparound sunglasses doesn't seem out of place.

Layla takes the stage to thunderous applause from the expectant audience. She is beaming from ear to ear and settled down at the black Baldwin piano after she treats the crowd to a dignified bow. She wears a form-fitting beige blouse which complimented her olive brown skin tone. A black miniskirt with dark black nylons and thigh-high patent leather boots finishes her sexy look. Her curly hair flows in cascades past her exposed shoulders.

Around her neck, the singer wears a copper-colored gris-gris, an Afro-Caribbean amulet given to her by her father. The gris-gris is believed to ward off evil while bringing good luck to the wearer.

Layla is in perfect voice. Her misty, jazzy renditions of the once only heavy metal tunes captivated the audience with her brilliant adaptations.

When she finishes her last song, the audience rises as one with prolonged waves of applause, whistles, and cheers. Her performance is nothing less than magical.

Practically in tears, Layla takes a long bow, fingered her gris-gris, and disappeared behind the pinkish curtains.

***

The houselights quickly come on as the crowd calls out for an encore. An announcement for the crowd to use the main exit of the showroom signals that there will not be another tune. The waitresses collects the cash and credit cards as the audience slowly fil out, murmuring about what they have just seen. The bartenders closed the bar patrons' tabs, and the staff begin cleaning the tables for the midnight show. The next crowd will be seated at 11:30.

Layla sits in the small dressing room; her eyes closed as she enjoys capturing the moment in her mind. She needs to gather herself and wind down after the ninety-minute performance.

Two of her friends arrive at the dressing room. A light tapping on the dressing room door takes Layla from her alone moment.

Rather than a full meal at the renowned 'Don't Tell Mama' restaurant, Layla instead chooses a small salad with grilled chicken, which she only picked at. She drinks nearly an entire large bottle of San Pellegrino water. Her friends, both ladies, know how to keep the conversation light after congratulating her on an amazing show.

The second performance is every bit as good as the first. It ends at 1:30 in the morning to even more thunderous applause. Layla does a meet-and-greet for a few of the late-night fans who hang around for selfies and autographs. Her two friends remain at Layla's side as they celebrate her last show at the nightclub with chilled bottles of Crystal champagne sent by the owners of the venue.

Feeling excited about the evening, the champagne doing its part, the three ladies decide to go to Chinatown for a little Dim Sum and a few more drinks.

The enchanted night over, Layla arrives alone at her apartment a few minutes before 4 a.m.

***

Layla fumbles with her apartment keys on the steps of her walkup apartment building. She is tired and a bit drunk from the after-show drinks and full of the Chinese food. As she approaches the front door to the building and inserted her key, the door moves open on its own. “Assholes,” she mutters to herself, thinking that one of the other tenants has left the door ajar. In the dark, she cannot see the scratch marks around the lock of the solid wooden door. Layla slowly walks up the darkened stairs to her third-story apartment. She is humming one of the songs she sang tonight, smiling about the loving response from her fans. Layla knows her career is now on its way to great things. Her confidence is higher than the moon.

At her apartment Layla can barely see the number 302 on the door. The place seems darker than normal, so she looks around and noticed that the hallway light is out. She finds the lock with her key and opens it.

Suddenly, Layla feels a tremendous force pushing her into the apartment. She falls to the floor in disbelief trying to turn to see what is happening, but all the young singer can see is a dark figure above her. She feels a sharp pain in her neck and tried to grab at the pain. She feels her body slump.

Layla’s eyes flutter as she regains semi-consciousness. She tries hard to focus her vison in the darkened apartment. She realizes after a moment, through her confusion, that she is in her bed and tries to move to no avail. An attempt to call out was to no avail. She is going in and out of consciousness. Layla can hear rustling around in her kitchen as mild panic begins to set in. It sounds like metal clinking against metal, and the water is running.

Layla focuses on her fingers, trying to move them one at a time with all her will. Nothing. She doesn't even have the ability to swallow, never mind screaming. Her eyes try to look down onto her body, and she can't see much except for the tops of her exposed breasts. She wonders if she has been raped.

Suddenly, the sound of the water running in the kitchen stops, and she begins to have a feeling of impending doom. A moment later, she senses the presence of someone in the room with her.

The bedroom light is flicked on, her eyes needing a few seconds to adjust. Above her stands a man with a surgical mask and square, tortoise shell glasses. The panic is now at its peak but her breathing never changes.

A monotone voice startles the young woman, but there is no ability for fight or flight.

"Hello, Layla. My name is Paul. You are an exceptionally talented woman. I was at your first show tonight. I would have stayed for the second show, but I had to come here and set things up. You have a real cute place here. Beautifully decorated. Very cozy."

Layla try to flash her eyes from side to side, but that doesn't happen.

"You know...it's a shame that someone as beautiful and artistic as you, with all your musical brilliance, has chosen to be part of the alphabet mafia. You are part and parcel of the homosexual and transsexual world, who keeps forcing your depraved lifestyle down the throats of those of us who believe your life is a sin against the Lord. You need to pay for your transgressions. It says so in the Bible, Layla. I am simply a servant of the Lord. Little by little, we must take back our normal society from the debauchery of people like you and prevent you all from destroying the family unit and poisoning the children."

Layla still cannot move a muscle. She understands what he is saying, but it is all surreal. She isn't a religious person, so she cannot mentally say any prayers to bring her solace. Her mother is an atheist and her father dabbles in the black arts, but only for his cultural connection.

"Layla, know that you brought this fate upon yourself. You will now go to a forgiving God. I hope he has mercy on your soul. I am going to put you down now. I'm a doctor, so you will not feel any pain. I will pray for your soul."

CHAPTER 4

NYPD Homicide Detective James McLaughlin arrives at his 5th Precinct desk in lower Manhattan promptly at 8 a.m. to do his 8 to 4 shift. The office is timeworn and musty, with old-fashioned beveled glass surrounding the tops of the cubicles.

Most days McLaughlin does fifteen hours or better, depending on his caseload. He is juggling only eight murders at the moment. One is about to be sent to the cold case file. It is approaching the three-year anniversary of a Yellow Cab driver, killed for twenty-eight dollars. No clues have led to the killer. The second, most recent homicide is only six days old. A known drug dealer in Tribeca was shot execution-style in broad daylight. The ever-present cameras couldn't give the slightest hint to identify the killer. The shooter is likely in the Dominican Republic spending the $5,000 he received to do the hit on lots of coke and chicas. The third homicide on McLaughlin's hot list looks like a lock. An office manager of a Fortune 500 company is stabbed to death in her office. The list of suspects is long, but McLaughlin and his partner, Detective First Grade John Miliotis, have a good hunch about who the stabber is. This one is five days old.

"Hey, Jimmy Cartoons, what do you want for lunch today?" Miliotis asks. McLaughlin loves to watch *Family Guy*, *Bob's Burgers*, and any cartoons that Disney has put out in the 50s and 60s. He doesn't just watch them. Jimmy Cartoons is obsessed. Even in the precinct, a small television in the muster room has cartoons playing non-stop while he is in the office.

McLaughlin looks down at his bagel and coffee. He used to start his day off with a shot of bourbon and a beer, but that is twenty years ago, before he entered Alcoholics Anonymous. He credits A. A. for saving his career as well as his life.

"You fat Greek bastard. This is why I'm a skinny fuck and you look like a before advertisement for Jenny Craig."

"Not Greek. For the thousandth time, you dumb mick, I'm born in Crete."

"Greek, Crete...you are still obsessed with eating. I know... let's have salads today," Jimmy blurts.

The give-and-take, good-natured banter continues for much of the morning.

Miliotis brought back two fully packed souvlaki gyros from a local Greek place for his lunch. Jimmy orders two slices of Sicilian Pizza delivered by 'Door Dash' and a diet Pepsi.

At 2 p.m., things change.

"Guys... in my office." Captain Frank Bortugno orders.

"Get over to 17 North Moore. A DOA. Our uniforms are there now. They say its messy."

"On it boss," Miliotis says.

The two detectives jump in their unmarked four-door Dodge Charger sedan and are at North Moore Street in minutes. They pull up and block the fire hydrant in front of the building. There are two double-parked 5th Precinct blue and white squad cars in front with their overhead lights flashing. A group of residents of the building and other bystanders stand in quiet disbelief as the detectives, their badges out in chains over their suit jackets, walk past them looking at the faces in the crowd. It is the kind of high-rent neighborhood that doesn't see much police activity.

McLaughlin points to the scrapes on the front door lock to get his partner's attention. They walk up the dark stairwell to the third floor and step around the yellow police tape at apartment 302 which is set up by the uniformed cops.

Patrolman Ben Rivera, with his long black notebook in hand, greets Miliotis and Jimmy Cartoons. At 6' 1", Rivera looks more like a model than a police officer, his muscular body filling out his blue uniform perfectly.

"What do we have, Ben?" Jimmy asks.

"It looks like the DOA, probably happened early this morning. Forensics is on the way. It's really weird. She's on the bed," Rivera points to the bedroom. "A friend of the deceased came calling an hour ago and found her like this. We have her in the apartment next door with a neighbor. She's a mess."

Miliotis and Jimmy don't say much as they take in the scene. It is as if they were taking everything in as they slipped blue surgical gloves on. They knew better than to touch anything until the other departments arrive.

"Look like she is dissected. Whoever did this knows what they were doing. I don't know what the captain meant, but I've seen a lot messier," Jimmy pronounces. There is a small amount of blood which seeped down both sides of the body and soak the light-brown bed spread. "I don't see any splatter. Nothing on the ceiling or walls," Jimmy utters. He looks around the floor looking for any blood stains or footprints on the area rugs and the polyurethane over the oak wood floor.

"What is that on her chest?" Miliotis asks.

"Looks like something from her insides. I can't tell what it is. I could tell you all the internal parts of a frog from high school biology but not so much on a human. The doc will know."

"I'll go interview the friend, after I rummage around to see who this poor kid is," Jimmy says.

Just then, both the forensic team and the coroner show up in front of the bedroom door. Forensics immediately begins their investigation. Prints, photographs, blood samples, and hair samples are taken from the body, which are pulled with military precision. Few words are shared. No one on the team is barking out orders. It is a somber and respectful procedure.

The coroner takes the temperature of the body. "Rigor has already set it. Not official but I'm putting the time at early this morning. Between 4 and 6 is my thought," she says. Susan Shepard has been with the coroner's office for nine years. She wears a white lab coat over a long-sleeved gray jacket and a below-the-knee black dress with opaque stockings. Her full brown wig and the way she dresses indicates she is of the Orthodox Jewish faith. In a few hours, Shepard will be home lighting Shabbat candles.

"Station house got the call at 1:30. We pulled up at 1:37. The DOA's friend was in the hallway, hysterical," Patrolman Rivera adds. The coroner notes his remarks in her book.

"Doc, what are those things on her chest?" Miliotis asks sheepishly "They're the size of almonds."

The coroner pauses for a few moments.

"Those are her ovaries, detective."

CHAPTER 5

Jimmy Cartoons knocks lightly at the apartment door next to the Layla Cole homicide scene, apartment 330. A stooped-over, elderly woman answers the door. A full white head of hair, and old-fashioned eyeglasses with a loop chain off each ear magnifies her red, tear-soaked eyes. She carries crystal rosary beads in her right hand and a crucifix around her neck. The yellow and green print house coat she wears reminds Jimmy of his beloved late Irish Catholic mother.

"Come in please, will ya," the elderly later speaks with a slight brogue.

"Thank you, ma'am. I'm detective James McLaughlin. Homicide, 5th Precinct."

"Right this way, please. The young lady is having tea in the kitchen trying to compose herself. She found the body, don't ya know?"

"That's fine, but I'd like to ask you a few questions first if you don't mind. May I know your name, please?"

"Certainly, young man. Katherine Walsh. I knew of the McLaughlin's in Inwood. Any relation to ya?"

"I'm from the Bronx. I have cousins in Upper Manhattan. Ya never know. Mrs. Walsh, did you hear anything early this morning? Say, after three? Any noises out of the ordinary? Any yelling or screams?"

"None. She was such a sweet girl. Never a problem. She was a singer, don't ya know? Always singing. Lovely music and never loud. I'd water her plants when she was away. Take her mail in for her. Poor thing. May God keep her soul."

"So, I suppose you have the key to her apartment?"

"Indeed, I do. It's hanging' on the kitchen wall."

"Do you know if Ms. Cole had any next of kin?"

"She spoke of her parents. But I never met them. Divorced." Mrs. Walsh whispers divorce like it was still a sin.

"Did she have many visitors?" Jimmy asks.

"A few lady friends are all. Never any male callers in the five years she was here."

"How long have you lived here, Mrs. Walsh?"

"Nearly fifty-five years. I raised my two children here. My husband went to heaven eleven years ago this Christmas. My apartment is rent controlled. I suspect the damn landlord is wishing it were me who was killed."

A sob comes out of the kitchen.

"Jesus, Mary, and Joseph, that poor girl. How could anyone want to take such a beautiful life?" Mrs. Walsh utters, fighting back tears. She kisses the crucifix on her rosary.

"Let's go into the kitchen, shall we?" Jimmy asks.

Sitting at the chrome kitchen table with four red metal chairs sits a young woman with her head in her hands, her body heaving in quiet sobs. Jimmy notices a tattoo sleeve on both arms. The girl's two-tone blue and brown hair was short, like a man's haircut. The white- and green-specked linoleum flooring is a throwback to Jimmy's grandmother's era. *'It's strange what things are noticed while preparing to interview a potential witness'*, Jimmy thinks to himself.

"Stephanie, my dear, this is Detective McLaughlin," Mrs. Walsh announces.

"I know it's not a good time but it's important that we talk now, Stephanie." Jimmy states in a soothing voice.

"Who would do such a heinous thing?" Stephanie utters. She raises her head to look at the detective.

"That's my job to find out. What brought you here this afternoon, Stephanie.... ahh......?"

"Stephanie Russo. I was coming to get Layla. We were going to..." The young woman breaks down in a torrent of tears.

Jimmy waits a bit until the young woman is able to compose herself. "Where were you planning on going?"

"Just walking around Soho. Layla needed a few new outfits and some shoes. It was to be a shopping spree to celebrate her record contract. I always helped her pick out her clothes. Then we were planning to meet friends in 'DUMBO' for dinner."

"When did you see her last?"

"This morning. I don't know. It was late. Layla appeared at a club, and after we went to Chinatown for a celebration and some food."

"Were you two alone?"

"No. Our friend Lorna was with us."

"Okay. I'll need Lorna's information from you, please. What time did you leave Layla?" Jimmy adds.

"Like 3:00, 3:30 this morning, I guess, maybe a bit later. We were all pretty drunk."

"How did Layla get home?"

"We took a cab. Lorna and I dropped her off and went home," Stephanie notes.

"Where did Lorna go?"

"Home with me. We're a couple."

"Okay. I see. Did you see Layla enter her apartment building?"

"No. Not really."

"Did she have any enemies that you know of? Former or current lovers? Any men in her life?"

"No men. Layla was gay. I don't know anyone that didn't adore her. She was so sweet...so talented."

"Do you happen to know her family?

"Not really. She spoke to her parents a lot, but I never met them."

"We have her cell phone. That will help us contact them," Jimmy says.

Jimmy and Miliotis spent the next three hours at the scene gathering Layla's personal effects and trying to reenact the homicide. Forensics has noticed that the kitchen sink has some moisture in it and a few droplets of liquid on the countertop. They took samples and photographs of the area. After a while, the coroner's staff bags and removes Layla's body. Mrs. Walsh stands in the hallway with Stephanie, both crying and holding on to each other.

Back at the precinct, the two detectives know they

have a lot of work ahead of them. Jimmy changes the television in the muster room from Fox News to MeTV for some cartoons. There are none, so he find a cable channel which has *The Simpsons*. Funny thing is, Jimmy generally doesn't watch the cartoons, but he find the sound to be comforting for some reason. Once in a while he would hear the cartoon and laugh aloud.

"She appeared at 'Don't Tell Mama' last night and early this morning. I'll go there and look at their videos. I'll see if there are any other cameras on that street that we can pull potential perps from," Miliotis volunteers.

"I'll track down the cab. Hope it wasn't a gypsy." Jimmy adds. "I'll look around North Moore Street for any video."

"Do we know where they were in Chinatown?" Miliots asks.

"I'll try to get it from her friend Stephanie. That time in the morning is dead, so if luck is with us we'll see if anyone followed them on street cams. I'll check on their credit cards too. I bet that the perp was inside the apartment waiting for her. Just a hunch, but the fresh scraping on the front door lock is telling."

"Let's go through her phone. Next of kin needs to be notified." Miliots states.

"I hate those calls, partner. Almost as much as I hate my ex-wife."

They track down Layla's parents, both of whom live out of town, to give them the unthinkable news. The grief-stricken pair are both making plans to come to New York City within the next day or two. The coroner usually takes a few days to release the body of homicide victims. This means that they have some time before the wake and burial arrangements can be made. Jimmy speaks with the father and Miliotis with the mother. Jimmy feels like going to the nearest bar and having his twenty sober years destroyed in a waiting boilermaker. Miliotis goes out and brings back six hot dogs...all the way. Jimmy's thoughts still go to the booze. Miliotis' to food.

The partners work the case until after midnight on every detail of Layla's life and specifically, her last three days. They have a 9 a.m. autopsy meeting at The Office of the Chief Medical Examiner on East 25th Street.

CHAPTER 6

"I found dinner last night to be very strange. The whole thing has me fucked up," Vic utters.

He and Raquel are holding hands while taking a stroll on their way to see Michelangelo's David at the Galleria dell' Accademia. The police inspector of Florence got the famous couple a pass to avoid the massive line to see the great marble masterpiece. Raquel wears a full-length beige knit dress with dark brown espadrilles and big Italian-made sunglasses with a white Panama hat. Vic has on a light blue linen jacket and fitted jeans finished by dark blue Ferragamo loafers without socks. He also wears sunglasses and a Lazio soccer cap so he cannot be recognized. They both enjoyed being well known while out in public, but sometimes it is a pain in the ass. Especially with Americans who want a selfie with the famous couple.

"What do you mean?" Raquel asks.

"The dinner was great, don't get me wrong. I've never tasted a steak like that in my life. And the conversation at the table was interesting about their lives in Switzerland and ours in New York. It was the stroll afterward that got me twisted. The Italian men don't think twice about walking arm-in-arm with another man. It's a sign of affection, I get it. But you and Gjuliana were walking ahead of us, and here I was with one of the greatest serial killers in history. Yeah, he helped us with his brilliant mind on five cases, but he is still the number one fugitive on the planet all these years later. And here is Vic Gonnella, detective extraordinaire, walking along with my arm entangled with his."

"I guess I can see your point, baby, but we have a pretty good relationship with him now," Raquel notes.

"I know. That's my point. It's just surreal."

"What were you two talking about?"

"He's starting to think about his mortality. A lot. He's cancer free, and that's a good thing, but he's in the 'last inning' as he put it. And he's bored to shit."

"Bored? Why?" Raquel queries.

"John Deegan needs action. He loves to figure out complex puzzles. Looking out at Lago Lugano just ain't cutting it for him. He can't write a book like we did. He can't go on the lecture circuit. If he shows a hair on his ass, they will throw him in a cell like that cannibal Hannibal Lecter. Until the day he dies."

"He needs a purpose," Raquel announces.

"And his options are very limited. He's not looking for acclaim. It's figuring out of things even before they happen and drawing the conclusions as he did with our cases. And no one in the world is even remotely aware of what he's done for us. Nor could they be."

"It's kind of sad." Raquel laments.

Vic sighs. "And here we are feeling badly for a serial murderer. He seems to garner that kind of sympathy."

CHAPTER 7

Jimmy and Miliotis meet at the 5th Precinct at 8 a.m. sharp. They went straight into Captain Bortugno's office to fill him in on the Layla Cole case. Bortugno is one of those men who nobody can read by looking around his office. Nothing hang on the drab, green-painted walls, no family photos, no plaques or trophies on the bare credenza, nothing that said, 'I have a life outside these four walls'. He is the hardest personality to figure out. If there are arrest charts and case names that his men are involved with, then you can assume that he is an analytical type who just wants the facts and nothing more. If there were some pictures of his kids or photos of him at golf outings or sports teams you could make conversation about how the kids were doing or his handicap, or just complain about the Giants, Mets, Yankees, or Knicks. There is no drawing Bortugno into any conversation. Just give him your verbal report, back it up with paper, and get the hell out of here.

"Whatdoyougot?" The captain asks while looking at his Dell desktop computer.

Jimmy looks sideways at Miliotis for a second and shrugs. Miliotis points at his partner as if he wants to say, 'The floor is yours, Cartoons'.

"The deceased is a singer. Just got a big record contract. Twenty-three-year-old lesbian with no record, nothing pointing to anything that would make her an obvious victim. It looks to us that the perp broke into her house. Robbery is not indicated, except for a missing voodoo type amulet she was wearing that night. Her friend said she was wearing it."

Bortugno interrupts. "Did she practice voodoo?"

"No, captain. Nothing like that. Her father gave her the talisman to remember her Afro-Caribbean heritage. It's like when Italians wear that gold horn around their necks for good luck," Jimmy says. Bortugno looks up from his computer and glares at him.

"No disrespect, captain. Just a simple analogy," Jimmy feels his face flush.

"We don't know the cause of death just yet. We are on our way to 26th Street at nine."

Miliotis speaks up. "It looks as though the perp had some medical background. She was, for lack of a better term, dissected from her throat to her pubic area. Her ovaries were removed and laid on her chest."

"Sounds psychosexual to me, detectives," Bortugno interjects.

"Yeah, could be. We are tracking down old girlfriends. Maybe she had a jilted male in her life. We have no way of knowing at this point if the killer was male or female, or ahh...transgender," Jimmy adds.

"Any video?"

Miliotis clears his throat before saying, "We have video of her on stage the night she was killed. Our people are scanning to view the crowd, inside and outside the venue.

We have her in Chinatown, her destination before she went home. Nothing out of the ordinary, but they are still analyzing that piece. She took a yellow home with her friends. Driver checks out."

"Come back to me after the autopsy," Bortugno mumbles. He starts typing something onto his desktop.

Awkwardly, the two detectives look at each other, rise, and leave the captain's office.

On their way down to the Medical Examiner's office, Miliotis cannot hold back.

"The cap is one strange motherfucker. He gives nothing. He reminds me of my ex-mother-in-law. He doesn't look at you, he looks through you."

"He was pissed at that Italian horn comment I made. And even at that he didn't show much emotion. Weird guy," Jimmy adds.

"I hope he gets promoted to 1 PP with the rest of the zombies." Miliotis blesses himself in the Greek Orthodox fashion.

***

Dr. Jennifer Bridwell starts the autopsy promptly at 9 a.m. She works from Dr. Shepard's notes, and today is the Sabbath. Sixteen other autopsies performed by twelve pathologists are scheduled today at the Manhattan ME's office. Seven victims are murdered, and the others are either suspicious deaths or otherwise warranted suspicion. Blood and tissue samples are already taken and are in the examination process.

Dr. Bridwell speaks into an overhead microphone as she proceeds with the three hour and sixteen-minute process. An assistant stands by, making notes and ready to put in any wounds or other descriptive markings on a body diagram. The two detectives stand by in rapt attention, ready to take their own notes as well. They both have witnessed hundreds of autopsies in their years at homicide, and it has become almost routine. Only the first ten or so kept them up at night.

Layla is as beautiful in death as she was in life. Her head is slightly elevated by the plastic block it laid upon, making it look as if she is watching the V-shaped incision the coroner has opened.

After forty minutes, Dr. Bridwell makes her first comment other than the clinical details such as general body condition and organ weights.

"Whomever did this has an excellent knowledge of human anatomy. My guess is that it's someone with OR skills. A surgeon, an OR nurse, someone like that. The victim should have bled out, which obviously didn't occur. Surgical clamps were used on the correct arteries. Generally speaking, in a sex-driven homicide, an incision on the abdomen is much deeper, and the ends of the cut are never straight like this. There is no real anger in this incision. It was almost as if it was a planned, well-thought-out operation if you will allow me to use that word."

"Very interesting," Dr. Bridwell continues. "The ovaries are removed with perfection. The wounds are even cauterized. It's as if the perp was planning on keeping the victim alive after the procedure. Well, at least for a while.

Very neat, very clean. Whomever did this had to keep the victim breathing."

The autopsy continues with more tissue samples being taken and sent to the ME's pathology lab. A soft, grumbling noise is loud enough for those standing around the waist high, slanted autopsy table. Jimmy thinks the sounds are gasses that Layla's body is expelling. Dr. Bridwell looks around the table and mutters, "I guess someone has missed their feeding time."

Jimmy looks at Miliotis, who is red with embarrassment. To keep the dignity of the autopsy in tack, Jimmy walks away from the procedure.

Near the end of the autopsy, Dr. Bridwell exhales in frustration. "No blunt force trauma, no asphyxiation. The heart is strong, and it shows signs of oxygen deprivation but certainly no sudden infarction. There are no wounds that would indicate obvious cause of death. My initial conclusion, and this is in no way official, detective, is that this homicide was chemically induced. I see some gross hardening of an otherwise healthy liver. There is a small hematoma on the back of the victim's neck. Nearly covered by the hairline. That could be where a chemical was introduced to the body. I cannot release this body to a funeral home until the pathology tests are completed and I can make a conclusive judgment."

On their way back to the 5th Precinct, Jimmy finally lets his laugh out. "You fat bastard. I thought her body was farting or something. When Doc said what she said I almost lost it right on the spot."

“What do you want from me? I missed my breakfast because of that mutt Bortugno.” The partners laugh together.

“I’d rather spend the entire day at the ME than ten minutes with our Count Dracula captain,” Jimmy announces.

“Perfect nickname, pally. Fucking Count Dracula. This one will stick for sure.”

***

Two days later, Jimmy gets a call from Dr. Shepard. The cause of death on Layla Cole is determined, and a report is sent to both detectives, Captain Bortugno, and a bunch of others at 1 PP. Some call the 1 Police Plaza headquarters of NYPD the Puzzle Palace, depending on who is in the room.

“My office,” Bortugno orders after he stuck his head into the homicide unit.

“Come to me,” Miliotis says, mimicking the Bela Lugosi paralyzing hand. Jimmy starts to walk to Bortugno’s office with a feigned hump like Igor.

“Whatdoyougot?” Bortugno asks.

“Cause of death was induced myocardial infarction.” Jimmy responds.

“I can read, detective.”

“Looks like someone in the medical profession had it in for the victim. So far, nothing we have is tying anyone like that to her. It could be someone with good human anatomy skills. This is not your average stab and slash

homicide," Miliotis replies. He could sense Jimmy's level of pissed off.
"Yes, and it could be just a sick bastard who enjoys killing," Bortugno retorts.
"Doubt it," Jimmy blurts.
"Doubt what, detective?"
Jimmy answers with attitude. "Your average sick bastard theory. Man or woman, whoever cut up and killed Layla Cole knew what they were doing and had an agenda. Why the ovaries? Why not the pancreas or the gallbladder? This fucker is making a statement. Removing a lesbian's ovaries because she doesn't need them. That's the key to this case, captain. With all due respect."
"Bring me something that isn't a theory. Dismissed," Bortugno seethes.

CHAPTER 8

ONE MONTH LATER

After his New York City debut, Paul Vogelbach went back to Milwaukee. He works at the hospital and at his private general surgery practice for four weeks. He goes to three Sunday services at the Unified Free Church of Truth, listening with great zeal to Reverend Christian Stewart's anti-gay, anti-transgender, anti-woke diatribe.

In one of his weekly sermons, Reverend Stewart calls upon the Bible to bring home his point, and this time he adds other sinners to his list of condemned souls. At a fever pitch, almost to the point of blacking out, the reverend screams the words "In 1 Corinthians 6:9-10, it is written; '*Do not be deceived: neither the sexually immoral, nor idolaters, nor adulterers, nor men who practice homosexuality, nor thieves, nor the greedy, nor drunkards, nor revilers, nor swindlers will inherit the kingdom of God'*."

Dr. Vogelbach takes these words to be the impetus to continue his work for the Lord. Even thinks, in truth, if his Lord was indeed Jesus, Jesus never did condemn any man or woman for acts which were homosexual in nature.

Jesus, even though he is considered God in the Christian faith, never fathomed the idea of transsexuality.

Vogelbach has prebooked a round-trip flight when he returned from New York to Los Angeles. He is to leave on the red eye that evening with a stopover in Houston.

Vogelbach's target this time is Gary Pose, a gay man who is in a long-term monogamous relationship with his husband Charlie Workman, a Hollywood feature film producer. Pose, a flagrant homosexual, is touted in People Magazine and on several social media platforms as 'the hairdresser to the stars. Every talk show clamors for an interview, largely because of his amusing and humorous stories. Pose's life story is part of a feature with photographs of a variety of mostly A-List actresses and actors.

Gary Pose's real name is Harold Bloom, an admitted mama's boy from Brooklyn, New York. He often brags in interviews about spending hours a day on the telephone and on Skype with his aging, long widowed mother Becky, who lives in, where else but, Boca Raton, Florida.

"If I don't speak with my dear mother every day, she won't get out of bed, and she will not eat. Never mind show up to play mah-jongg with her gaggle of widows," Gary joked. "And Mom really loves my husband. Especially because he sends her his financial statement every year end."

Gary Pose's studio, POSE, is on Wilshire Boulevard in Beverly Hills and is strictly by appointment only. The name is etched within the gray marble facing at the top of his single-story stand-alone building. A burly man in a black suit and black tie with Secret Service-like ear buds stands at the entrance to POSE to chase away any overzealous Paparazzi from taking unwanted photographs of Gary's clients. On film sets, Gary insists on his own trailer to do touchups and blowouts; otherwise, he won't work. He can work anywhere in the world where his devotees work, so long as his fees and expenses are paid in advance. First-class accommodation of course. A-Listers have Gary's trailer built into their contracts. His list of non-artist clientele reads like a Who's Who or the heavyweights of the Forbes Fortune 500. Gary Pose is the bomb in hairdressing, and he also has his own line of hair products and cosmetics that catapulted him into being one of the wealthiest gay men in America.

Among Gary's many neuroses — of which there seems to be no end, riding as a passenger in a car, or sailing on any boat, from a rowboat to a 4,000-person passenger ship — is that the hairdresser to the stars will get motion sick and remain ill for days. Air travel is fine so long as his noise-reducing headphones are always on his head. Elevators, escalators, heights, dogs, cats, subways, (somehow trains are okay), and crowds are all taboo, and it seems like he is inventing more phobias as he ages. Big stores and concerts just recently popped up on his list of no-no's.

Gary Pose drives a yellow Lamborghini Huracan with a powerful V10 engine. He will never go over fifty miles per hour, what seems like a waste of horsepower to everyone who knows him. Of late, Gary will only wear shoes or sneakers without laces. He finds them too constricting, as he does with neckties. He wears Ferragamo loafers, which he has in every color, and Jordans, without their laces.

Charlie Workman thinks all these foibles his partner has are cute. He said so in the People article.

Paul Vogelbach studies Gary Pose. From magazine and television interviews, Facebook, Instagram, Tik Tok, and all the rest, it is easy to become familiar with his next target. For four straight days, Vogelbach trails Gary Pose from his home to the salon, to lunch, dinner, and back home. During the week, Gary has a boring life. No parties, and his housekeeper is not a live-in. There is a gardener, but she only works in the mornings. The neighbors are far enough away from Gary and Charlie's home, and there are plenty of trees and hedges for privacy around the six-bedroom English Tudor once owned by Rudolf Valentino, or so they said. "This place has seen its share of fucking and sucking. Just a little different now." Gary jokes in his lispy cadence.

The Thursday evening of Vogelbach's visit to Los Angeles, Gary and Charlie are in bed by 10:30. Vogelbach is prepared to jimmy one of the rear doors, but the couple makes it easy for him by leaving the door that opens out onto the pool area unlocked. Slipping the lock pick set back into his black medical carry bag, Vogelbach gives it one last check to make sure the tools of his craft are all there. Dressed in a bulky cloth, mid-waste jacket and a hoodie this time, his wig is blond with hair down well past his neck. Vogelbach wears dark aviator glasses and a surgical mask.

The stealth killer spends some time preparing the items he will need on the large kitchen center island's beige and blue granite counter. He checks his watch. It is 12 a.m. As if on cue, a cough comes from upstairs.

Vogelbach moves away from the night-lit counter and waits in the dark. He can hear steps coming slowly down the highly polished oak staircase. Charlie Workman, stifling another cough opens the refrigerator door, not seeing the items left on the countertop. The light from the fridge illuminates the kitchen. The killer steps from his hiding position and drapes a wire garrote around Charlie's throat. They are butt to butt and Vogelbach pulls his unwitting victim over his shoulder, a foot above the Terrazzo marble floor. Charlie makes a grunt, his feet kicking into the inside of the refrigerator until Vogelbach takes two steps forward. Vogelbach is much taller than his victim, and the routine workouts makes him enormously strong. Blood runs down the front of Charlie's naked body onto his shaved pubic area. In a couple of minutes, the killer feels his victim go limp. The body is slowly brought down onto the floor. Charlie's eyes, wide open after death, are red with blood and bulging from his skull.

Vogelbach uses a surgical towel from his black bag, wiping his head and face of any perspiration. Taking the bag up the stairway, the killer walks slowly to the second floor, where he finds the main bedroom where the sleeping Gary Pose is tucked neatly under a red satin sheet. Taking a syringe and a chemical vile from the bag, Vogelbach administers the drug into Gary's neck. The unsuspecting Gary makes a slight move with his hand to his black night eye cover but the hand never makes it. His body twitches, and Gary goes into deep nothingness.

Vogelbach checks his watch. It was 12:56. Gary is now naked on top of the sheets, his eyes rapidly blinking as he comes to near consciousness.

"The great Gary Pose, hairdresser to the stars," Vogelbach whispers. "So nice to finally meet you."

Gary is frozen. His body will not and can not respond, but he hears the voice clearly.

"This whole gay lifestyle must end so that our Lord and Savior will re-enter a world without the disgusting filth that is being pushed upon American society. I saw a television commercial the other day with two adult men, in bed, without their tops, looking down at their playing children who were of mixed race. I almost vomited, Gary. This is not what our children need to see, and they see signs all over the place that it's okay to lay down with another man and have sexual relations. You are Jewish, and your Old Testament makes it truly clear that it's simply not acceptable to behave like this. I'm shocked at your deviant behavior."

Vogelbach digs into his bag and begins preparing for Gary's surgery. "Now, if you were a woman, I wouldn't be here to do the Lord's work. But, because of my skills I can accommodate you, well, at least figuratively. Only God selects your gender. Man can make believe, but it is unacceptable in the Lord's eyes. So, Gary Pose, I will now send you off from this world, mocking you and your unholy lifestyle."

At 2 a.m. an hour and four minutes later Gary Pose's heart stops.

CHAPTER 9

A month after the Layla Cole murder, detectives Jimmy Cartoons and John Miliotis have nothing. Other than a possible male suspect there is no DNA evidence, no fingerprints or blood splatter, and no video evidence except for a guy in a leather jacket, fake beard, a surgical mask, and wrap-around sunglasses that they saw at the bar when Layla performed at 'Don't Tell Mama'. That same guy is seen on a building camera walking near 25 North Moore Street in a hoodie. So far, he is the prime person of interest, but no one has another clue as to who he is. They are running down leads of doctors, medical students, operating room nurses, and anyone else that could have known Layla or ever had a run-in with her, as far back as high school. "Nothing, nada, zero, zilch," as Jimmy Cartoons so aptly puts it.

The detectives have three more cases to go after Layla's murder. Fresh meat with real possibilities to make a collar. They have done all they could so far and are still being haunted by the Cole case. The voodoo amulet her father had given Layla is indeed missing. Likely taken as a souvenir by the killer.

"Every time we review our case file with Count Dracula it's the same thing. When we get to the Cole homicide, he makes this smug face like we are total losers. If this is his way of motivating us, I guess he's gotten into my head," Jimmy whispers. The duo is having a hamburger at Pete's Tavern on Irving Place.

"He's right. We suck on that case. How can there be nothing? Nothing whatsoever? I'm sure we've missed something," Miliotis utters as he dips three fat French fries into the red blob of ketchup on his plate.

The tavern is old school. Built before the American Civil War, Pete's doesn't look like it ever has seen a real renovation, although it was closed for a time for 'alterations'. The long rosewood bar on the left side of the restaurant and wooden tables and booths, tin ceiling, and original lighting fixtures brings back an almost haunting feel. Cartoons and Miliotis sit in the very booth where William Sydney Porter, a.k.a. O'Henry, wrote his famous tale 'Gift of the Magi'.

"Listen to me, John. Her apartment is scoured by forensics, like they do with every case. They may be the best forensic team in the entire country, as good or better than the FBI. We may suck, but we did everything by the book. Followed each and every lead ad nauseam. We both burned the midnight oil until we were shot. Look, seeing a beautiful and talented young girl killed just when her dream was about to come true is enough motivation for me. And that thing with her ovaries. Holy shit, that's sick. The tox reports showed she had this paralyzing drug in her system. We checked out the hundreds and hundreds of doctors who have access to that shit. Talk about a needle in a haystack. Yeah, we could get lucky, but so far, we are the opposite. Somehow, I think that's the key to this one, and sometimes shit happens and there is no solving a crime. Sometimes it's a dead end, and thirty years from now some a cold case asshole will find out who this killer is."

"And we will both be dead," Miliotis adds. He takes a huge bite out of his burger.

"You will be dead in five years if you keep eating the way you do, you Greek slob," Jimmy blurts before he choking on his Pepsi.

***

The word of Gary Pose and his husband Charlie Workman's demise hits the news wires an hour after their distraught housekeeper discovers their bodies. Police arrives, and within minutes, so does the paparazzi. How the cops and the paparazzi don't crash into one another is sheer luck. These photographers have people within the police department who sell the information on the rich and famous for three hundred bucks. There is an unwritten scale for information. Depending on who is involved the prices could easily soar to $10,000. Morgue and autopsy photos will be much higher, of course.

When the coroner's van pulls up, and not knowing what goes on inside Gary and Charlie's home, the rumor mill starts with a double suicide. Perhaps a lover's pact because Charlie had been in the hospital for a week. Then, it moves on to just plain old murder-suicide because one caught the other cheating.

Homicide Detective Bill Barutis, a near retirement,

by-the-book cop in his late fifties, is assigned to the case. Forensics is all over the place when Barutis gets there. Since the Nicole Simpson/Ron Goldman slaughter, this department is bound and determined not to screw up another case. Everything is checked, double checked, and checked again. The supervisors and their supervisors are at the scene especially for a high-profile case like this.

Barutis notes that there is no obvious forced entry. First thing on his mind is that the victims perhaps knew their killer. Maybe they have a key or the code to the garage where the Lambo and Charlie's Range Rover are parked. When the homicide detective walks inside to the kitchen, photographs of Charlie's body are being taken. It looks like a choke-out to Barutis. He has seen many of them in his years at LAPD Homicide. He takes his time looking over the scene. He notes that there are some small cuts on the victim's feet from kicking on the interior of the refrigerator, and a few of his manicured fingernails are broken from trying to pull the garrote away. He also lost his urine and bowels most likely after his struggle because there are no footprints in the mess.

Barutis makes his way to the upstairs bedroom. He walks slowly, looking closely for any hints on the oak steps. All the forensic people and Barutis himself wear paper booties and surgical gloves.

Gary Pose looks like he is resting in his bed. His hands are folded over his chest in a peaceful manner. Both his eyes and mouth are open, and the body is in the beginning of rigor mortis according to the Medical Examiner. The time of death is called between one to three a.m. There has been a lace doily that evidently is taken from a nightstand. Each of the two nightstands have an identical doily. It is placed over Pose's private area. The doily has a stain of blood on it. The dark blood has already dried. The ME has already removed the doily and exposes the desecration left by the killer. There is some blood that has seeped down onto the satin sheets but not enough to point to a brutal slash and stab. It is clearly a controlled environment. According to the ME, it is much like a surgical procedure. Neat and clean.

Barutis has seen a lot of murders in his day, but this one is shocking, even with all his experience. Gary Pose's penis is flayed open, almost in half, with a precision cut from its tip to the testes. It is neatly sutures to the victim's lower abdomen to resemble a vagina.

Pose's testicles are removed. The medical examiner soon finds them tucked under Gary's folded hands.

CHAPTER 10

Vic Gonnella and Raquel Ruiz have been back from their trip to Florence for two weeks. They had the time of their lives. Lots of great food, exceptional wine and coffee, great sight-seeing, and fabulous sex. Just what they needed after their intense book promotion tour.

Vic is watching a Yankee game at his New York City townhouse when he gets a call which reads UNKNOWN CALLER on his cell phone. It is either someone with the latest scam from India or a call from John Deegan. It turns out to be the latter.

"Back at the grind, I imagine," Deegan opens.

"Easing back into it," Vic replies. "My staff kept the place afloat. They started a bunch of new cases."

"And how is my Gabriella?"

"Growing up fast. Hey, by the way, after we had that fabulous steak dinner, we didn't see hide nor hair of you and the missus."

"We drove back north the next morning. You know I can't stay in one spot for too long. I enjoy my freedom too much," Deegan answers.

"To what do I owe this call?"

"I think there is another case brewing. I guess you don't

follow things in the States as closely as I do. I'm always looking for an opportunity to get busy, Vic."

"Are you just looking for work so hard that you may be out on a ledge this time?" Vic queries.

"Nonsense. In the past two months there has been a murder in your city and one in Los Angeles with some common denominators. Smells serialist to me," Deegan says. He is taking Vic's temperature. Throwing something out there as he has in the past.

"No idea what you're referring to. Besides that, how do you get these things all the way from your perch up in the alps?"

"I have friends in high places, or I just read a lot. I never reveal my sources," Deegan teases.

"You know better than to classify two murders as a serial killer. Even the FBI wants to see three with similar footprints."

"The FBI? Don't make me laugh. Those bureaucratic assholes have their own pot of shit to be concerned about these days."

"So, what do two murders 3,000 miles apart have in common that make you so cocksure there will be another?"

"I'll guarantee it."

"Okay, Mr. Genius, let's hear your story."

"The next one will be in about two, maybe three weeks if I'm correct. And Vic, when have I not been correct? And, my dear young friend, after the next one, and there will be a next one, you will likely get a call from those idiots in Washington. Their profiling department with that messy woman, what's her name again? Oh yes... Gail Gain. They call her GG correct? That's unless they've locked her up in a loony bin somewhere. There is no way they will find this one. When they call you, you can call me. I'll say I told you so, and then we can go to work," Deegan brags.

The phone call goes dead.

"That son of a bitch always does this to me," Vic says out loud.

CHAPTER 11

"I heard from our friend," Vic blurted. He and Raquel are having a nightcap before turning in at the townhouse.

"About what? He always calls for a reason."

"Mr. John Deegan is hot after a possible serial killer case."

"Where?"

"One here and one in L.A. Didn't say much about it, except he knows there will be a third," Vic says.

"I have an idea. Why don't we try to get in front of things for a change?" Raquel offers.

"Go ahead. What's your plan?"

"Let's put Chris or Emilio on it or maybe both of them? Let them research all the murders in the two cities and search for similarities. If John is right, we will shock the shit out of him and have a jump start if we are called in to consult by the feds," Raquel offers.

"Okay, first thing in the morning."

Raquel reaches for her cellphone. "No way. I'm putting them on it now. Time kills deals, you know that. Besides, if Deegan calls us, we will have trumped him for once."

"It's 10:30, sweetie."

"And these guys need practice. This 9 to 5 crap will get them nowhere. I like them competing with each other."

***

Detective Bill Barutis finally receives the e-mail from the Los Angeles Medical Examiner's office. The official cause of death for Charlie Workman is asphyxiation by strangulation. Toxicology tests comes up normal....as far as Hollywood normal is concerned. Cocaine, Xanax, marijuana, traces of amphetamine, Amplodine, Previcid, and Ambien, but not at levels that would contribute to his death. Charlie was the typical stressed out Hollywood medicine cabinet. Gary Pose is a different story. No stimulants or depressants of any kind are found in his blood samples. Not even Tylenol. Another phobia the hairdresser developed was taking anything foreign into his body. *'My body is a temple'* and *'My bubba was a hundred and three when she died and she never took a pill, never smoked a cigarette, never drank alcohol, and her skin was as smooth as a baby's ass'*, Gary had said in various interviews.

The only foreign substance in Pose's toxicology report is vecuronium bromide with a ketamine chaser. And plenty of it. His heart gave out because of too much of it. There is also a hematoma on his neck, likely where the drug is injected.

Barutis thinks for a few minutes after reading the reports. He has no idea what vecuronium bromide is, but he has some idea about ketamine. He makes a note to fully research the drugs. Aside from the obvious, which is that the murder of these two gay men are premeditated, he wonders to himself why only Gary Pose's body is desecrated. *'Definitely a hate crime, definitely planned out, perp possibly knew one or both victims',* Barutis thinks to himself.

The detective has never known a crime scene without something left behind. Some tiny something that could blow a case wide open. Barutis has seen quite a few murders of passion in his time at L.A. Homicide. Almost every case has vengeful multiple stabbings. The kind where the victim is slashed and stabbed as much as fifty or sixty times. If a firearm is used, the victim is often shot in the genitalia, or the cranium of the deceased is shot repeatedly until the head was gone or the face is unrecognizable.

The victims have no known enemies. There are no lawsuits pending other than a few of the normal business issues by bottom feeders suing over a cosmetic skin burn, but they are overseen by the corporation attorneys and generally settles out of court.

Barutis, not known to give up on a case, is totally frustrated. And the media is all over him and the LAPD. At least with O.J. Simpson, the entire nation saw the car chase and the arrest. The seasoned detective knows that his department had screwed up that case at every turn. Barutis recalled the trial in his mind and the not guilty verdict when everyone knew who the murderer was. He also remembered the crowd of blacks screaming '*WE WON*!' outside the courthouse. In the Cole-Workman case, the gay community is scared out of their wits but there will be no demonstrations or at least not yet.

***

By 3 p.m. the next day, at Vic and Raquel's Centurion Associates, LLC headquarters at 56th Street and Park Avenue, Chris Papa and Emilio Ramos, the criminal justice graduate students and full-time investigators in training, are ready to present a preliminary report.

In the main conference room sitting at the long mahogany table high above the Manhattan streets, only Vic and Raquel will be privy to the information found by the two trainees.

Vic senses that the two men are a bit nervous. Chris's hands are shaking slightly, and Emilio is perspiring, his forehead shiny with moisture.

"Okay guys. Before you start, I'm Vic, and this is Raquel. I know you know who we are, but we are just two former NYPD assholes who got really lucky. Just relax and tell us what you found," Vic says.

Chris chuckles and Emilio throws his head back and exhaled. Chris starts the report.

"First of all, we would like to thank you for this opportunity. Secondly, and it's a bit personal, but we want to tell you that we have skin in this game. We are both gay men with our own partners. We feel a kind of a kinship to these homicide victims. This being said, Emilio will run down what we have discovered so far."

Raquel smiles. She known they are both gay, and she likes them both. Vic just stares with his best poker face. He doesn't know of their sexual preference, and he doesn't care. Vic hasn't had any interaction with them to date.

Emilio clears his throat. “We have the cases side by side in a handout. You will note, although the homicides are separated by three thousand miles and by a month, the M.O. is too alike to be coincidental in our opinion. The similarities include surgical procedures with the use of the exact same nerve-blocking anesthesia, determined by blood samples on the victims. The lack of pre and post blood loss on the deceased indicates advanced surgical room experience. Also...”

Vic blurts out “Typo. Paragraph four. Should say, ‘removed’, not ‘remove’.”

Emilio blanches and Chris grabs the document off the conference table.

“So sorry, Mr. Gonnella,” Emilio says. Chris looks at Emilio. His face reddens.

“Vic. Call me Vic. Mr. Gonnella was my dad, and he passed long ago.”

“Sorry, Vic. As I was saying, we found something that may have been overlooked,” Emilio offers.

Chris takes over. “I spoke with NYPD and LAPD detectives who are on the case. We were trying to see if there are any other things that have the fingerprint of a serial murder. The victim, Layla Cole here in Manhattan, had a broach or talisman, which she wore around her neck the day of her murder. That was the only thing taken from her. Nothing else was missing from her apartment, so robbery was not a motive. The victim, Gary Pose, in Los Angeles, had a golden hairbrush and comb missing from his bureau. It was a keepsake gift from the mother of Mr. Pose, one of the victims, and was under a crystal container. In our opinion, these souvenirs point to a serial killer mentality."

"You are wrong about one thing, Chris," Vic says. He takes a long pull on his iced tea with lemon. "You said the only thing taken from her was the talisman. Let's not lose sight that he also has taken her life," Vic adds.

Chris is set aback. "Yes, sir. That's correct."

Raquel is trying hard not to look at Vic and ask him what he is thinking like, *'What the hell Vic?'*

"Okay. So, I think I know what Raquel wants to say something, but I'll go first because I'm a few years older than her. You two did a respectable job in the little time you had on these cases. And you recovered well from my interruptions. I'm not breaking balls, but I do like reports to be concise and as near perfect as possible. Look, get back to it. Let's meet when you have some more data. I agree with your supposition that this is a serial killer's work. But know one thing. Soon, in a couple of weeks, there will be another similar killing with the same M.O. I'm certain of it."

Emilio looks puzzled. "How can you be so sure, Vic?" he asks.

"A little old birdy told me," Vic replies.

CHAPTER 12

Paul Vogelbach makes an afternoon appointment to meet with Reverend Christian Stewart. He intentionally makes a light schedule at his practice and makes his rounds at the hospital quickly. At 4 p.m., Vogelbach arrives at the church and makes his way to the Reverend's office at the side of the building.

Dressed in his typical conservative blue suit and necktie, Paul is surprised to see Reverend Stewart in a pair of fitted blue jeans and a plain white collared pullover shirt. Stewart wears a pair of worn and scuffed brown Crocs. The reverends office has a white faux leather sofa with two fabric maroon wooden framed armchairs facing it. An IKEA dark walnut coffee table separates the sofa and chairs. Photographs of church picnics, celebrations, and outings inside plain brown wood frames dot the walls. On the other side of the office is an old oak wood desk with a desktop computer on top and a high-back black leather chair behind it. The reverend's diplomas hang on the light gray painted wall. Stewart is not into creature comforts or foolishly spending the church members' contribution dollars.

Paul is used to seeing the reverend standing at his lectern peering down on his congregation in his black suit and black tie. He realizes Christian Stewart isn't a tall man, but he seems much shorter and smaller in his casual attire.

"I'm so happy you called, Paul. Please, make yourself comfortable," Stewart says, gesturing to the sofa as he makes his way to one of the maroon armchairs. "How about some coffee or a pop?"

"No thank you, Reverend. I'm fine," Paul replies.

"You must be busier than a one-armed paperhanger at the hospital." Stewart starts making small talk.

"Yes, we have a very active hospital. I enjoy the challenges and try to keep myself fit to manage the stress," Paul offers.

"I suppose between the insurance companies, Medicaid, and Medicare regulations, the hospital personnel and your office staff must be overwhelmed."

"The secret is to have the right staff who know how to get things done and...well..."

"And offer the best medical care for your patients," Stewart finishes.

"That's correct, Reverend Stewart."

"So, Paul. To what do I owe this visit?" Stewart gets to business.

"I am so happy to be part of your congregation, Reverend. The way this country is going, I look to your sermons as an oasis for my soul. I wouldn't miss one of your Sunday services for the world. It's refreshing when you preach that the Lord made only two genders, and those genders have a duty to behave in a certain manner not to offend Him. I find myself clinging to your every word, and I wanted to thank you by donating to your ministry."

"Well Paul, you have been the most generous congregant in the years you have been part of our flock. My only wish is that you could spare the time to be more involved with our church. Our youth could benefit greatly from your presence, for example," Stewart says.

"Yes, making time is difficult, but I am not all that outgoing, as I'm sure you have already noticed. I prefer to make my donations anonymously and watch the Lord's work being done by such a great man."

"I'm humbled by your kind words, Doctor."

"I want to give you my annual tithe in full today and another special tribute so you can carry on the enormously important work you do for this community. My tithe is a bit more than last year, and my second contribution is for you to do with as you please," Vogelbach announces. He hands a sealed envelope to the reverend.

"I am again humbled by your generosity, Paul."

Stewart opens the envelope and places the two checks on his lap. His face shows both shock and gratitude.

"I can only think of the teachings of the bible at moments like this, Paul. From Luke 6:38, *'Give, and it will be given to you. They will pour into your lap a good measure, pressed down, shaken together, and running over. For by your standard of measure it will be measured to you in return.'* Paul, your generosity is overwhelming."

"Reverend, I too would like to quote scripture. It was something you said in a sermon earlier this year that struck me. Acts 20:35, *'And I have been a constant example of how you can help those in need by working hard. You should remember the words of the Lord Jesus: It is more blessed to give than to receive.'"*

"And indeed, you are blessed. But Paul, I must ask. Why now and why so much?"

"Reverend, I am a man alone. I have no need for the trappings that having money brings. I don't see myself having a family. In many ways this church is my family. This church rewards my spirit in so many ways that I cannot even put it into words. I look around your office and see that you do not squander the parishioner's tithes and donations on frivolous things, as so many clergy do in America. I see so many modern-day preachers using their congregation's money in such vile self-serving ways. These so-called television evangelists ought to be...Well anyway, you, Reverend Stewart, are a true servant of the Lord."

"Paul, forgive me, but I want to understand why a person of your talent, with your brilliant mind and love of scripture, doesn't see himself being a father. In Genesis, the Lord said *'I am God Almighty: be fruitful and multiply. A nation and a company of nations shall come from you, and kings shall come from your own body.'* Perhaps your offspring can make a difference in leading our future generations."

"I prefer to be fruitful in a spiritual manner, Reverend. I have prayed for this for many years. I will continue to do the Lord's work until I no longer can," Paul utters. He looks down at his hands, which are on his lap.

Reverend Stewart can see that Vogelbach is troubled by his question.

"Perhaps we can pray on this together one day, Paul."

"But someone will say, *'You have faith and I have work. Show me your faith apart from your works, and I will show you my faith by my works,'*" Paul responds. He stares hard at the reverend.

"Hmmm. From the book of James. And what do you consider to be your true work for the Lord, Paul?"

"Perhaps we can pray on this together...someday." Vogelbach replies.

***

Two weeks later, after another sermon from Reverend Stewart, this time with more fire and brimstone than ever before, condemning the woke culture and the transgender and gay lifestyle to the eternal fires of hell, Paul Vogelbach is once again on an airplane to do what he believes to be the Lord's work.

CHAPTER 13

ONE WEEK LATER.

Blake du Mont comes from a mega-wealthy family, what we call today, old money. In 1800, his fifth-great-grandfather and his family immigrated to the United States from France. One of Pierre Samuel du Mont de Nemours's sons, Éleuthère Irénée du Mont, started a gunpowder manufacturing company in Wilmington, Delaware. The company grew to be one of the most successful chemical companies in American history. Unlike several of his family members, Blake didn't attend MIT and never worked in the family business. He flunked out of the University of Delaware in his sophomore year.

Famous for doing nothing but having an incredibly large trust fund, Blake du Mont is a socialite, a jet setter who is a stapled-on page six in the tabloids and a familiar face in all the fan magazines. One day in the Hamptons, the next day in Aspen or Palm Springs or Key West or Monte Carlo, Blake's dyed spiked blond hair is a magnet for the paparazzi.

He works out just enough to keep his rippled six-pack and to fight off the dreaded handlebars. The du Mont heir looks like a cross between Robert Downey, Jr., and Drew

Barrymore, and very often his female persona comes out in a flamboyant flourish.

Open about his bisexuality and confirmed bachelorhood, the only thing Blake hasn't done, at least so far, was do a pornographic video like Kim Kardashian has done, which brought the talentless, surgically altered woman to celebrity status. Blake is already a celebrity. He seems to be born for fame, except he never accomplished a damn thing in his thirty-four years. He cannot think of embarrassing his philanthropist mother and father by showing his not so remarkable assets on film. A walk-on appearance on Real Housewives of Los Angeles is as close to acting as Blake has ever tried on video.

***

'Milwaukee is far from everywhere', Paul Vogelbach thinks to himself. He'd briefly contemplated driving, but the twenty-five-hour trip is just too much to deal with. It isn't that a car trip that long would be lonely. Paul is comfortable being by himself. He has taken many trips abroad over the years to see and experience the great sights of the world. He doesn't need to be with anyone to share his experiences. Paul didn't need to turn to someone when he saw the Mona Lisa at The Louvre in Paris and gave his opinion or ask for one. For that matter, when he saw the Great Pyramids in Egypt, he just took it all in and stared for a while. He never took one single photograph at the Vatican or the Grand Canyon, or at the Great Wall of China, or anywhere.

The three-hour and forty-five-minute flight to Las Vegas will give Paul a welcome nap in his wide, comfortable first-class seat. He always books a window seat, and he will never engage in conversation with the person in the next seat, no matter how they try to engage him. Paul doesn't care if the person is a stripper going back to her money pole or a widowed grandma going to see her grandkids. He doesn't watch television, read, or taste one bite of the food or take a bottle of water. He will tell the flight attendant not to disturb him for any of the amenities that are offered. His noise-cancelling earphones with soft classical music from his laptop and extra dark sunglasses are all he needs for the flight.

Paul never traveled to Las Vegas before. This city is the closest thing to the biblical cities of Sodom and Gomorrah Paul can imagine. Vegas is not the kind of place a God-fearing person will visit under any circumstances. Except, of course, to do the Lord's work.

Blake du Mont posted a message on his Instagram page. *'I'm off to Vegas to do some gambling and to see my great queen friend Carla perform in RuPaul's drag race at the Flamingo. Remember, what happens in Vegas stays in Vegas'.*

That is all Paul Vogelbach needs to know. He packed a carry-on bag and checked his trusty medical bag and is off to Sin City.

Some people do stupid things when it comes to putting their lives on social media. Blake du Mont, to keep himself relevant, telegraphed his every move on Instagram. His three million followers all but know when he is going to the toilet. Blake loves the attention of being a celebrity. If a post on Instagram tells his followers he will be at Jimmy's Pizzeria in Red Bank, New Jersey, sixty to one hundred teens will be poking their heads into the windows to get a glimpse of Blake and clamor outside for an autograph and a selfie.

All Paul Vogelbach has to do is click on Instagram to find out where his prey is at any given time. Today, Blake du Mont is holding court at the pool in the Venetian Hotel and Casino. Vogelbach makes the correct assumption that Blake would be staying there.

Arguably, Las Vegas has more video cameras per square foot than any place on the planet. Between the casinos and the hotels, the Strip, the restaurants, the street cameras for the police to monitor, a person's every move is being videotaped. Vogelbach decides to wear a disguise that will make him stand out in a crowd and potentially draw the eye of law enforcement after he completes the Lord's work.

Wearing a pair of blue jeans, a red sequined shirt, and a brown vest topped off with a combed mid-chest blond beard, a gray fedora, and thick horn-rimmed sunglasses, Vogelbach looks more like a member of ZZ Top than the actual band members. To add to that, he feigns a badly injured right leg by displaying a severe limp which slows up his gait to a near crawl.

The rest is easy, if he can get close enough to Blake du Mont and pull him away from his adoring minions.

Paul walks slowly by the du Mont cabana. Blake is sitting inside of an eight-person cabana poolside at The

Venetian. "Hey, you look like one of those guys in that band. What was it...yeah, ZZ Top. That's it," Blake announces.

"Yea, I get that a lot," Paul mumbles. He is limping by the cabana, paying no attention to Blake or his guests.

"So, are you one of the band or not?"

"Dude, those guys are like seventy. I just like the look," Paul says. He keeps walking slowly.

"And you look great. I never meant to insult your age, dude."

"No worries."

"I'm Blake Du Mont. Why don't you join us for a beer...or something?" Blake offers. He points to the white billowy drape covered cabana.

"Hell, everyone knows who you are, Blake. Even a nobody like me. Anyway, I need to take the weight off my damn leg and put this fucking bag down for a spell. Well, I can only stay a bit. Any idea what time it is?"

Blake looks at his wristwatch. "Yeah, it's time half-past the cow's ass. You gotta chill, man."

"Pretty old watch," Paul notes.

"Yeah, an antique goes back in my family like a hundred years. The last owner was a cousin or an uncle, I forget. We du Monts have thousands of relatives. Anyway, he was a whack job and shot a dude up and killed him. He died in prison. We have a lot of nutty people in the family. They say it's from inbreeding."

"Happens in the best of families."

Blake points at Paul's leg.

"What happened. What did you say your name was? Looks painful." Blake asks.

‘I’m Curt…Curt Henning. I could say I broke it skiing, which would sound sexy, but that would be a bold-faced lie. Truth is, I tried to ram my foot up in this dude’s ass but I broke my foot instead.”

“What the fuck? Why?”

“He called me a fag, that’s why. My sexual preference ain’t none of his concern, don’t you agree?”

“Yep. I would have smashed his head with something. I have no time for a broken bone.”

Blake and Paul, a.k.a. Curt, hit it off and stay in the cabana for most of the day. Curt pretends to make a call on his cell cancelling several appointments. Curt intrigues Blake, especially when he is led to believe that Curt is bisexual and isn’t sure which gender he preferers. Blake is of the same persuasion.

After a while, Blake shoos away all the hangers-on to be more private with Curt in the cabana. As dusk approaches, Blake stands and removes the two tasseled cords which keeps the cabana’s front flaps open.

Blake moves in for a kiss, which Vogelbach allows. “Take those jeans down and I’ll show you a billion-dollar good time,” Blake whispers.

“I can be freaky as hell, but I don’t care to do that right here. Anyone can walk in.”

“All the better!” Blake answers.

“Nah, I’m too private, dude. Must be my Christian upbringin’.”

“Let’s take this party up to my suite,” Blake offers.

“Sure ‘nuff. Lead the way, darlin’.”

Blake offers to carry Vogelbach’s black bag. The killer

thinks it is poetic and thanks him as he limps toward the hotel lobby and to the bank of elevators.

Once inside the suite which has a view of the Las Vegas Strip second to none, Vogelbach takes his bag, saying he has to freshen up as he limps
to the bathroom.

"Let's shower together!" Blake announces.

"That's for after."

"Are you going to play hard to get, Curty boy?"

"No way...I can't wait to see what a billionaire is really made of. Just give me a minute."

Once inside the enormous bathroom complete with a bubbling hot tub, double shower with ten jets, and marble everywhere, Vogelbach removes his beard, hat, and sunglasses and quickly opens his black bag. He takes a syringe and pulls a long dose of rocuronium bromide into it. He grabs a manual inhalator in his other hand. He opens the bathroom door and calls out.

"Blake, can you gimmie a hand with this?"

Blake saunters into the bathroom and is quickly spun around by the much taller and stronger man.

The heir to the du Mont fortune feels a sting in his neck and begins to droop down to the marble floor before he has any idea what is happening.

The unsuspecting and paralyzed Blake du Mont is awakened by a voice he is unfamiliar with. His eyes flutter. He is on his bed naked as the day he was born.

Vogelbach speaks in his normal voice. "I must say,

Blake. That kiss you gave me was absolutely sickening. So...I rebuke you in the name of our Lord and Savior. I point you to the New Testament. The First Letter of Paul to the Corinthians *'Or do you not know that the unrighteous will not inherit the kingdom of God? Do not be deceived: neither the sexually immoral, nor idolaters, nor adulterers, nor men who practice homosexuality, nor thieves, nor the greedy, nor drunkards, nor revilers, nor swindlers will inherit the kingdom of God'.*" He parrots the words he had heard from Reverend Stewart.

Blake is in and out of consciousness, but he knows he is screwed. His life begins flashing in his mind.

"I must tell you, I enjoyed our long discussion about music and Instagram and the rest of your useless, unwarranted fame and the folks you had sex with. You have achieved nothing in your life except being an expert in debauchery. I truly believe I am doing our society a blessing in removing you from this earth. Now, I will begin the providential procedure. But first, a quick removal. You should feel no pain. The Lord will administer the pain you deserve quite soon."

Vogelbach takes a stainless-steel pair of forceps and a scalpel out the black bag. He easily pried open Blake's mouth and grabbed his tongue, pulling it as far forward as possible. With the scalpel the physician cuts the muscular organ away with little force. Blood splatters onto the surgical gloves and onto the victim's chin and chest. All Blake can sense is the sound of his tongue being cut and the feeling of his blood oozing down his throat. His eyes blink uncontrollably as his brain tries to process what is happening to him.

Vogelbach then administers a lethal dose of ketamine, closing Blake du Mont's eyes forever. The killer takes the family heirloom watch from the wrist of his third victim.

CHAPTER 14

Late the next afternoon, Chris and Emilio are chomping at the bit to speak with either Vic or Raquel. Preferably both. The two burgeoning investigators have received news over the ViCAP program of another murder that looks to be the serial killing they have anticipated. ViCAP, the FBI's Violent Crime Apprehension Program, has been managing the communication and coordination between law enforcement agencies to track and apprehend violent serial offenders. Three is the magic number for the FBI to begin profiling a serial killer.

Vic and Raquel are out of pocket for the remainder of the day. Their daughter Gabriella is on the Chapin School varsity basketball team. A scrimmage is being played at the home campus on East End Avenue. This will be the first time Gabby will wear the school uniform in a game. The Chapin School will be playing a rival school from the west side of Manhattan, Avenue: The World School. While Chapin is a girls only, Avenue is co-ed and part of a muti-city, multi-country organization. Both private schools' endeavor to make future thought leaders and innovators by growing their students academically, emotionally, and socially. Well, that's what the website for Avenue says, so it must be true. The annual tuition at Chapin is $64,500. Avenue is a tad higher.

Vic, Raquel, and her mom Olga are being driven to Chapin by Pando, the ex-NYPD detective who has been with the firm for years.

There is an outside chance that Gabriella will play today. She is still a sophomore but makes the varsity team because of her ball-handling skills and quickness. Vic and Raquel, both season ticket-holding Knicks fans, know the game. Olga has no idea how the game is played, nor the rules, but wants to see her granddaughter in her Chapin uniform.

Olga and Raquel are having a discussion in the car. A discussion in a lot of Puerto Rican families can quickly turn into a full-blown argument. Vic knows a storm is brewing and wishes he would have driven himself or had taken an Uber. He sits in front of the BMW 760i with Pando. The ladies sit in the rear.

"Mama, all I'm saying is the old neighborhood is no longer a place you should be going to every week. We have been through this before. Vic and I see the crime statistics from that precinct. It's a war zone. Day or night, no one is safe there. It's been bad for years, but now it's simply unsafe for you to visit your friends anymore," Raquel preaches.

"They are my friends, Raquel," Olga replies. "What am I to do, just drop them? No, I won't." Her voice has a tinge of, get ready for the screaming.

"Listen, please. We can bring your friends to you. I'm sure they wouldn't mind a trip into the city. I'll arrange lunches, trips to museums, plays, movies—just tell me what you want."

"What am I, a snob? Just because you have money, it will be like me bragging. Unlike you, I haven't forgotten where I come from. Besides, I like the Spanish stores in my neighborhood. And my church too," Olga declares. Her pitch was rising.

"We can have your food, the fruits, and coffee and anything else you need delivered. You can pick from several great churches near us," Raquel offers.

"Impossible. No."

"Vic, will you please tell her how dangerous it is on Southern Boulevard and Tremont these days?"

"It's dangerous, Abuela," Vic utters. He really doesn't want to weigh in on this.

"Of course, you will agree with your wife, who has become a Borinquen snob. She wants me to tell my friends my daughter is rich and famous so I can't come to see you anymore. I will never do that!"

"Mama! Please! Even Pando doesn't want to sit in the car waiting for you over there, and he's a big guy and carries a gun."

"I'll take the subway. Coño!" Olga hollers.

"Sure, the subway. That really makes me feel secure. My old mother taking the worst subway system in the world so she can get robbed and stabbed or worse," Raquel states.

"I go with my Lord and Savior. If it's meant to be then it's meant to be. *AND DON'T CALL ME OLD!*" Olga shouts. "Cállate la boca! I want to see my granddaughter play basketball." Olga stares out of the rear passenger side window fuming and avoiding eye contact with her daughter.

"Tienes cabesa de burro. We will take this up at another time."

"No, we will not, and you are not getting the last word, daughter," Olga screams. Vic and Pando jump in their seats. Raquel feels like bashing her own head against the rear driver's side window.

Pando makes an illegal broken U-turn near Gracie Mansion to the other side where the Chapin School is. Every cop in the precinct knows Pando and knows the car. There is no chance the car will be pulled over for a ticket. Deep down, Vic likes that kind of recognition and respect. Raquel thinks it is silly.

Vic's cell phone rings as they approached the school. He sees UNKNOWN CALLER on the screen. He knows it is John Deegan and almost hits the red button to end the call but takes the call to encourage the argument between Raquel and Olga to end.

"Vic Gonnella." Answering the call would hopefully shut the two in the back seat down. It does.

"I will begin this call by telling you I told you so," Deegan says.

"I'm in the car with some people at the moment," Vic replies.

Deegan ignores the comment. "An incredibly famous guy from a bigshot family is killed last night in Las Vegas. Same mess. This time the perp surgically cut out the victim's tongue and with great precision sewed it to his forehead. Real medical procedure, like the other two."

"I'm going to see my daughter play in a basketball game right now."

"And get this. The entire world knows it. The deceased is admitted bisexual. See a pattern yet? Oh, and a souvenir was taken from the crime scene. Wanna guess what it was?" Deegan teases.

"I don't have the slightest idea."

"Okay, Vic. The two kids you have on the case will fill you in. They are pretty good, by the way. Very thorough." Deegan replies.

"And just how do you know this?" Vic steams. Raquel can see Vic's neck redden and his jaw tighten. She knows it is Deegan from the start of the call.

Deegan ignores the question again. "I've already figured out the motivation. I can now better predict the next one. And there will be a next one! Four weeks from now. I'll tell you all about it when the game is over. Kiss Gabby. I hope her team wins." Deegan ends the call.

Vic wants to throw his phone out onto East End Avenue.

CHAPTER 15

Vogelbach finishes his work quickly in Las Vegas. He didn't have to stalk his prey this time. It was easier than he thought to meet up with Blake du Mont and to dispatch him to the nether regions, the abode of demons and evil spirits.

Not wasting very much time getting out of Sin City, Vogelbach recalled a bible verse of when Lot was fleeing Sodom and was told by angels not to look back, *'But Lot's wife looked back as she was following behind him, and she turned into a pillar of salt'*. He has no intention of looking back to Las Vegas. Paul also doesn't want to leave and immediately return to Milwaukee and telegraph his moves that would make it easier for law enforcement to track him. Instead, he purchases a one-way plane trip to San Francisco.

Vogelbach has spent a week in San Francisco when he was in medical school. The city is different now; urban decay has destroyed this once regal city. On any given day addicts can be seen shooting heroin into their arms or smoking deadly fentanyl-laced drugs from foil packets. Paul recalls how much he had loved the city for all its tourist attractions — the Wharf, Alcatraz Island, the cable cars, the great restaurants, China Town, and Haight-

Asbury — but Paul will have an experience in San Francisco that he always will regret. He promised himself back then that he would never return, but something pulls him back to the City by the Bay. Paul knows that with the Lord's help he could face his demons and forever clear his conscience.

***

At the National Center for the Analysis of Violent Crime in Quantico, Virginia, the FBI is aware of the three murders that have crisscrossed the country. The evidence they have compiled on the Layla Cole, Gary Pose-Charlie Workman, and Blake du Mont homicides is enough for the Bureau to declare that a suspected serial killer is on the loose.

Special Agent Dean Salerno oversees the Child Abduction/Serial Murder Investigative Resources Center. Inside his fourth-floor office, Salerno and his staff of agents and profilers work closely with the ViCAP program to hunt down serial offenders.

Salerno is the poster boy for an FBI Special Agent. Tall, with light blue eyes and close-cropped reddish-brown hair, Salerno, born and raised in Providence, Rhode Island, the son of first-generation Sicilian parents, his dad rose to the rank of an Army Lieutenant Colonel. Salerno insists that his male staff always be dressed in dark suits and ties, without facial hair of any kind. He also insists that no red-colored neck ties be worn. The female staffers wear dark pantsuits or conservative knee-level skirts. Every one of the twenty-seven agents who work under Salerno have homicide investigative experience and are adept at analyzing the massive database that the FBI has compiled for serial violence.

Inside the 'bullpen', as the workroom of (CASMIRC) is called, are individual workstations with desktop and laptop computers, state-of-the-art telephone communications, with no personal photos or memorabilia allowed on desks. It resembles a military operation that Salerno's dad would have been proud of.

A large overhead white board and several monitors will display photographic evidence which included crime scenes, victims' snapshots, morgue photos, autopsy reports with graphic details, and, hopefully, when they get to that point, photographs of the suspected perps.

Salerno holds a morning and afternoon staff meeting. He works the floor of the bullpen most of the day. The only offices in the unit with glass doors were Salerno's and his second-in-command, Special Agent Cecilia Burns. Burns was once an NYPD Homicide Detective in Brooklyn's notorious 75th Precinct. She was involved with nearly two-hundred homicides in the ten years before the FBI swooped her up after she received her Doctorate degree from John Jay College of Criminal Justice. The unmarried, diminutive agent looks as if she is in her early twenties. Her strong Brooklyn accent adds to her no-nonsense attitude. Cis, as she is called, is married to the bureau.

"Ladies and gentlemen, we have our ninth active serial killer in the United States. So far, there are only two of the nine that have persons of interest. We need to step it up, people. On the monitors are the latest cases on which we will focus. One homicide in New York City, one in Los Angeles, and the latest a few days ago in Las Vegas. So far, that is the trifecta. It seems our suspect travels a long way to his victims. Our field offices in those cities have assigned agents to the respective cases. So far, the perp is very careful and extremely elusive. The monitor shows a split screen of surveillance video in New York on the left and another altogether different disguise on the right. He or she, and the smart money is it's a male perp, has left no hard evidence at any of the homicides, except each victim was given lethal doses of the muscle relaxant rocuronium bromide. On the surface it seems the perp has extensive knowledge of surgery and has operating room ability. Each killing took place within a month of each other, so there is a distinctive pattern of behavior. Any questions so far?"

A few arms shoot into the air. Salerno points randomly to one.

"Can we begin to make some broad-based assumptions?"

"Such as?" Salerno replies.

"The perp obviously can afford to take trips to the various cities. Is anyone checking on flights in and out of those cities?"

"Thanks for volunteering, Larry. Use whatever pressure you need on the airlines," Salerno orders.

Another agent is called upon.

"What do we know about this rocuronium. How readily available is it, and what can the manufacturer tell us?"

"Another good one. You are on it, Ben. Let's see if we can narrow it down, although I think this is a widely used drug throughout the country. I'm assuming nothing."

Salerno is distracted by a wheezing phlegm-filled cough from someone standing in the rear of the bullpen. It is Gail Gain. Salerno inherited her from the prior agents in charge. Gain is not an FBI agent. She is a civilian with twenty years on the job. She is considered difficult to work with but an expert in profiling who has been instrumental in closing more serial cases than anyone in the bureau's history.

"GG, would you like to add something?" Salerno asks.

Gain looks up at the ceiling above Salerno's head. She has difficulty making eye contact with anyone. Her hair is like a gray and black rat's nest. Uncombed and unkempt. Her anemic looking pale skin and un-ironed, multicolored peasant's dress made her stand out in this room of meticulous agents. She has a Diet Coke can in her dark brown nicotine-stained fingers.

Salerno waits for her response, which takes an awkwardly thirty seconds.

"What hand did the killer use?" GG finally asks.

The agent in charge is stumped. "I think the reports were silent on that. Tell me why that is germane, please?"

GG coughs up some mucus which she swallows with a sip from her drink. Some of the agents need to look away.

She wipes her nose with the sleeve of her dress.

Again, a long pause.

GG looks down at her sleeve.

"In the United States today there are over 30,000 surgeons. Assuming from the postmortem reports, and I know it's just an assumption at this point, let us imagine for argument's sake we have a surgeon killer. Forty-eight percent of surgeons are women, and around fifty one percent are men. Let's hope that the killer is left-handed. Only ten, maybe fifteen percent of the population is left-handed. That narrows the field a bit. It's a detail that should be part of the profile." GG sneezes into her hand and looks sideways at it.

GG's many eccentricities are well known among her colleagues. However, she is greatly respected as a brilliant profiler.

"Okay...good point, GG. Let's run this through our database. Perhaps surgeons with prior felonies. Maybe we get lucky?"

GG coughs again, signaling she isn't finished.

"Yogi Berra once said, '*Little things are big*,'" GG announces.

Salerno pauses and keeps himself from chuckling by biting his lower lip.

"And that's an important lesson to everyone in this room. Don't ignore the little things. The devil is in the details."

CHAPTER 16

The Chapin School's varsity basketball team wins their game by three points. Gabriella Gonnella never got a chance to dribble the ball but she is thrilled her team won and cheered them on from the bench. She decides to stay at the school with a study group. The competition for good grades at Chapin is demanding, and Gabby wants to prove herself to the teachers and her parents.

Pando is waiting outside the school with about ten other chauffeurs waiting to pick up the other well-heeled students and their parents.

"I'm getting in this car under one condition," Vic announces. "No arguments!"

Raquel gives him the dirtiest look she can muster.

"They could have put her in at least for a minute," Raquel whines. She is disappointed her daughter didn't play in the game.

"Gabby has to pay her dues, honey," Vic retorts. "It's like anything else in life."

Olga sits stone-faced, looking straight ahead with her arms folded across her chest. She is still pissed off at her daughter over the old neighborhood discussion and totally confused by the basketball game. Vic thinks, *'It's cold enough to hang meat in here'.*

When arriving at the townhouse, Olga storms into her room like a petulant child. Raquel puts on a pot of Café Bustello coffee. She is deciding between pizza or Chinese takeout for dinner. Vic gestures for Raquel to join him in the study.

"Time to call Deegan," Vic says. "Let's hear what pearls of wisdom he has to offer."

"It's after midnight in Switzerland, Vic."

"He never sleeps. Most geniuses sleep three of four hours a night."

Vic calls the number under Genius in his contacts. He puts the call on the speaker.

"Did they win?" Deegan answers on the first ring.

"Yes."

"How did my niece do?"

"She sat on the bench."

"She's paying her dues," John says.

"Great minds think alike." Vic makes a face at Raquel.

"My bucket list includes coming to see her play in a game," Deegan offers.

"You may have to wait until next season," Raquel blurts.

"I'll make the coach an offer she can't refuse," John says in his perfect imitation of Don Corleone in *The Godfather*.

"So, I suppose you want to know about the newest serial killer in the states?" Deegan asks.

"We're all ears. Like you can hear, Raquel is on the call with us."

"Okay. So, here is my supposition. I've figured out the front part of the equation. The killer is an anti-gay, anti-woke, anti-everything religious fanatic. Pretty sure it's a man. He is going after fairly well-known victims. His pattern is going down the alphabet mafia," Deegan offers.

"The what?" Raquel asks.

"The alphabet mafia. LGBTQ and so on."

"Never heard them called that before," Raquel replies.

"At first, they didn't like that term. Now they think it's cool. Gives the gay-lesbian and trans-world power. Anyway, let's look at the killings one by one. First killing, the one in New York City. Layla Cole. Lesbian for 'L'. First initial of first name. Then, in Los Angeles, a gay man. First initial 'G'. Gary Cole. His husband was collateral damage. The latest in Las Vegas. 'B' for Blake du Mont. An admitted bisexual. LGB so far. With me?" Deegan queries.

"Farfetched at best," Vic replies. His tone is a matter of fact.

"Really? Way too much of a pattern to ignore, folks. This guy is planning his victims precisely to make a statement about alternative lifestyles. To him they are unacceptable. Probably a Bible thumper. He takes trophies, like most serial killers do. The amulet, the golden brush set, and now an antique watch — a family heirloom."

"Where did you get that information, John?" Raquel asks.

"From the reports. It's right there in black and white, guys," Deegan responds.

"I'm not even going to ask how you have access to this stuff," Vic blurts.

"So, the next will be a transexual?" Raquel states.

"Pretty and smart, too, Vic. You need to marry this one."

Vic ignores the quip.

"And where do you suppose he will hit again?" Vic asks.

"In a month, we will know. There are a lot of transexuals in the world right now. You must focus on a trans with the letter 'T' in his or her first or last name. Following the pattern, likely the first," Deegan instructs.

"I guess we have to check the global transexual directory for that one," Vic says. His voice is dripping with sarcasm.

"Put Heckle and Jeckle on it, why don't you? It's a good graduate school study. They figure it out, they get a bonus. Or call your FBI friends. They keep records on everyone," Deegan matches the sarcasm.

"Why religious fanatic, John?" Raquel asks.

"Very good question. The average gay hater isn't so smart. Just a hater, or likely should be on the list themselves. The murders all have a psychosexual motif. Ovaries removed because Layla wasn't going to use them naturally. Gonads removed on the hairdresser because they were superfluous in his life, and finally, the tongue sewn on the forehead. A great symbolism from the Bible. Look at James 3:9 '*with the tongue we praise our lord and father, and with it we curse human beings, who have been made in god's likeness*.' the alphabet mafia are all made in god's likeness, and they transgressed. get the religious theme now?" Deegan asks.

Vic and Raquel stare at one another.

"Is that religious enough, my dears?"

"You're getting warmer," Raquel states.

"I can go on and on, Raquel, until you are convinced. *'A person who speaks in tongues is strengthened personally, but one who speaks a word of prophecy strengthens the entire church.'* 1 Corinthians 14:4. It's the whole Holy Spirt thing. I'll go out on a limb and say this guy's church has lots of believers that speak in tongues. The Greeks used the word tongues to mean languages. These bible-beaters fake speaking in tongues pretty good. Elementary, my friends," Deegan insists.

"You are building a good model for your supposition John," Vic admits.

"Class dismissed for the day." Deegan drops the call.

CHAPTER 17

Detective Jimmy 'Cartoons' McLaughlin gets to the 5th Precinct at ten minutes to 4 p.m. for the 4-12 shift. He places a two-liter bottle of Pepsi on his desk.

Detective John Miliotis sits at his own desk, facing his partner. He has just unwrapped the aluminum foil from an overstuffed bacon egg and cheese sandwich on a hard roll.

"I think the Dominican chick at the deli around the corner likes me. She loads this thing up with extra cheese and bacon. I may marry her," Miliotis mumbles as he chews the first bite of his meal.

"Yeah, she likes her men fat and near death. She gets a lifetime pension after you croak," Jimmy laughs.

"Nah, the ex-wife has dibs on that. I'm trapped like a rat."

"Hey, something's bothering me about that Layla Cole case. That guy from Vic Gonnella's place keeps calling me. He said it's now considered a serial killer case. I looked at ViCAP last night. Two more after Cole. We better take another pass through our reports. Maybe we missed something," Jimmy says.

"Sure, let's drop the other eight cases and deal with Count Dracula."

Almost as if he heard his name mentioned, Captain Bortugno appears in the doorway like Bela Lugosi without his cape.

"My office, ten minutes. FBI is on their way. The Cole Case. I have the files on the off chance you are looking for them." Bortugno, his voice dripping in sarcasm, vanishes like the Count.

"Here we go! Back to Castle Dracula," Miliotis utters. He takes a second bite of his sandwich, then wraps it back up in the foil.

"Agent Cooper, this is Detective McLaughlin and Detective Miliotis. They handled the Layla Cole case."

Handshakes all around as Captain Bortugno eyes glaze over.

Agent Samuel Cooper stands well over six feet. Probably 6'5" or 6'6". Born and raised in the Bronx, Sam Cooper has a certain familiarity about him. The offspring of an African American father and a Puerto Rican mother, Cooper played basketball for the St. Raymond High School for Boys Ravens and for the Fordham University Rams before going to Fordham Law on a full scholarship. The FBI swooped him up before he could even think about working for a New York law firm.

Bortugno clears his throat in an authoritarian alert.

"Agent Cooper is the field agent the bureau has assigned to the case. The Cole homicide is now being investigated as a serial case, as you already know. Please afford Agent Cooper every and all courtesy, gentlemen. Let me know if you need my assistance." Bortugno raises from his desk, signaling that the meeting has ended. "By the way, copies of the files have been e-mailed to you, Agent Cooper."

Sam Cooper stands up slowly, feeling a bit awkward at the captain's quick dismissal. Bortugno doesn't offer him a handshake, and Sam doesn't push it.

The trio goes directly to the muster room, where some afternoon cartoons are playing at very low volume. Jimmy glances at the television for a second or two.

"So, Agent, where would you like to start?" Miliotis asks.

"Start by calling me Sam."

"Great. I'm Jimmy, this is John. You already met the Count of Darkness, so we're all set," Jimmy offers.

The three men break out in friendly laughter.

"He'd be perfect in the New York Field Office," Sam jokes. "I'm told you two have loads of experience in homicide cases. Tell me, how is this one different from the others you've been on?"

John looks at Jimmy and nods.

"Clean. I mean absolutely nothing to go on. Not a fingerprint, a hair, a smudge, a flake of dandruff. It was like the killer worked in a sterile environment. We didn't even find a fiber from the wig he wore earlier that evening. That's assuming he was still wearing it at the scene," Jimmy informs.

"Tell me about the wig, please." Sam asks.

Miliotis replies. "You will see in the video surveillance in the club where the deceased sang. There's a guy at the bar with a thick wig, hat, sunglasses, and dark jacket. The same guy is seen on video from a condo near the victim's apartment a few hours later."

"I'm not here to break balls, guys, but I'm gonna need some more details. Give me a timeline. What time was he seen at the club, then what time at the condo?"

Jimmy jumps in. "We hear you, Sam, and we are not taking it any way but positive. We've done all that detailed stuff, but we are no way near perfect. Okay, from memory, and John will correct me as the reports can. The victim's first show was from eight until 9:30. She was there a couple of hours early. The show is where the potential suspect was seen at the bar. We ran down some of the other bar patrons and the bartender. There was no conversation. He ordered a couple of ginger ales. No booze. Paid cash. He left, and the second show started at midnight. The suspect wasn't seen on video outside when the show ended at 1:30. He was seen walking past 25 North Moore Street at 12:14 a.m. That's on the same street as the victim's apartment. There were scratch marks on the building door lock."

"So, the disguise. What did he do with it?"

John takes over. "He may have put it in his bag after he entered the building or dumped it. Forensics did the usual sewer and garbage search. Nothing. Certainly, they could have missed it, or he was lucky enough not to lose a hair from that wig."

"What do you make of the ovaries being removed?"

"Freaky. Maybe he was a spurned boyfriend who wanted her to have his babies. She was on the other team," Jimmy blurts.

"And the cut and the ovary removal were a professional job. Clean as can be. Very little blood from the incision," John adds.

"What do you make of the voodoo necklace. Any weird shit going on?" Sam asks.

"Nah. That was a one-off. Gift from her dad. Strictly ethnic thing," Jimmy replies.

"Do you have an approximate height and weight on the perp?" Sam inquires.

John shoots back. "6-1, 215-220. Muscular build."

"That matches the dimensions on the Las Vegas killer. Could be coincidental, though," Sam replies.

"Oh, I bet it's the same guy. Who else goes around with a surgical kit, set up lopping off parts and sewing them up. Jesus Christ, this guy is a sicko like I've never seen," Jimmy proclaims.

"Guys, I appreciate your details. I want to review your reports before I leave here. The profilers at Langley are all over the reports too. Anything I'm missing?" Sam asks.

Miliotis speaks up. "Yeah. You never asked us where this guy stayed. Does he live nearby? Was he in an Airbnb? A hotel? An SRO? Did he sleep in a park? Did he sleep at all?"

"Good point. What did you discover?"

"Absolutely nothing," Jimmy replies. "Every move he made was smooth, neat, and calculated. Even our facial recognition surveillance came up empty. Let me give you a heads-up Sam. You seem like a nice guy, like one of us, if you know what I mean. Vic Gonnella's people are on this case, too, for some reason. They keep calling for dribs and drabs, and we are more than happy to provide that to Vic. Maybe you want to give him a call. Ya never know."

"Thanks, Jimmy. I will. I think I may need approval to do that. The bureau is very skittish these days."

CHAPTER 18

San Francisco is nothing like Paul Vogelbach remembers. He has lodged with friends of friends right outside the rough-and-tumble tenderloin district at the end of his first year of medical school.

When he arrives at the airport, he hires a driver to take him into the city. He remembers the address where he is going to stay and has given it to the driver. "Pretty crappy neighborhood," the driver said. "I don't think you're gonna stay anywhere near that dump unless you have some kind of grudge against yourself."

"I just want to see the place and then check into a decent hotel somewhere."

When they arrive at the address, Paul cannot believe his own eyes. There are homeless people everywhere. Huddled under makeshift tents or crammed into large cardboard boxes, it looks like the city of the dead and near dead. Some are just lying on makeshift beds with bags of clothing and other personal items which they clung to. The building he had stayed in has been converted into a four-story single-room occupancy hotel that was likely a crack house or a brothel, likely both. Unkempt men and women hang around the entrance to the building in ragged clothing. Some are leaning to the point of falling to the ground, but they don't drop. Paul opens the car window, but the stench of human waste forces him to immediately close it.

"Told ya!" The cabby said. "Seventy percent of the crime in this city happens right around here. Murders every other day, it seems. Listen, mister. I have kids. I'm getting us the fuck out of here or you can get out."

Paul tries to remember something about the time he spent there, but he can't recall anything. There is nothing, not a store, not a building, not the bar his friends hung out in, nothing at all familiar. Even the street signs seemed different. The street is like a battle zone. This is what is happening to my beloved country. This is the moral decay and sin that Reverend Stewart preaches about, he thought. Paul closes his eyes for a few seconds, and the event that has occurred to him returns in a flashback. He breaks out into a cold sweat.

"Sorry, man. I've seen enough. Take me back to the airport," Paul blurted. He reaches his hand over the driver's shoulder and puts three hundred into his hand. He put his head back and closes his eyes, trying hard to forget the past and what he just saw.

***

Back at Vic and Raquel's office, Emilio and Chris are dissecting every inch of the ViCAP reports. They learned very quickly that the Gonnella name is like magic in the law enforcement world. *"We generally don't give out this information, but for the Gonnella group we are more than happy to oblige,"* and answers like that shows the pull that their bosses have.

"How come we didn't catch that?" Emilio asked Chris. They are ensconced in a breakout room off the company's main conference room. They have a makeshift wall board with photos of the three victims, the similarities in their lifestyles, and their murders.

"Catch what?" Chris replied.

"The whole LGBTQ thing. How the killer may be going down the alphabet mafia concept? When Vic and Raquel gave us that theory, I almost shit myself," Emilio said.

"Pure genius. When Vic told us they were two cops who just got lucky, they didn't mention they were also brilliant. There is no substitution for smart."

"This is why they are who they are. With all the serial killer cases they worked, it's no wonder they are on the top of the law enforcement food chain," Emilio added.

Little do they know that the theory came from the most notorious serial killer and still wanted John Deegan.

"I've been staying up nights thinking of the next victim. T...for transexual if the theory is correct. Where will the killer strike again? Who are the most well-known trans people in the country?"

"With the letter T in their name, no less," Emilio added.

"There is always the possibility that the killer will stop now," Chris guessed.

"Doubtful. In general, serial killers have a message to convey. This guy certainly has a problem with people who are, let's say, different from the mainstream."

"Do you consider us unique?"

"Not within myself...no. And not within our circle, but in society I feel apart from most of the general public."

Chris becomes quiet before he continues the conversation. "I remember when I came out to my family. What a battle that was. My Italian father went nuts. I thought he was going to drop dead on the spot. And my Sicilian mother wanted to take me to this woman she called 'la storpu.' This old, crippled woman from her small town in the mountains near Palermo. Apparently, this lady can cure her faggot son." Chris didn't laugh. "She even called over there and started to make plane reservations. What a mess."

"My family always knew," Emilio remembered. "My mom said I always acted feminine and played with dolls. It was no surprise to them. It's as if I just grew up to be gay."

"But today, if a boy picks up his sister's Barbie one time, the parents are ready to declare him transexual and all that shit that goes with it. Before he knows it, they are chopping off his junk," Chris added.

"Hey, do you think our killer is gay? Or maybe he's gay and doesn't want to admit it?"

"That entered my mind. I'm sure there are millions of dudes like that. Talk about a needle in a haystack! But how many would just start murdering people?"

"So, we are looking for a possible surgeon or nurse, who may be gay or is gay or...this is getting too crazy."

***

At the Child Abduction/Serial Murder Investigative Resources Center in Langley, Virginia, Special Agent Dean

Salerno and his next in command Cis Burns go to Gail Gain's office on the first floor of the FBI building.

GG cannot have an office above the first floor. It is another one of her eccentricities. She hates elevators and is deathly afraid of fires. She wants a quick exit in case of the latter. Her office is the only one in the entire building, and maybe in the entire FBI system, which grandfathered her smoking.

Special Agent Salerno taps on the glass office door and opens it.

"Hi, GG. Got a minute for us?" Salerno asked.

GG stares above his head with her usual delayed response. Her eyes flutter before she noticed Agent Burns. She nods her head up and down.

"Just wanted to stop by and bring you some information on the new case," Salerno stated.

No response.

"It seems the perp is right-handed. The theory is, he or she worked from the right side of the victim's bodies. They were lying in their beds, and incisions are made from the right side. If the perp is a lefty...well, he or she would have had to climb onto the bed to make the cuts from the victims' left sides. There was no indication of that happening in the photos from the scene," Cis Burns informed.

Making no eye contact, GG replies, "Makes sense. That widens the field of suspects."

GG's desk is covered in papers, photographs of crime scenes, and crumpled up packs of empty red Pall Mall cigarettes. Red is for full strength. A large glass ash tray is filled with more than a pack of smashed cigarette butts.

Her metal desk has burn marks on the edges, where she apparently placed her burning smokes. Burns notices three large fire extinguishers in the 8x12 office. The agent also notices that GG is in the exact same outfit she wore at the meeting the day before. Just a few more food stains around the belly area. A pungent body odor emitters from GG.

GG looks down at her hands and speaks in a monotone voice. “I’m thinking there is a message he — and I’m sure it is he, as I’ve said — wants the world to know. I’m thinking he has a religious background of some kind. Maybe a Jesus freak. Maybe a former clergy. But definitely a surgeon. The way he operates and the use of the paralyzing chemical proves that part of the equation to me. Why he is separating the killings by a month is yet to reveal itself. Perhaps it’s his vacation time, or it coincides with his days off? I’m running a report on the Zodiac calendar to see if there is a correlation.”

“That adds to the profile for sure,” Salerno replied.

“GG, if he strikes again, would you care to visit the crime scene yourself?”

GG stares above Cis’s head. It seems to Agent Burns for a second that GG’s eyes are going in different directions.

“No. I don’t fly, and I don’t like to travel.”

“We can setup a video call to see the scene. It may help you,” Cis uttered.

Another long pause. Salerno is getting ready to exit the office.

GG begins opening a fresh pack of Pall Malls, whipping the red band off the top and using her greenish-tinged teeth to open the cellophane. She spit the refuse to the side of her desk.

"Suit yourself. I like you, Agent Burns. You are nice to me."

CHAPTER 19

When Paul Vogelbach returns to Milwaukee, he is on the verge of despondency. Seeing Las Vegas and all that went with that place, and then San Francisco's huge dive into decay, is enough for him to realize that what he is doing in the name of the Lord is righteous. As a medical doctor, his Hippocratic Oath is directly opposed to his fanatical actions. But the Lord's work trumps all.

Vogelbach counts the days until Reverend Stewart's next service. Finally, Sunday arrived, and the serial killer gets to the Unified Free Church of Truth earlier than anyone in the congregation. Sitting tall in the rear of the church like he always does, Paul revels in the quiet of his safe place. Alone with his thoughts and his God is all Paul needs to be happy.

After a while, parishioners begin to file in and take their seats. Without one bit of guilt about the three murders he has committed, his actions don't even enter his mind. Vogelbach has a slight grin of satisfaction on his face as he watches his fellow believers fill the pews. He recognizes most of the congregants from the weekly services. He watches the older couples, some with canes or walkers or leaning onto one another for support, families with their young children, all neatly groomed in their best Sunday services clothing, well-mannered teens who don't seem to resent being in church or being with their families. Paul Vogelbach feels his spirit return to a calm state.

"Dr. Vogelbach, I'm so sorry to disturb you," a voice came from behind him, temporarily startling him.

Paul turns around to see an attractive young woman in her late twenties whom he hasn't noticed before. She is dressed in a long, cascading, flowery dress and wears a green hat that nicely framed her flowing blond hair and light green eyes.

"My name is Rebecca Sipes. You don't know me. Actually, I live in Wausau now. I moved away from here about eight years ago. You treated my father, Ronald Sipes. I wanted to thank you for saving my dad's life," Rebecca whispered. Her eyes glimmer as she smiles broadly at the doctor.

Vogelbach is nonplussed. He has to look away from Rebecca for a moment and regain his composure.

"Yes, of course. Mr. Sipes. I understand he is at home now."

"Thanks to you he is. My mom went to the Lord a couple of years ago, and I thought we were going to lose him. His doctors didn't hold out much hope for him, but you came along, and with the help of our Lord he is recovering nicely. Again, Dr. Vogelbach I'm sorry to bother you."

Vogelbach offers an awkward smile, "You are welcome. May the Lord bless you both." He turns his head and focuses on the cross at the front of the church. He feels uneasy that someone actually spoke to him. He always avoids eye contact with anyone at the church and is the first to go quickly to his car at the end of services.

A few minutes later, Reverend Christian Stewart comes from the rear of the church and walks down the middle isle as he always does. He carries his Bible in his right hand and moves with a quiet resolve to his lectern. It is as if he can't wait to begin the service.

"Brother and sisters in the Lord. I bring you to Matthew, chapter 6, verses 3 and 4. Follow in your bibles please." Stewart waited a few moments as the shuffling of pages from the assembly sounded like dry leaves blowing in the wind. "'*But when you give to the needy, do not let your left hand know what your right hand is doing, so that your giving may be in secret. Then your Father, who sees what is done in secret, will reward you.'* You may ask, Reverend, why are you bringing this to us this morning? Brothers and sisters, we are blessed more than you can imagine. The Lord has brought forward one among you who has given our small but growing church a magnificent endowment that will carry us forward with plans to bring the word of God beyond these church walls. Only the Lord can heal the sick and the infirmed, but we are now able to bring His word to those in our community who cannot be a physical part of our church. I rejoice as you should and bless the anonymous donor who the Lord will compensate here on earth and in when the Lord calls, also in heaven."

Vogelbach feels butterflies in his stomach and an enveloping warmth that comes over him like never before.

Reverend Stewart, as he usually does, starts his sermon low and slow. Some in the assembly crane their necks to hear him. This morning, his voice is so low, it seemed Stewart is even more nervous than ever about speaking in public. This is his way of building momentum to get his assemblage caught up in his words.

"I don't care what the politicians say about alternative lifestyles. I don't care what the liberal left opines about gay men, lesbian women, and the freaks of nature that change their genders. I don't care if the print and television media condone homosexual behavior. I only care what our all-powerful God says about this deplorable life they have chosen. In last week's sermon, I quoted chapter and verse where the Bible condemns the homosexual lifestyle, and these people will have no salvation. The Bible states clearly, they should be put to death, yet some so-called Christians say we should embrace and understand them."

Stewart paused, looking out at the filled pews in front of him. He raises his right hand, pointing his forefinger to the ceiling. He raises his voice and yells, "The subject of homosexuality as a sin has nothing to do with the Constitution of the United States of America, nothing to do with free speech or human rights, but it has everything to do with the word of our one true and living God. They should perish into a lake of fire. EVERY SINGLE ONE OF THEM!" Stewart screamed. The assembly was awestruck.

"Parents...If you permit your children to watch television, to go to a movie where Cinderella is a man, or that new catch phrase non-binary...whatever in God's good world that means. If you permit your offspring to watch MTV or encourage them to have friends of homosexual parents, you are condemning them to accept the Devil's work. And so...you are condemning your own flesh and blood to eternal damnation. Not three miles from here, a so-called Christian church... is... marrying... homosexuals. Did you hear what I just said...MARRYING HOMOSEXUALS," Reverend Stewart yelled and he continues.

"I am telling you all right here and right now...these people are condemned by the very word of our Lord. I will be leading a group of us to boycott this mission of the Devil. I will fight this debauchery and this disrespect of God's will with every fiber of my being. I can no longer countenance this evil being spewed within our community. I am unafraid of these anti-American, anti-family, anti-God freaks of nature and the media that want to ruin our core values."

Stewart is sweating profusely. His eyes seem to be popping from his head. He wipes his brow with the back of his leather-covered Bible. The dramatic effect sends shivers up the spines of many of the worshipers.

"Remember these words, my dear brothers and sisters in the Lord. From Romans 13:4: *'For he is God's servant for your good. But if you do wrong, be afraid, for he does not bear the sword in vain. For he is the servant of God, an avenger who carries out God's wrath on the wrongdoer.'"* Steward steadies himself, putting his left hand on the lectern while grasping his Bible with his right. He walks slowly and enters a door directly behind the lectern.

The rest of the service would be officiated by one of the deacons and the head of the choir.

With Stewarts words, Paul Vogelbach knows that the Lord ordains his mission. He no longer has any doubts.

CHAPTER 20

Olga made scrambled eggs and toast for Gabriella's breakfast. Pando picked up Gabriella at the townhouse promptly at 7:15 as usual for her early morning study group. After her granddaughter left, Olga brews the Café Bustello in the old-fashioned percolator pot on the stove. When the coffee is ready, the distinct nutty and almost caramelized aroma fills the house, as it does every morning. The Abuela insists on grinding the fresh beans herself each morning. The sound of the coffee mill usually wakes Raquel. Olga turns off the jet and goes back to her room. Raquel and Vic just have to warm it up a bit before they take off for the office.

"She's still pissed off at me from that Bronx argument," Raquel said. She and Vic are having their first cup of the strong Bustello coffee, standing at the speckled green and white granite-topped center island in the kitchen. Vic is checking e-mails and text messages on his cell phone.

"She'll get over it," Vic responded. "Or she won't."

"I can tell when she's up to something. It wouldn't surprise me if she went up there today. She is incredibly thick-headed."

"And for sure she isn't Calabrese. They are the most testa dura of all the Italians," Vic chuckled.

"She should not be allowed to go!"

"Allowed? Raquel, you can't tie her to a tree. Olga will do what Olga wants to do," Vic uttered.

"Pando knows to let me know if he's taking her to the Bronx, right?"

"He does. Why? So, you can sit and stare out your office window and worry all day? C'mon, let's get going. I have a conference call at 10."

Raquel's intuition is correct. Olga is going to the Bronx today, except she decides to get an Uber ride rather than call Pando. Which means Raquel would have no idea her mother is going, and Pando wouldn't be around to watch over her, nor be around for the return trip. Olga is very plotting when it comes to her independence.

By 10:15, Olga is walking alone on Tremont Avenue near Southern Boulevard. She is shopping on Tremont for a few things before going to the apartment of her long-time lady friend Gladys Ramos. They raised their kids together in that neighborhood. The ladies planned to walk to their parish church, St. Thomas Aquinas on Crotona Parkway. Once there, they would meet another old friend, Maria Nunez, who lives next door to the aging church. Maria has type II diabetes because of her weight and her high-carb diet. Olga and Gladys are always on her for her choices of food when they went out together. After a planned late mass, they would have lunch, probably at Cosmo's Restaurant, their regular eatery.

Olga always insisted on picking up the check with the company credit card her daughter has given her. After all, Maria and Gladys are women alone, barely making ends meet with their Social Security checks and zero help from their grown children. Olga is always ready with some cash when these two elderly ladies are in a bind. Raquel and Vic give Abuela a generous allowance, as it should be for people with money. Olga also gives a nice fat envelope to St. Thomas Aquinas church each time she goes there.

The neighborhood at that time in the morning is quiet and very pleasant on this warm sunny morning. No blaring Spanish music, no kids out yelling in the streets just yet. Olga is used to the soda and beer cans and bottles of cheap booze from the night before all over the gutter. Paper refuse strewn along the concrete pavement and on the black tar roadway is part of life in the neighborhood. It seems her people just threw their papers and other junk on the ground so someone else could pick it up. Olga thought the Dominicans were at fault because she had forgotten the dirty streets when only Puerto Ricans lived there.

It seems that every other store is permanently closed or is boarded up by the landlords. Covid has ravaged the area. A few stores are still trying to make a go of it. The woman who ran the botanica is sweeping the sidewalk of her storefront. A small Dollar Store had just opened, and a few people are going in for the inexpensive personal items, a corner pizzeria is getting ready to sell slices for lunch, and a shoe store has a GOING OUT OF BUSINESS sign in English and Spanish in the window. Very few cars ride by on Tremont Avenue this early, unlike the weekends where the street is bustling, and double parking is part of the culture. A few mopeds zoomed by with drivers without helmets. In many ways the streets resembled Puerto Rico or the Dominican Republic.

Olga passes a Korean-owned fruit and vegetable store, making note of the nice yellow and dark brown plantains and dark green 'aguacate' which are on display in boxes outside the store. Before she returns to Manhattan, Olga will buy some and a homemade Dominican guava cake for twenty dollars from a lady she knew.

Being from the neighborhood, Olga knows to keep her pocketbook strapped from her shoulder and in front of her to avoid tempting any drug-addled purse snatchers from ripping it from her. It is just the way it is.

"Gladys, what a pretty dress!" Olga stated as she meets her friend in front of Gladys's building. Olga's outfit is a Caribbean looking multi-flowered sundress. She held her pocketbook the same way Olga did.

The two friends embrace one another.

"And look at you!" Gladys announces. "You look like a Manhattan model. How do you stay so slender, my friend?" Olga has on a green knit pantsuit and fake white pearls.

"Nonsense, I'm at my heaviest in years. I don't walk as much anymore. Let's hurry and meet Maria. Father Lopez isn't going to hold up the mass for us."

The two old friends step up their pace as they make the turn onto Crotona Parkway. They see St. Thomas Aquinas Church and immediately spot Maria. Maria waves and Olga and Gladys wave back, all with big smiles.

"Maria, you are on time for once," Gladys declared.

Unexpectedly, out of nowhere, a dark blue BMW with tinted-out windows roars by. The rear window is lowered, and automatic gunfire is sprayed almost in front of the church. A dark Hispanic man in his early twenties is the intended target. He drops to the ground and pulls a handgun from his waistband in one motion. The car comes to a stop and the gunfire continues, this time from the front and rear passenger windows of the vehicle. The target pops off a few shots and half rose to flee. He drops to the ground again for a second before rising to his feet to run. As he is fleeing down Crotona Parkway, he slams directly into Olga. The Abuela is splayed onto the concrete sidewalk. She hits the ground hard. Everything happens so fast that Olga never knows what hit her. Gladys begins screaming for help in Spanish and calling on Jesus for his protection. Olga tries to rise from the sidewalk but cannot. She feels a searing pain in her hip. The shooting stops as the deafening roar of the BMW's motor is engaged. Almost immediately the sound of nearby police sirens fill the air.

"Olga, don't move. Stay down, the police are coming," Gladys screamed. Olga knows she is badly injured.

Suddenly, Gladys wails again. "Ay dios mio! Oh no...Sweet Jesus, NO!" Gladys noticed her friend Maria.

Maria is in a sitting position. A chain link fence along the side of the church holds her up. The front of her cotton dress is soaked with blood, and she is dazed. Maria's lips are moving as if in silent prayer.

Vic gets an emergency call interrupting his meeting. Raquel is busy in her office with Emilio and Chris reviewing the serial killer case.

"Vic, it's Joe Myers at the Four Eight. There's been an accident. She's okay, but your mother-in-law is being taken to Barnabas by EMT. She got knocked down in a drive-by. She asks for you." Captain Myers knew Vic for the entire time he was on the job.

"Jesus Christ, Joe, was she hit at all?" Vic blurted.

"No, not at all, but a lady friend is. Doesn't look good for the friend, Vic. She's on route to Barnabas, too," Myers advised.

"I'll be there in twenty," Vic advised.

Vic calls Pando. "Hey, get the SUV, now. We gotta get up to the Bronx. Olga is hurt."

Gonnella walks into Raquel's office. "Baby lets go. Abuela was hurt in the Bronx. She's okay. Let's move now!"

Raquel's olive skin turns almost chalky white. She feels her stomach flip over twice. When she rises from her chair, she is so light-headed she nearly drops to the floor. Raquel regains her composure quickly. She and Vic take the stairs to the street two at a time. Pando is outside the office building in the Escalade.

"Barnabas Hospital, Pando. Lights and sirens."

CHAPTER 21

The tires on the shiny black Escalade squeal on the pavement, leaving a puff or white smoke as Pando put the pedal to the metal. Raquel and Vic sit together in the rear seat. Raquel reaches out and holds Vic's hand tightly.

"Did Meyers say anything else?" Raquel's voice is quivering as she sits on the edge of the black leather seat.

"All he said was Olga is being taken to the hospital. Let me try and call him and see what else he knows," Vic said. He reaches for his cellphone.

Pando is going north on the FDR Drive, zigzagging between cars. He was pushing eighty-five miles per hour as he heads up to the South Bronx to the Sheridan Expressway. The Escalade is outfitted with flashing red and blue lights built into the front and rear bumpers. The siren has an NYPD-approved loud warning system that moves cars out of the way on the busy New York City roadways.

Vic puts the call on speaker.

"Joe...It's Vic. Any news on my mother-in-law?"

"She's pretty banged up pal. I just pulled up to Barnabas. I have a few of my uniforms there just to make sure the docs know she's VIP," Joe Myers stated.

"Is she conscious?" Raquel blurted.

"Oh yeah. My guy said she is more worried about her friend who is hit. I have no intel on that but like I said, doesn't look good."

"Thanks, my friend. We are getting onto the Sheridan. Be there in ten," Vic noted.

"This is the nightmare I was trying to avoid. How many times did I have to warn her about that shithole neighborhood," Raquel seethed.

"Let's not do the 'I told you so,' baby. You know how she gets. Let's just hope she's okay."

Pando hits 95 mph on the Sheridan, making short work of that roadway. He gets off the ramp at the West Farms exit, going around traffic and through three red lights. He zooms past Tremont Avenue, where Olga was shopping earlier that morning, and headed onto the side streets to Barnabas Medical Center. On Southern Boulevard, Pando has to veer off to avoid a city bus and winds up driving on the sidewalk for almost half a block. Raquel and Vic are being jostled in the back seat because of the beat-up streets and Pando's swerving.

Pando pulls the Escalade on two wheels into Barnabas' emergency room entrance on Third Avenue.

Vic and Raquel jump from the SUV and run into the ER. There are cops and plainclothes detectives everywhere. Captain Joe Myers meets them inside.

"The doctors are with her now. Raquel, you knew this is a level two trauma center. The level ones, Lincoln Hospital is crowded, and I thought Jacobi was a bit far. The staff here is pretty good. We bring our guys here," Myers offered.

"Thanks, Joe. Let's see what they have to say, but if she needs surgery…it won't be here," Raquel choked up.

"Agreed. We are here for you…you know that," Myers added.

With all the cops around the ER, out of respect for Vic and Raquel, it is reminiscent of when a cop is shot or injured. The big difference is that when a cop is shot, NYPD brass and the mayor shows up for a soundbite. No matter what, Vic and Raquel are always NYPD family.

Olga is behind drawn curtains in the ER. Gladys is standing next to the unit. She rode in the EMS ambulance with her friend. Raquel embraces Gladys and starts crying holding her tightly.

"We are all in the Lord's hands," Gladys spewed.

Raquel enters the unit without Vic. The doctors are taken aback for a second.

"I'm her daughter. How is she?"

A short, heavyset doctor in gray beard wearing a yarmulke steps in front of Raquel.

"I'll be out in a minute. Please let us finish the examination of your mother."

Raquel backed up out of the unit. It is not a good time to argue.

Dr. Sol Wasserman pushes the curtain aside and comes out with a serious look on his face.

Vic stands next to Raquel.

"She will be fine. I want an MRI taken immediately. I'll see to it that she is not in any real pain. I'm guessing without the MRI, but I'm fairly certain her right hip is fractured," Wasserman stated.

"Oh my God!" Raquel responded. She puts her hands to her face.

Dr. Wasserman reaches for Raquel's shoulders.

"She will be fine. I don't see any signs of internal injuries or brain trauma, but at her age I want to be cautious. She has a strong will and even joked with me. She said she likes Jewish doctors and accountants," Wasserman smiled.

"She didn't!" Raquel blurted.

"She did." Wasserman replied.

"That's Olga for you. Doctor, how is the woman with the gunshot who came in?" Vic asked.

"I'm not on that case but I know they took her straight upstairs to the OR. I will follow up with the surgeon. In the meantime, I suggest you give your mother some time for us to take the tests. We may need a couple of hours. You can go in now to let her know you're here. By the way, I loved your book."

Raquel moves quickly into the unit with Vic tailing her.

"Mama? We are here," Raquel said.

"My loves. I'm okay. I should have listened to you, my baby girl."

"Don't worry about that, Abuela. Let's just get you better," Raquel replied.

Vic noticed the crystal rosary beads intertwined in Olga's hand.

"I am praying for Maria. Her daughter lives way out on Long Island and her son moved to North Carolina. That poor woman," Olga said.

With that, a gurney was pulled into the unit to transport Olga to the MRI. One of the nurses asks everyone to go into the waiting area.

***

Vic has asked one of the uniformed men to take Gladys home, but she refuses, wanting to stay and waiting for news on her two injured friends.

"C'mon Raquel, let's grab a decent cup of coffee," Vic insisted.

They left the ER on Third Avenue and walked half a block to Arthur Avenue. The street is busy, with the outside tables filled with the lunch trade at Enzo's and Mario's restaurants across the street. Cars are already double parked, as shoppers go in and out of the bread, pork, pastry, and fruit and vegetable stores. A few diners are waiting on the sidewalk to get into Dominic's Restaurant.

Dervish, the owner of La Parisian Café, comes out onto the street to greet Vic and Raquel.

"Mr. Vic and Missus. Haven't seen you in so long," Dervish said in is slight Albanian accent.

The couple sits on the aluminum chairs at a small square metal table on the sidewalk.

"Dervish! I'll have a MacCallum's 15, and Raquel will have..."

"Double espresso please. We have to be quick," Raquel added.

They downed their drinks in minutes, Raquel is anxious to get back to Barnabas. Hurry up and wait.

As they walk back, Raquel laments, "A few weeks ago we were in Florence at a café without a care in the world...now this."

"Life is a hard story of twists and turns," Vic added.

***

Two hours later, the NYPD presence gone, Vic and Raquel wait in the Barnabas ER, watching the steady stream of sick and injured people entering for care. Maria's distraught daughter comes in. She never notices Raquel. They grew up as little girls together, but the daughter is too intent on finding information on her mom's condition. A minute later, Father Lopez from St. Thomas Aquinas Church walks into the ER. He looks pale and confused as he approaches the desk. The attendant points to a bank of elevators as Father Lopez disappears to check on Maria.

"I hope he's not here to give the last rites," Raquel quipped.

"Positive vibes, baby. Let's think that he's here to give her a blessing," Vic replied.

"These bastards shooting up the streets will never, ever stop. They are predators killing their own. Innocent old ladies, kids. I've had enough of this sewer of a city," Raquel bemoaned.

Vic stays quiet.

CHAPTER 22

Paul Vogelbach is spending his spare time researching his next victim. He enjoys this part of his calling to help the Lord. His internet research indicates a few cities that are known for an active and growing transgender population. The cities are San Francisco, Portland, Boston, New York, Austin, and New Orleans.

Vogelbach will never return to San Francisco under any circumstances. He also isn't enthusiastic about returning to New York City. Been there, done that. He narrows his search down to Austin and New Orleans.

It takes him a day or two to figure out what, to him, is a meaningful target. And the city Vogelbach selects is New Orleans. He finds a potential victim that is fitting all his criteria.

Teri Arceneaux, a well-known transexual activist in her early fifties, with Cajun roots, is to be Vogelbach's next victim.

Teri's family dates back to the mid-1700s in Acadia, Canada, from where they were forced to flee from British domination. By way of New Brunswick, then Montreal, the Arceneaux clan and tens of thousands of others made their way to Louisiana, settling in the Bayou.

Teri is born, raised and still living in Pierre Part, a town of less than 3,000 inhabitants, an hour and a half by car, due west of New Orleans. The Arceneaux family have been trappers and fisherman since the first of them arrived in Louisiana.

Born a man, Teri was the seventh son of a Roman Catholic family. He always felt like a woman despite him being a tad over six feet tall with a bulky frame. He is built country strong, as are all his brothers.

Because of the strong religious practices that followed the family from Acadia, Teri formerly, known as Terrence, waited until both his parents had passed before he began his transitioning to a woman. Using the pronouns, they/them, Teri's hero is Kaitlin Jenner, formerly the Olympic Gold Medal winner Bruce Jenner, whose transition captured national media attention.

"From as long as I can remember, I felt the pull to be a woman," Teri said in one of their weekly podcasts, which Vogelbach sees on YouTube. "When my brothers would skin a gator or bring home some trapped nutria for their furs, I had to do all to not pass out. Killing these creatures was more than I could stand."

Teri, a vegetarian, is an advocate for not only transgender rights but for the ethical treatment of animals. A vocal spokesperson for PETA, they (Teri) became estranged from their six brothers and their entire family. They live alone in a small, two-bedroom beige aluminum sided house they have built on property inherited from their parents.

Continuing with hormonal treatments, Teri already has breast implants, grew their graying dishwater blond hair to shoulder length, and has regular electrolysis to remove unwanted hair on their face and body. They visited a gym regularly to tone their masculine body, which is a difficult if not impossible challenge. To soften their facial structure, several plastic surgeries are performed with remarkable success.

A tenured professor of Sociology at Nicholls State University in Thibodaux, Louisiana, Teri is a favorite of both male and female cis-gender students as well as the LGBTQ+ college community.

In the main gymnasium, where a rally for LGBTQ+ rights is being held, Teri speaks from a 10-person dais with a fervor that captivates their students, friends, collogues, and invited media. They wear a red top with a fine black border and matching skirt with black prim pumps. Around their neck is a gold chain and crucifix and a gold Mother Theresa medallion. Teri is self-conscious about their height and never wears high heels. Their size 12 shoes are difficult to source locally but easy to find on Amazon.

"Nowhere in the New Testament did Jesus condemn alternative lifestyles. Jesus loves you; he just doesn't love your sins, and I am here to tell you that being gay or transitioning from one gender to another is in no way a sin. Your life is yours to do what you desire. Many of you in this room have families who experience the forced removal of their families from 1755–1764 by the brutal

British during the Déportation des Acadiens. When a government tells its people how they must live, how they must behave, who they must be, how they must think, that is considered a totalitarian state. Thankfully, we live in a place in this hate-driven world which allows an individual to express themselves as they see fit. To be free to be whatever they want to be. I am not embarrassed to say that soon...very soon, I will finish my transition to completely express my total femininity. Let me say to each and every one of you...I love you all for the magnificent heartfelt support...for the solidarity you have shown me from the day I became a professor here at NSU. I pray I have been a beacon to those of you like myself who have gone away from the traditional gender identification into which we were born. I will not deceive anyone who decides to transition. Breaking the shackles of a once suffocating society and smothering religions is not an easy path. I was never a man. Not even one single day of my life. Let me be clear. This whole concept of being assigned a gender at birth troubles me. There are two socially accepted physical genders at birth: male and female. I was born a male because of my penis and testes and assigned as a male. Emotionally I am female, but it took me time to understand there were options I could take. My entire life, I knew I should have been born a woman. But when should I have declared my gender? Is my choice to become a woman a reassignment? I don't think so, but I believe using the words assigned at birth further alienates the transgender world, making us even more misunderstood by society. The grueling path to my true identification was not unlike my ancestors fleeing for their lives from Canada. The big difference between me and them is simple. I fled for my very soul."

The entire rally of over 700 people rise as one in an ocean of thunderous applause. All except for one lone figure sitting on a gray metal folding chair next to the rear door of the gymnasium.

CHAPTER 23

Gjuliana sits on the veranda overlooking Lago Lugano on the Switzerland side next to her infamous husband John Deegan. The lake is reflecting the clear blue sky and shimmering with the late-day sunlight. A lake breeze brings a slight mist, refreshing the elderly couple.

"I waited so many years for you, my love. I think you don't realize how difficult it was for me being so alone for so long. Maybe that's why I find it so difficult when we are apart," Gjuliana said. Her tone is sad yet understanding.

"You have been the most special person I have ever known. Truly, you are the love of my life. It's difficult to be away from you Gjuliana, but..."

"No need to say any more. I know your mind needs to be challenged. You wouldn't be you if you were content to sit here every day and look at this magnificent view. Or drive into Italy for lunch. I know you are not much for shopping, and of course you must stay under the radar. If we traveled the world, that wouldn't be enough for you. But I must be honest. I fear you are around real danger on these escapades of yours and worry that you will be taken from me. After all, you're not chasing shoplifters, John."

"Nah. They have to worry about me!" John announced. He mimics a gorilla pounding his chest.

"You're not fifteen anymore, my love. You aren't playing handball or basketball with the boys on the Aqueduct in the Bronx," Gjuliana uttered.

"I betcha I can still play," Deegan joked.

"John, I see how you pick up your socks to toss them in the clothes hamper. The age is catching up, my dear."

"Numbers. That's all age is, my precious. I feel better than ever, except for the bag of pain old age had brought," Deegan laughed.

Deegan continues. "These escapades of mine, as you call them, are what keep me sharp. Okay, I'll admit it, but only to you, my love. I can't move like I once did, but my mind is sharper than ever. This is what's keeping me focused on life. I have to keep active mentally as well as physically. Mind over matter, Gjuli. It's elementary, my love."

"At any rate, I insist you call me often from the States. Every day would be nice," Gjuliana appealed.

"I promise. Now, let's have a snack together so I can get on the road. I'm sure I won't have any decent food until this case is solved."

Deegan isn't big on long and tearful goodbyes. There is very little sentimentality in his genius mind.

Once the light dinner — a potato and egg omelet with some onions, topped off with Beluga caviar — arrives, John insists on pouring Heinz ketchup on in his plate to dip the egg and potatoes. Gjuli has baked some semolina Italian bread. They share a nice bottle of Antinori Chianti Classico and finish with homemade Baklava, from a recipe given to Gjuli by her Albanian grandmother.

Deegan gives his wife a quick peck on the cheek, and he is off. Gjuliana takes it in stride, saying a silent prayer which she memorized as a child even though her family was Muslim. *"O Glorious Saint Christopher; you have inherited a beautiful name, Christ bearer, as a result of the wonderful story that while carrying people across a raging stream you also carried the Child Jesus. Teach us to be true Christ bearers to those who do not know Him. Protect all of us that travel both near and far; and petition Jesus to be with us always. Amen."*

John's regular driver takes the best route from Lugano to Milan, making the 51-mile trip in 50 minutes. Having access to the tarmac for private planes and having avoided the security check-in, John is aboard the leased Learjet 36A in no time. The driver places Deegan's two suitcases in the hold, while John carries his old St. Nicholas of Tolentine High School gym bag onboard with him. Deegan has owned this bag for 59 years, first using it during his freshman year. This is the first time he took it back on an overseas trip.

The Malpensa, Milan to Teterboro, New Jersey flight was 3,995 nautical miles, with a stop to refuel at St. John's International Airport in Newfoundland and Labrador. The Learjet 36A needs a bit more fuel capacity to make the trip nonstop, but John isn't in a hurry. The case would wait for him.

***

Raquel's mom is already transferred to Lenox Hill Hospital in Manhattan for hip surgery. Dr. Sol Wasserman explained the basics to Olga, Raquel, and Vic at Barnabas Medical Center in the Bronx, but the orthopedic surgeon at Lenox Hill wants to explain things his way.

Raquel thought it is important to tell Gabriella of her abuela's injury so she would understand the process. Understandably, Gabby was hysterical when she was told the news after Vic and Raquel had Pando swing by at the Chapin School to pick up their daughter on the way to Lenox Hill. It took a few minutes to calm the young woman down.

Once at Lenox Hill, where many of the rich and famous and the biggest professional athletes in the world are treated, the head of orthopedic surgery, Dr. M. Stuart Adler, met with Vic, Raquel, and Gabriella in his office. Olga is scheduled for surgery within the hour.

"Let me go through the basics with you, and I will speak in laymen's terms, so you have a clear understanding," Dr. Adler begins. In his office stands a plastic model of a hip and pelvis. He points to the model as he speaks.

"This is a very serious injury. A fractured hip, like Olga has, is a complete break of the femur, what is known commonly as the thigh bone. See here where the femur meets the pelvic bone. This is where the MRI shows the damage is. She also has some osteoporosis, which is relative to her age. The surgery ideally must be done as soon as possible to prevent complications, especially in a person of Olga's age. Now I need to tell you some things that may be shocking to you, but before I do I want to tell you that Olga is in very good shape physically, and I expect her to experience a full recovery. After surgery of this kind, Olga can expect to stay here for ten days to two weeks. I suggest she stay here or be admitted to one of our affiliated locations for rehab. Now when I say full recovery, I want to be totally transparent with you. Only one in four patients fully recovers from a hip surgery at your mom's age. Also, you need to know that twenty percent of patients die within the first year."

Raquel covers her mouth with her hands. "*Oh God*!" she exclaims. Gabby starts to cry again.

"That is worst case scenario, but you need to know this because the three of you need to be there to help with the recovery and rehab. There is another important component to this injury. Depression and the loss of independence becomes a major factor. We need to make sure that, psychologically, Olga doesn't feel as if her quality of life is diminished."

"Any questions so far?" Dr. Adler asks.

"What about pain, doctor?" Vic asks.

"It's no walk in the park, Mr. Gonnella. We will manage the pain the best we can post op. The rehab is rougher for some people than others, but she seems feisty and determined. She will do well in my opinion, but you guys must be her cheering section."

"Will she limp after this?" Raquel asks.

"I hope not. Let's see how she tolerates the surgery and how she takes to rehab. I have patients older than Olga who have done great and some that immediately take to a wheelchair, but I must tell you it has a lot to do with how the patient reacts emotionally to the experience. I promise she is in the best of hands here. You are in the right place. We really know how to do our jobs."

"Money is no object, Doctor Adler," Raquel blurts.

"It's nice to be financially well off, but that is the least of our concerns. Olga is on Medicare. Her hard work as an American is the least the country owns her. Put it out of your mind. Now, Gabriella, let me go fix your grandma."

***

Barnabas Medical Center in the Bronx is just nine miles from Lenox Hill Hospital on Park Avenue and 77th Street. The difference in the neighborhoods is like two different worlds. So is the medical care.

Maria's daughter couldn't get information on her mother's condition. She became so distraught that she passed out, collapsing on the floor of the emergency room waiting area. The nurses wheeled her in and set her up in a unit for evaluation.

Along with the normal medical emergencies at Barnabas, victims of two more shootings and a stabbing were rushed in by EMS, along with two wounded uniformed NYPD police officers.

The ER became bedlam. At least 10 police officers and detectives are milling around the lobby of the emergency room and around the wounded officers. One of the shot-up patients watches by the detectives is in critical condition and rushed to the operating room. One of the cops, shot just below his Kevlar amour, is in serious condition. He is also in the OR.

Captain Joe Meyers is waiting for the NYPD brass from Bronx Command and One Police Plaza HQ and the Mayor of the City of New York, who are in route. Media trucks are already on 3rd Avenue outside the hospital. A small crowd of onlookers stands behind the reporters as they did their soundbites.

"What do we have, Lu?" Meyers inquires of one of his supervisors.

"One of our undercovers got a lead on this morning's shooters outside Aquinas Church. Our guys found the blue BMW on Clinton Avenue near 180th. We moved in with five squad cars, a few undercovers, and the SWAT unit. Shots were fired. Nelson will be okay, a graze to the leg. Ray Briggs is in bad shape. Got him right here," the lieutenant pointed to his lower abdomen.

"Any other perps?"

"Two. They surrendered. We have them at the four eight. The detective unit is interrogating them."

Meyers saw Dr. Sol Wasserman heading to his wounded police officer.

"Hey, doc? How are my guys?"

Wasserman points to the unit where Patrolman Nelson was being attended. "This guy will be fine. Superficial wound. The officer upstairs is critical. The surgeons must see the extent of his internal injuries. Too soon to tell," Wasserman replies. "It's been insane all day. From this morning's shootings to this. And it's not even dark out yet."

"How is that lady we came in with?" Meyers asks.

"I'm just about to see her family. She's in an induced coma. I'm told she has considerable damage to her large intestine. Her spleen and gall bladder were removed, plus there is some liver damage. Peritonitis is always a concern with injuries like this. It's touch and go. The next forty-eight hours will tell the story," Wasserman replies.

CHAPTER 24

GG calls Special Agent Salerno for a meeting in her office. It is difficult for her to go up onto the higher floors, although she does so when absolutely necessary. She attends the daily meetings mostly by Skype, occasionally walking up the stairs and staying in the rear of the bullpen.

Salerno and Cis Burns go to GG's office immediately.

"Hi, GG. I hope you don't mind that he dragged me along?" Burns asked.

As usual, Gail Gain stares above her visitors' heads and doesn't reply for an awkward twenty seconds.

"I...I always like to see you, Cecilia," GG muttered into her hand.

Cis is floored that GG calls her by her name.

"So, what do you have GG?" Salerno asks.

Again, no eye contact and strange silence from Gain.

"Well, I received a call this morning. I tape all my incoming calls, so I want you to hear it with your own ears," GG offers. She fumbles with her desktop clicking away until she found the right file. "Here it is. I've listened to it five times."

"Ms. Gail Gain. I am calling in regard to your recent serial killer case if you can spare a moment," the male voice said. The accent clearly had an Irish brogue.

"Who is this?" GG asks.

"You will never in a million years guess, and in your case, it would truly be just a guess. Never mind that for now. I want to give you some clues on the alphabet mafia killer."

"Clues?"

"Well, if you don't want them, I can always just tell one of the news networks. Don'tcha know the one having a field day with the corrupt FBI."

"Explain alphabet mafia, please." GG asked.

"Oh, ya know what I'm referring to, GG. Ya know full well."

"I'm listening."

"The next one the surgeon will be doing is in the lovely transexual community. And if I'm correct, as I normally am, the victim will be a woman transitioning into becoming a man."

"And how are you so sure?" Gain asks.

"It's a gift me love. God-given gift at that. Anyway, that's all the time I have at the moment. All the best to ya." The line goes dead.

GG looks at the ceiling above Salerno and Burns' heads.

"Prank call?" Salerno asks.

"No," GG replies.

"Then, what?"

"I know who the caller is," Gain replies.

Another awkward moment passes.

"In his own way, he's putting us on the right track. He wants to make sure the Bureau is moving in the right direction. It's because he sees the FBI as his competitors, and he thrives on winning. This is all like a game of chess to him. He makes his moves based on the killer's moves and our moves. It's a sick, twisted game," GG stated. She looks a bit flustered and pulls a Pall Mall from its package. Fumbling with a book of matches, it seems Gail Gain's hand trembles slightly.

"You know who he is, Gail?" Cis asks.

"I'm certain about it."

Burns can tell Salerno is losing his patience. She eases the answer out of GG.

"Is it someone I would know?"

"It's someone everyone knows."

"Do you want me to guess, GG?" Cis smiles.

GG looks at her strangely. The Pall Mall hangs limply between her chapped lips.

"It's John Deegan," GG announces.

Salerno and Burns look at one another as people do when something is either funny, silly or sad.

"John Deegan? The serial killer John Deegan?" Salerno offers.

"Yes." GG says nothing more to substantiate her theory.

Salerno shifts his weight in his seat.

"Okay, GG. What makes you so sure? Did you do a voice screen? Have you checked the incoming call log?" Burns inquires.

"I don't have to. It's Deegan."

"Respectfully, GG, Deegan hasn't been seen or heard from in nearly ten years. Even Interpol had no clue of his whereabouts. He may even be dead for all we know," Salerno advises.

"It was Deegan. It's the game he plays. It's classic Deegan. He wants us to fish for the killer so he could call again and say I told you so. He's already predicting the next homicide and likely has the next one already figured out."

"And the brogue?" Salerno asks.

"It's one of his favorites. He loves disguises. His clothing and his accent. Deegan is a master chameleon. He's uses that brogue many times before. I've thought a lot about this. The accent he uses is in tribute to his Irish ancestors. He pulls that trick in Dublin where he murdered two people. It's Deegan alright, and he will call me again," GG blurts.

"Let's get Tech Support down here to wire up your phones, GG." Salerno orders. "Maybe we can pull him in."

"Well, that would make big headlines for you," GG says, with more than a hint of sarcasm. "He's already figured out that move. And he's two steps ahead of you. Respectfully, we are all amateurs when compared to Deegan." GG declares.

CHAPTER 25

"I will never return to my old neighborhood again. Never!" Olga pronounces from her bed at Lenox Hill Hospital on swanky East 77th Street in Manhattan. "I'm praying so hard for Maria that my rosary is worn. I pray the Blessed Virgin will intercede with her Holy Son to save Maria's life."

"Mama, the best thing right now is to relax and heal. "We are so blessed that you are still here with us," Raquel says. Vic and Gabriella stand at the front of the bed while Raquel sits in a chair next to her mother, holding her hand.

"You tried to tell me so many times, daughter. Years ago, when you were a little girl, the area was rough but not like today. These animals go by shooting at each other while good people wind up hurt or God forbid for Maria...dead."

"Times change, mama. The police don't even have the ability to stop these bad people. You have a beautiful home with us forever, and we need you around us," Raquel added.

"Abuela, after all, who is going to make us Bustello in the morning and cook all that great Puerto Rican food," Vic laughs.

"My daughter is capable. I taught her from when she was eight years old."

"Abuelita, now you need to teach me, and I'm a slow learner," Gabby offers.

"Yes, my love. I will teach you the old ways from the island, as my grandmother and mother taught me. It's the best way for you to remember me. As soon as I get out of here, your lessons will start."

"Mama, the doctor said the surgery went perfectly. After you are healed the rehab starts, and we will be with you every step of the way," Raquel says.

"What do you hear of Maria?" Olga asks.

Vic speaks up. "She is resting. The doctors are doing everything they can. Her daughter and son are at the hospital and staying at her apartment. Everyone is praying for her."

"You brought me here because it's a better hospital. Can we bring Maria, too?"

"Mama, we offered to help but it's not a good time to move her," Raquel states. She glances quickly at Vic.

"I think you are lying to me. For all I know, Maria can already be with Jesus."

Gabby moves to be next to her grandmother and took her hand from Raquel's. "Abuelita, we would never do that. Maria is in intensive care and fighting hard. I promise to tell you even if the worst happens, but right now, she is still with us. Jesus will have to wait."

"The Lord will take her when it's her time, baby girl. I'm also asking Him in my prayers to save her."

***

Emilio and Chris are getting frustrated with the investigation. They asked to meet with Vic and Raquel, mostly for their guidance but really to use the couple as a sounding board. When the couple returned from seeing Olga, they all met in the firm's conference room again. Emilio and Chris brought their laptops, which are filled with data, to the meeting.

"Any new ideas, you guys?" Vic asks.

Emilio clears his throat. "Just to review Vic and Raquel, we've poured over every report, every photograph of the autopsies and the crime scenes. Nothing at all connects the victims with their telephone records or backgrounds. We are certain the victims never knew each other. The only common denominators are ketamine, the muscle relaxant, and the precise surgeries. The drugs aren't easy to track. Virtually every hospital and surgical center in the country uses these drugs or variants like them. This guy is not only clever but he's very careful. He hasn't made one mistake."

Raquel interrupts. "Yet... He hasn't made a mistake yet."

"Correct," Vic adds. "He will kill again, and all we can hope for is that one mistake that may lead us to him."

"It's bizarre that we are waiting for another human being to be killed," Chris blurts.

"But we know he will hit again, and this time the T for transexual will be the target," Raquel says.

"It's a big country, and he has traveled all over the United States," Emilio offers. "There are more transexuals than we can imagine."

Raquel follows up. “Frankly, we just need to wait and hope for a clue. Sometimes, but not very often, a serial killer wants to be found. In the Deegan case we were given plenty of clues. Let’s hope that we’re good enough to decipher one.”

***

Teri Arceneaux isn’t going to be an easy target for Paul Vogelbach. Paul isn’t at all familiar with the Bayou, and for the first time the killer needs to use the fake identification he has made a while ago. It was his fallback in case he is ever pulled over by law enforcement. To get back and forth from the school to Teri’s home, Paul needs to rent a vehicle. No public transportation would work in that part of Louisiana, so he needs a driver’s license to obtain a rental. He would pay cash, of course, but Paul is very conscious not to leave any loose ends.

Teri’s life is generally a simple one. Teri would drive the 45 minutes to work from their home in Pierre Mont in Assumption Parish to Thibodaux in Lafourche Parish. From time to time, they make a doctor’s appointment and have a weekly visit to their esthetician for hair removal and makeup. For the most part, Teri’s life is boring. They aren’t ready to take on a love interest, wanting to get themselves completely set as a woman before starting the next leg of their journey. They crave intimacy but wants to wait for the right time and the right person who would accept her for who she is.

Paul tracks Teri for four days, selecting that Friday night to make his move. He has rented a nondescript Jeep

Wrangler from a local rent-a-car spot near the college and would return it there before he went to the New Orleans airport by taxi to return to Milwaukee. He expects to be home in plenty of time to make Reverend Stewart's service on Sunday. The killer will do everything he can not to miss a sermon.

After Teri's classes ended at 4:45 in the afternoon, they milled around with a few of their students and have a coffee. It isn't until 5:30 that Teri finally approaches their car in the facility parking lot. Vogelbach is waiting patiently in his Jeep near the entrance of the lot. He follows Teri back to Pierre Part as he did the prior three days, being careful not to tail them too closely to arouse any suspicion.

The 45-minute ride ran an hour and fifteen as Teri stopped to pick up their dinner at Cyril's Roadside. Every Friday, Teri likes to reward themselves with a cold one and a couple of Cyril's famous Shrimp Po Boys. The counter help at Cyril's never looks at Teri with judging eyes or raised brows, and they appreciated that. They may have talked about Teri after they left, but they never showed a hint of disrespect.

Vogelbach is momentarily thrown off from Teri's daily routine of going straight home. In the past three days, Teri never once stopped the car. Not even for gasoline. Vogelbach waits on the road outside Cyril's small gravel parking lot. When Teri returns to their car, the sun is setting, and dusk is drawing near.

Vogelbach stays a reasonable distance away from Teri's secluded home as they pulled into their driveway. He waits a while until it is completely dark outside. Taking his trusty black bag, the killer walks slowly toward Teri's home passing by a few times to see if they were alone in the house. They were. Only one room was lit, and Vogelbach could see Teri walking around inside in what he assumed was their kitchen.

Paul taps lightly on the screen door, which covered the white wooden main entrance of the home. He could hear his victim shuffling to the door. Teri turns the outdoor light on over the main door, leaving the screen door closed. Almost immediately mosquitoes, flies and a large moth made their way to the light.

"Can I help you?" Teri asks.

"I hope you can, ma'am.' I believe I'm kinda lost. That GPS is not too much help in these parts. I'm looking for the Rossi home. Can you direct me please?"

Teri looks at the tall, handsome, well-groomed, clean-cut man who is wearing a pressed blue blazer and crisp white shirt. They sense and see no threat.

Teri opens the screen door quickly, stepping outside to keep the bugs from entering their home.

"Well, there aren't many homes around here." Teri points with their right arm toward the right of her property. "A way down the road there is another family. I don't think they are Italian, though. Real Cajun family."

Vogelbach attacks quickly and with great force. He grabs Teri's right arm and tries to twist it behind their back. The killer has a syringe in his left hand, which he planned to plunge into his victim's neck. Teri instinctively tried to pull themselves away from the intruder. Not being a small person, Teri still has deceptive man strength. Knowing that screaming wouldn't be of any help in this desolate area, Teri makes their move, running toward the marshy backwater about 60 yards from the front of their home. Teri figures they know the terrain better than this cretin; whomever he is. They are in their stocking feet and could feel the boggy ground seeping through their toes. Vogelbach is all over Teri, grabbing Teri with his strong right arm around their neck. Even that is a challenge to get around Teri's bulky neck and shoulders. Panicked, Teri gras his arm with both hands, attempting to free themselves from his vice like grip. Teri feels a sharp sting in their neck and suddenly realizes they were falling to the ground.

***

Teri starts to regain some semblance of consciousness. They sense they are in their bed, but their vision is blurred. They kept passing in and out until they heard a man's voice. Their body is completely paralyzed except for their ability to breathe, and they are laboring to do that.

"Wasn't too easy dragging you back in here. You certainly aren't a small woman...Or is it a man? I'm still not sure about what you call those of you who decide to break God's natural law," Paul said. His tone is a matter of fact. The killer busied himself with the contents of his black bag.

Teri is trying to make sense of his words but cannot focus.

"I know you have a Christian background, but I can't phantom how you would take it into your own mind to change what our Lord designed you to be. After all, you, like me, were made in God's own image and likeness. So, are you telling the God of us all made a mistake with you? What is so wrong about being a man in the first place? And look up at that crucifix you have hanging on the wall. How can you be a follower of Jesus and make yourself into something you are not? I say that is hypocritical."

The murderer knows he isn't about to receive an answer from his stunned victim. He continues to play around in his black bag, which he has placed on Teri's bureau. Paul has placed a white sheet, which he pulled off Teri's bed and placed it over their naked body.

"I watched your lecture at the school. I had all to do not to vomit from the adulation you received from the students. Did you ever realize you are poisoning the younger generation with your own sexually deviant thoughts? How could you defy the Bible with such evil? I am convinced that what you and others like you are doing is far worse than what was done at Sodom and Gomorrah. I truly believe you are evil and are doing the work of Satan to destroy God's work on earth. This is why I am sending you to Him for judgement. If the Lord decides to forgive you after you are judged, then he will be the loving God I have come to embrace. I am simply doing His work. But I don't believe that will be the case. Anyway, this will not be painful. I abhor when people have pain."

CHAPTER 26

Rumors have begun to swirl among the LGBTQ community after the third of Paul Vogelbach's murders and the awful desecration of the victims' bodies.

Not since 1981 had rumors in the gay community been as rampant, when gay men had symptoms which appeared to be immune system disorders. Young, actively homosexual men were dying from what was first termed to be the 'gay men's disease'. The *New York Times* had run an article entitled 'Rare Cancer Seen in 41 Homosexuals'. Doctors were initially confused by the unique symptoms and concerned that the disease could be contagious. After a while, undertakers wouldn't even handle the bodies of gay men. They generally sealed the bodies in body bags and would not perform embalming or have open viewings. Panic had set in.

The gay community experienced the outbreak of HIV and AIDS in the 1980s and 1990s, even though the disease originated a few decades earlier. Nearly thirty-five million people have died from AIDS since its inception.

Only three murders, and the LGBTQ community are looking over their shoulders waiting for the next victim to be taken. It was reminiscent of the Son of Sam murders in 1976 and 1977, when a serial killer had killed six innocent young people. The streets of Brooklyn, Queens, and the Bronx were virtually empty in the evenings as young lovers, especially brunette women and their boyfriends, awaited word of the next victim, until David Berkowitz was apprehended.

This killer has a much wider field, crossing from New York to Los Angeles to Las Vegas. The next murder could be anywhere where there is a person with an alternative lifestyle.

***

John Deegan has plenty of time to think about where the next victim could be as he traveled from Milan to New York. He knows for sure that the next homicide would be a transexual person, but even his genius had come up short in predicting where it would occur. Deegan checked into a suite at the swanky five-star midtown Manhattan Loews Regency Hotel on Park Avenue and 61st Street, within walking distance of Vic and Raquel's townhouse.

The wanted international serial killer called Vic's cell phone after ten o'clock the evening of his arrival.

"Mr. Gonnella, so nice to hear your melodious voice," Deegan announces himself.

"We were watching a ballgame, but I can see that's not going to happen now," Vic jokes.

"Put me on speaker if Raquel is around."

"Done...She's here," Vic states.

"Hello my lovely!"

"Hi, John. Hope you are well."

"I am well and even better hearing you two. I'm in Manhattan, and hopefully we can see each other. I have some great disguises to try out on you both."

"Can't wait," Vic offers with more than a hint of sarcasm.

"So, we are just a day or so past the witching hour. The next murder hasn't been reported unless you two know something I don't, which I highly doubt," Deegan chuckles.

"No news is good news. Maybe he stopped," Raquel states.

"Nope. It just hasn't been reported. As sure as night follows day, this guy has already left a body somewhere. His pattern is steady, and his objective is clear. He will go down the alphabet mafia until he runs out of letters," Deegan lectures.

"So, tell us. What is his objective?" Vic asks.

"Elementary, my dear Watson. To me, he is clearly making a religious statement, or on the other hand, he is gay or one of the other elements of the LGBTQ... without the L."

"You sound sure of yourself," Vic replies.

"Only because I am, Victor."

"So now we wait?" Raquel blurts.

"What else is there to do? In my opinion, he has already killed a transexual somewhere within the last 48 hours. Hopefully, he will slip up so maybe we can figure out his next move," Deegan replies. He takes a deep breath and continues. "I have decided where his next one will be after this one. I did a lot of research. I guess you really must be a serial killer to figure one out."

"So, tell us what you're thinking," Vic says.

"Raquel, how is your mom? Is she resting after the surgery?" Deegan asks, ignoring Vic's question.

"How did you know about that?"

"I'll bring her some flowers and some snacks." Deegan ends the call.

"That son of a bitch. Just once I want to get him to tip his hand. He hangs up the phone and I want to bang my head against the damn wall," Vic shouts.

CHAPTER 27

On Monday morning, Professor Teri Arceneaux doesn't show for their 8:10 class at the school. They had a perfect attendance in all the years they were a professor, sending up a red flag. Teri's department head is notified and immediately begins calling their cell phone. The phone goes directly to voicemail. Their home phone goes to an answering machine after six rings. Something is wrong, and it isn't just car trouble.

The Assumption Parish Sheriff's Department is called upon to a do welfare check at Teri Arceneaux's home. Sargent Clint Deveraux is dispatched at ten o'clock that morning. Deveraux knows the Arceneaux family well. He has played high school football with two of Teri's brothers and is a drinking buddy with two others. Everyone in Pierre Part seems to know one another.

Deveraux approaches the house with his two-way radio, the microphone snugly attached under his uniforms epilate. The sergeant notices Teri's car in the driveway. He rings the doorbell and heard the chime from inside. Getting no answer, he taps on the screen door, announcing himself. Still no answer. Deveraux opens the screen door and pounds on the wooden front door. He checks the front door. It is locked.

Deveraux moves around the house, looking for any signs of Teri Arceneaux. The home is neat and orderly, not even a dish in the kitchen sink or papers on the counter. He notices an unopened bag from Cyril's and an open bottle of beer on the kitchen table.

The sergeant calls his headquarters to report his findings. After a short wait he is told by his lieutenant to await backup and then enter the house through any easy access he could make. He thinks about calling one of the Arceneaux brothers to see if they had a key but decides not to involve the family, knowing there was a rift about Teri's lifestyle. Deveraux double-checks the ground floor rooms again through the windows in case he missed anything while he awaits backup. Ten minutes later, a sheriff's department SUV pulls up with two patrolmen. One male, one female.

"Best way to get inside is through the back door. It enters into the kitchen. We can break a panel of glass and open the door. I hope we don't find her dead on the floor," Deveraux says. Each officer checks their bodycams to make sure they were all operable for the record.

Deveraux takes a baton and taps on the glass until it shatters. He pushes the glass fragments away with the baton, put his hand inside, and easily opens the lock on the door. All three officers enter the home.

Immediately, a strong stench greets them. The cops are no strangers to the odor of a decomposing body. "Damn, that's nasty," the male patrol officer blurts. Deveraux chokes at the smell. The female cop takes a handkerchief from her back pocket and holds it to her mouth and nose.

Deveraux gets on his two-way. “Come in, Charlie.”

“Go on, D.”

“We have a DOA here at the Arceneaux home. We haven’t seen the body yet, but it’s ripe in here. We’re moving upstairs. Send some Vicks, will ya.”

“Roger that. Confirm DOA.”

“Roger... stand by.”

Deveraux slowly leads the two others up the wooden steps to the second story. The closer they get to the bedrooms, the worse the odor is. On the second story landing both the bedroom and the bathroom doors are closed.

The female patrolman uses her handkerchief to open the first bedroom door. What they see makes them all take a step back.

On the bed is a bloated Teri Arceneaux. Their abdomen is at least three times its normal size. Their skin has turned a leathery brown, almost black color, with flies and maggots crawling all around their head. A sheet covers the torso, filled with crawling insects. Two discolored mounds were on top of the sheet just under the DOA’s neck.

“Looks like foul play. Those things look like silicone,” the female officer notes.

Sticky-looking fluids run from under the bloated body, dripping onto the beige carpet. Teri’s jaw is wide open, with a bubbly stream of maggots pouring in and out and through their nostrils. The window and draperies in the tidy room are covered with flies and other flying bugs. The male officer rushes from the scene down the stairs and outside into the backyard, where he put his hands on his knees, gasped, and vomits.

"Come on, Charlie," Deveraux calls the dispatcher.

"Go ahead, D."

"Body confirmed. Send homicide. This is ugly," Deveraux gasps. His eyes and nose are running like faucets from the vile stink of death.

***

Deveraux, the homicide detectives from the Sheriff's department, and the Parish coroner could do nothing but wait until the FBI and their forensics team arrives at the scene. The Baton Rouge FBI office made it very clear that the case is under federal jurisdiction due to the serial killer status.

Special agent Salerno and Cis Burns took whatever information they have and went to see Gail Gain in her ground floor office.

"GG, we have some news," Burns opens the conversation.

Cis and Salerno immediately notices a change in GG's appearance. She is wearing a fresh flowery print dress and actually had her hair done. It appears as if she went to a salon. It is an old-fashioned cut, and there is a bit of auburn color added. It is still a bit of a rat's nest, but the degree of messy had lessened. There is still the ever-present plume of cigarette smoke from her Pall Malls. GG holds the butt to the point where it is about to burn her fingers. The top of the straw in her can of Diet Pepsi has a ring of red lipstick, and GG's cheeks are smeared with two red blobs of rouge. It is the first time anyone has seen Gail Gain with makeup. Cis thought she looks a lot like Bette Davis in the classic movie 'What Ever Happened to Baby Jane?' it was startling. In fact, GG looks more like the Countess Aurel from Madwoman of Chaillot, played by Katherine Hepburn in the 1969 film.

GG stares at the ceiling above Cis's head but this time offers an almost bizarre smile.

"I like your new outfit and your hairdo, Gail," Cis Burns offers. She is trying to be polite.

Again, the strange ceiling look and delay reaction from GG.

"Thank you for noticing," GG murmurs. She seems flattered but it is hard to tell her real feelings.

Salerno interrupts. "There's been another killing with the same fingerprint as the others. Our field office in Baton Rouge is on the scene. We should have details soon."

GG looks down at her cracked and nicotine-stained fingernails. "A transgender, I suppose. A man to a woman, I will predict."

"Seems that way. Another brutalization of the corpse. This time the victim's silicone breasts were removed," Salerno adds. Another pregnant pause from the master of serial killer profiling.

"That fits his pattern," GG blurts. "With each victim he's makes a statement. With Layla Cole, he took her ovaries. He took her ability, at least symbolically, to procreate. With Gary Pose, he effectively took his penis away, making it something else of no use to him, and then his testicles. Pose had no need for them, in the killer's mind. Remember with Blake DuMont he took his tongue, the ability to tell which way he was swinging. And now with this latest victim he took her breasts. Why? He deemed she never needed to nurture another person. Fake breast, ergo fake persona. The religious symbolisms are clear. His God would approve, as the victims all have mocked the natural laws of humanity by being LGBT.... the next will be Q. He likely will begin all over again back to L, as he believes what he is doing is pleasing to the divine. And most of all, like many serial killers, he is enjoying himself."

Salerno feels himself staring at GG. Her analysis is brilliant. What he doesn't know is that the infamous serial killer John Deegan had figured this out weeks ago.

"Your theory sounds spot on, GG," Cis Burns says.

GG smiles and looks down at her hands again. "To me, the theory is only good if we apprehend the perp and learn something for the future."

CHAPTER 28

Seven hours after the FBI agents and their forensics team arrive at Teri Arceneaux's home, they begin sending field reports by e-mail to Special Agent Dean Salerno at the Child Abduction / Serial Murder Investigative Resources Center in Langley, Virginia. The state-of-the-art technology on which the FBI spent hundreds of millions of taxpayer dollars would have made J. Edgar Hoover proud.

The Assumption Parish Sheriff's office personnel are relegated to being spectators, as the FBI controls the case, but the agents are sensitive to their feelings, asking them to set up perimeters and asking Sargent Deveraux and the two other officers to stay around to be debriefed. The cops are happy. They would be clocking in for much needed overtime, which normally they wouldn't have.

Salerno already disseminates some of the reports to his key agents, including Cis Burns. The bullpen is humming with activity. Salerno calls for a staff meeting at 8 p.m.

"Cis, your job will be to get GG up to our bullpen. Don't take any shit. We need her. She's going to be kicking and screaming," Salerno warns.

"I'll offer to walk her up the stairs, and I'll run to CVS to get some nicotine gum and a vape. That should keep her calm for a bit," Burns blurts.

"I noticed something in our last meeting with GG," Salerno fishes.

"What was that?"

"I think she likes you."

"What can I say? I'm a likeable kind of gal," Cis laughs.

"I mean *like* like."

Cis pauses to take in the comment.

"Like? *Like*...Like?"

"Yup. She has a different look when you are around, and I can see she's trying to impress you."

"And the new look? You think that's for me?" Cis asks.

"Pretty sure, Cis. She looks at you even when she's talking to me," Salerno says.

"Please put my transfer in to Fairbanks, Alaska, or Bangor, Maine," Cis kidders.

"We can get a hell of a lot out of that genius mess if you can tolerate it."

"I sure can, boss. My job is to help the team find this maniac. I'll do what I have to do...within limits of course."

At 7:45, Cis went to collect Gail Gain. She is greeted with a gray plume of Pall Mall smoke and the aroma of musky, cheap drug store perfume.

"Meetings in 15 minutes, Gail. I bought you some special gum and a vape so you feel comfortable, and I have Diet Pepsi on ice," Cis offers.

GG looks at her like a deer caught in a car's headlights. Well, she actually looks above Cis's head before looking into her face.

"I appreciate you. You are a very nice person. I really hate these meetings. I think everyone in that room is staring at me and judging. Making fun of me like when I was in elementary school," GG mumbles.

"That's because they are in awe of you. Your reputation as a profiler precedes yours. It's like when the rookies get into the locker room with Tom Brady?"

"Who?"

"Never mind that. It's a football analogy. Gail, you are respected and admired so much by everyone, and they may be a bit intimidated. I'm really surprised you didn't figure that out. C'mon, let's walk upstairs."

GG stands up from her desk and takes a long pull on her Pall Mall. Smoke came out of her mouth and both nostrils. She seems confused and looks around the room and at her desk as if she isn't going to return for a week. Finally, she walks toward the door, Cis taking her gently by her elbow.

When they arrived upstairs to the bullpen, Salerno notices GG and Cis and is ready to go. He announces the meeting is in session.

"Okay, gang. Thanks to ViCap we were notified almost immediately after the murder in Pierre Part, Louisiana, was reported.

"There is no doubt that the victim was killed by our guy. First off, as Gail Gain predicted, the victim is transgender...male to female. There was a neat surgical removal of silicone breasts, with little blood spilled. Blood test results and official cause of death will be completed by the morning, but it's a safe assumption there will be ketamine and rocuronium bromide in the blood. There is also an injection mark into the victim's neck, even though the body was badly decomposed."

"Jim, what have you gleaned from the early reports I sent you?" Salerno asks his go-to agent.

"I think we may have our first real clue. Forensics did a great analysis doing a fine-toothed comb job. Retracing the scene, it looks as though the victim ran from the house and headed toward the marsh in the Bayou. That was evident by the boggy wet dirt between the victim's toes. The toe dirt matched the soil samples near the marsh, and there were some deep footprints in the mush signifying that the victim is carried back to the house. The perp has to be strong enough to carry a two-hundred-plus pound dead-weight individual without dragging the victim back into the home. Forensics confirms that the perp has to be over six feet tall to put the drop on the victim, who is also over six feet. This matched the height of the perp that we saw on the videos from the New York City and Las Vegas killings. Most importantly, we have boot prints. There were a few of them in the marsh. We found prints of the victims' bare feet and clear boot prints."

"That's huge," Salerno blurts.

"Yes, sir. Molds are being sent up to us tonight, but there is a clear logo on the middle of the souls of the boots. The manufacturer is Thursday Boots."

"Have we been able to find out about the company? Anyone ever hear of them?"

No one replied. A few agents shake their heads.

"Sir, I had asked Lois to track down intel on Thursday Boots," Jim announces.

Lois, a tall, short dark-haired agent rises from her cubicle.

"The Thursday Boots have a variety of styles. From what we can see, it looks to be their Captain style. They have a unique twelve circles imbedded on the sole and three on the heal. The Thursday logo is imprinted with the logo on the back of the sole. Forensics measured the size as a men's 13. The company boasts that their products are made in the United States, but a deep dive suggests a small percentage are made in Arkansas and the majority in Guadalajara, Mexico. The leather is all sourced from tier one U.S. cattle. Here is some more positive news. The company has only one store in New York City. There are no other retail stores in the country. They are largely an online store."

"Good work, Lois. I want agents from our New York Field Office at that store in Manhattan the minute they open in the morning. We have seven field offices in Arkansas. Lois, please find out which office covers where these boots are made and have agents there at first light. We need a list of all sales of the Captain, size 13 for the past two years, and then we start looking at anyone who bought them. I have to assume the online sales are all done by credit card. Let's not assume the owner is in Louisiana, based on the killer's penchant for traveling to his victims," Salerno orders.

Gail Gain coughs, signaling that she wants to speak. The nicotine vape hung from her red lips.

"GG? A comment?" Salerno asks.

GG looks up at the monitor screens which had photos on the forensic findings. Her usual pause, and then another smoker's cough.

"This is an unusual mistake for a killer who has been so careful with his work so far. But a mistake, nonetheless. I would narrow the search down not only by size but try to determine a religious affiliation as well. He is, in my opinion, someone who has a religious motivation for his killings. Also, cross-reference to a physician or someone who has operating room experience."

GG looks at Cis Burns and smiles.

"One more thing," GG blurts. She seems startled by the loudness of her voice. She puffs on the vape as if it were one of her trusty Pall Malls. "I want to know if anything was missing from the deceased's home. If the killer took a souvenir, I want to know what it is."

Cis looks at Salerno, who makes a mental note.

"Good strategy, GG. We have our work cut out for us. Cis, I want you at the point on this please. Push everything we get from the Thursday Boot Company through our database, and make sure GG reviews the data. With all the negative stuff flying around about the Bureau these days, a collar on this killer can turn things around a bit for us," Salerno declares.

CHAPTER 29

Paul Vogelbach leaves the Louis Armstrong New Orleans International Airport early Saturday morning for his return home to Milwaukee. He has taken his time cleaning himself up from the wet marshy soil that is caked onto his boots and on the bottom of his slacks.

Vogelbach's boots are an important part of his daily exercise routine. He finds these particular boots more comfortable than others he has owned. Paul enjoys the hiking trails at Three Bridges Park in Milwaukee along the Menomonee River. He loves the solitude and the much-needed cardio exercise on the rolling hills of the park which was once an abandoned commercial zone. The views of the Milwaukee skyline are somehow soothing to Vogelbach, who works at a frenetic pace at the hospital and at his practice.

Before leaving Louisiana, the killer went through his medical bag, making a mental note. He needs to refresh his supply of ketamine and rocuronium bromide from his surgical cabinet at the hospital. He is thinking about using vecuronium, another muscle relaxant that he had uses in surgery, but his go-to for the hour he needs is rocuronium. There aren't enough chemicals in his travel bag to complete his next task. He also needs to discard the empty chemical phials which he has left in the bag as a macabre reminder of his work.

When Vogelbach arrives home, the light on the answering machine in the living room is blinking. A red LED number 3 told how many messages awaited. The first is a solicitation from the local Republican Party for the next election seeking funds. Paul quickly hit the delete button. The second is his office manager/secretary reminding him of an early surgery on Monday. The calendar on his cell phone already notes the time and patient's name. Finally, the voice of Reverend Stewart fills the room. "Hello Paul, Reverend Stewart here. Hope to see you at services on Sunday. I'm actually calling to invite you to have dinner with me Sunday evening at five at Milwaukee ChopHouse on North 5th. Please let me know after services if you can make it. I hope you can. Bye for now."

Vogelbach smiles. It would be an honor to spend some time with the reverend, he thought.

At 6 a.m. Sunday morning, Vogelbach dresses quickly in a black Nike jogging suit with thin white stripes running down the sides of his legs and arms. He bent down to lace up his boots from Thursday Boots. Paul drove to a different park for an invigorating five-mile hike. Havenwoods State Forest has a variety of trails through trees, wetlands, and grasslands. The scenery is beautiful, and the aroma of wet grass in the morning is refreshing. The trails are not at all boring like he is walking around his neighborhood or around the hospital complex. Paul wore air pods so he can hear his choice of Christian contemporary music or recorded sermons of Reverend

Stewart. Sometimes he would listen to a surgical seminar, depending on his mood.

Dark sunglasses help to prevent him from making eye contact with the early morning dog walkers but especially to ignore any young women joggers or bicycle riders who may offer a flirtatious smile.

After a hot shower, Vogelbach shaves and dresses in his usual Sunday services attire. As usual, he arrives earlier than anyone in the congregation to sit and clear his mind before another one of Reverend Stewart's memorable sermons.

Reverend Stewart stands behind the lectern. He came twenty minutes late intentionally to build his usual anticipation. The eagerness within the assembly is palpable. Stewart's vibe is very much like any great orator, and he has studied his craft well. Again, he begins his sermon quietly, almost as if he has even more than his normal anxiety about speaking in public.

"Brothers and sisters in the Lord. I am a student of history, as many of you know. Biblical as well as modern day history. Joseph Goebel's Nazi philosophy of propaganda followed a basic tenet. If a lie is told long enough and loud enough, eventually most people will believe it." Stewart pauses to let his parishioners absorb his words. "Long enough and loud enough!" He pauses again for dramatic effect. "Haven't we heard the lies from the gays and liberals long enough? I, for one, am sick and tired of their diatribe."

"Homosexuality is a deceptive perversion. It is an abomination, a sin that is open rebellion against the divine pattern. In both the Old and New Testaments, it states in no uncertain terms that one man and one woman is a marriage covenant." Stewart now begins to raise his voice.

"Marriage is a relationship for life that is indeed the divine pattern which is historically sound. I am speaking ONLY about man and woman marriage. Not man and man nor woman and woman. The Lord created men and women to complete each other. To procreate, to nurture, to teach and to do His work on Earth. God's will works! Just think for a moment." A long pause again. Stewart's eyes seem to look at each and every man, woman, and child, and he scans the crowd.

"Every civilization has been built upon the institution of man and woman marriage and is the underpinning, the very foundation of a moral society. The happiness of couples, the nurturing and growth of our children, the propagation of the faith, the well-being of society, and the orderliness of civilization are all dependent upon the stability of marriage. When this God-given pattern is undermined and thrown into chaos, the whole of society becomes imbalanced. Any deviation from the divine pattern invites disaster. Look what we have being thrown down our throats by the media and by the freak show we all see in Washington, D.C."

Reverend Stewart opens his bible and slams it shut. Many of those in the congregation jump from the sudden sound.

"Armageddon is what I see, brothers and sisters. Yes! The end of days because of this homosexual abomination that is being forced upon our beloved American culture is a satanic plot against the Almighty. I am convinced America is the new Sodom and Gomorrah, and the Lord will destroy us rather than see the sins that are being glorified by the mainstream media. This rebellion against the will of God will bring His rath upon all of humanity because of the radical homosexual agenda that these foolish far-left liberals are advocating."

"I see an intentional silencing of middle America's moral fiber. This is the beginning of the end of America's religious freedom by the merciless gay rights juggernaut."

Stewart folds his arms and begins to scream.

"These satanic interlopers have already conquered our educational system with their so-called liberal-thinking teachers and professors. They have destroyed the entertainment industry with same-sex and multiethnic invective, shoving these alternative lifestyles down our throats and into the souls, the very fiber of our children's lives."

Suddenly, Reverend Stewart begins to weep. "Oh heavenly father, help us to stop those around us who will destroy your divine pattern. I beg of you to send a message to these faithless, filthy souls to have them come back into your fold."

Stewart takes a few minutes to compose himself. Many of the assembly are crying and wiping their eyes.

"Pray...pray, my brothers and sister like you have never prayed before. Rebuke those evil people who think politics are of the world, something Christians should stay out of. Since God created the institution of government, would He want His people to stay out of it? No. If Christians don't 'render to Caesar' Matthew 22:21 and don't function as 'salt' and 'light' Matthew 5:13-16 in the arena of government, then we disobey the commands of Christ and allow Satan to prevail by default. I say again that we must rebuke all forms of homosexuality and the debauchery that it brings into God's divine plan. I beseech you, Lord in heaven... Help us all!" Stewart was clearly overcome by his own words.

Suddenly, Stewart's face twists and reddens. "Shommbala sundana malakaa mullabena shista sangusa...." Stewart is speaking in tongues.

Stewart seems to lose his balance. It looks as if his knees have buckled. Some men instinctively lunged forward in their seats to come to the reverend's aid. Women cried out in sympathy. A few among the worshipers have passed out. Most of the worshipers began cheering after the reverend's sermon.

Dr. Paul Vogelbach jumps from his rear pew and dashes up to the front of the church. He put his arm around Stewart and, using his size and strength, neatly carried the reverend to the exit door toward his quarters.

***

Reverend Stewart recovers quickly from the episode that overcame him this morning. Dr. Vogelbach attends to the reverend, making sure his vital signs are stable before he leaves the residence. Stewart insists that they keep their dinner plans for that evening despite the doctor's advice to stay quiet and rest.

Promptly at 5 p.m., Paul Vogelbach arrives at the Milwaukee ChopHouse. The restaurant is dark inside, intentionally made that way by low-wattage bulbs inside ornate lamps mostly with an English country theme. The walls are dark mahogany wood panels dotted with prints and paintings, mostly of hunting scenes, and portraits of bearded old white men, reminiscent of aristocratic 18th century British life.

A college aged, pretty woman in a tight black miniskirt and a black spandex off-the-shoulder top escorted Dr. Vogelbach to the table where his host awaits. Paul pays no attention to the blond goddess. By the time he reaches the table, his eyesight has already adjusted to the darkened room.

Vogelbach is stopped in his tracks at what he sees. Sitting at a round corner booth with Reverend Stewart was a young woman dressed in a tailored blue knit suit. One string of white pearls hangs around her neck. He feels his face go flush and has to consciously close his mouth from the unwanted surprise. He recognizes the woman.

Stewart rises from his seat to greet Vogelbach and heartily shakes his hand with both of his. Paul looks at him with incredulity.

"Here is the man who came to me in my time of dismay. In The Book of Psalms 34:17. *'The righteous cry out, and the Lord hears them; he delivers them from all their troubles.'* My dear friend Paul Vogelbach, I believe you have already met Rebecca Sipes. You two met at services one Sunday."

"So…so nice to see you again, Ms. Sipes," Vogelman stammers.

"Ms. Sipes sounds too formal, unless you want me to call you doctor all evening," Rebecca chuckles.

Stewart, sensing Paul's dismay, tries to ease his shyness. "I have to tell you both that I don't do this very often, but when I see two wonderful people in my flock who are unattached, I play the matchmaker. Rebecca has now moved here permanently from Wausau to be with her father."

A waiter hands out menus to each of them.

"Ms. Sipes…I mean Rebecca, how is your dad feeling?" Vogelbach inquires. His voice has a slight quiver.

"He's terrific, Paul. We have you to thank, and believe me, you are in our daily prayers. The other physicians painted a bleak picture, but you saved his life." Rebecca smiles, dimples on her cheeks add to her alluring beauty. She looks deeply into Paul's eyes. Paul's discomfort begins to lessen.

"The Lord did his will through me. Evidently your father has more work to do here on Earth," Paul replies.

"Hallelujah! His will be praised," Stewart offers. Rebecca continues, "Honestly, I thought I was returning home to bury…" She gets choked up at the thought and couldn't continue her words.

Paul hands Raquel a cloth napkin from the table, which she takes and dabs at her eyes. "So, have you decided what you will be doing here in Milwaukee?" Paul asks. He decides to change the subject of Ronald Sipes's health. Like the first time they met in church, Vogelbach is taken by Rebecca's stunning beauty.

"I don't have anything yet, but there are a few possibilities. I'm a special needs teacher, and two schools have shown interest, so I don't think I'll be unemployed for too long."

"Special needs. That takes a certain amount of patience and devotion," Paul says.

"It's automatic for me. I think the Lord put me on Earth to do His will, and I do my work in His name."

"Interesting. I feel the same way about medicine. From a boy, I seemed to have a calling to what I do, and that was the hand of the Lord guiding me."

The reverend put his menu down. "Rebecca, Paul...I feel my work here is done. If you both don't mind, I think I will leave so you can get to know one another. I'm still feeling a bit weak from today's sermon." The reverend knows his presence as the third wheel would not work toward his goal as matchmaker.

CHAPTER 30

Vic Gonnella and Raquel Ruiz typically have their lunch delivered to the Centurion offices around 12:30 or 1 o'clock in the afternoon. After lunch they would run over to see how Olga is doing at physical therapy. So far, she is way ahead of the curve. Her mood is terrific, and that is half the battle.

Raquel usually has a salad with grilled chicken and a vinaigrette dressing on the side. Vic opts for a veal or eggplant parm hero. They would eat in Raquel's office, as it has a better view of Manhattan. She also has an authentic Italian-made professional La Marzocco espresso machine installed. To remind them of Italy, they loved an after-lunch *caffé corretto*, a coffee corrected with anisette or sambuca.

But today, Vic has invited his girl to have lunch at one of their favorite spots, Il Tinello on West 56th St. They walk hand in hand the 10 blocks to the restaurant. Vic has a surprise for Raquel. He actually has a double surprise.

No menus are necessary. John, the owner of Il Tinello, would have the chef prepare a special luncheon for the power couple. Their regular waiter, Carlo, is thrilled to see them. He has a secret crush on Raquel and kept his eyes off her cleavage the best he could. Raquel is wearing a short tan skirt and a white frilly top which had a Mexican peasant theme, off the shoulder with a bit of a plunge. Her natural skin tone compliments the delicate gold cross she wears around her neck.

Like most days, the restaurant is crowded. The lunchtime business crowd occupied every table. In the 80s and 90s, Il Tinello was the place for businessmen to have a delightful authentic Italian meal and the proverbial three-martini lunch. These days there are as many businesswomen in the place as men. Glasses of Aperol Spitz and French Rose wine have taken the place of the martini.

After they shared an appetizer of squid ink pasta with cuttlefish, Vic tells Carlo to space out the next course. He wants more time to spend with Raquel and await a guest.

Vic orders his regular MacCallum 15, and Raquel asks for a Prosecco. The tables at Il Tinello are spaced out, so it was difficult to overhear anyone's conversations, but there was enough chatter to make the background noise pleasant in the elegant setting.

Vic kept glancing at the front door, and Raquel picked up on his distraction.

"Expecting someone?"

"Nah. It's just an old habit from my cop days. I always sit with my back against a wall and my eyes ready for action. Old habits die hard, baby. Sorry."

"Is this where you took your dates before you met me?" Raquel chuckles.

"First of all... no. Second, I could never afford a place like this. My go-to spot for my dates was White Castle on Boston Road in the Bronx."

"Classy. And I'm sure you got laid if they had a double cheeseburger with onion rings."

A man approaches Vic and Raquel's table. He is obviously an Orthodox Jew with the long black overcoat and a black fedora-type hat. He wears a fairly long white beard, and his white hair peeks from under his hat. Black-rimmed glasses were down off the bridge of his nose. The man carries a black leather shoulder pouch that so many jewelers carry. After all, only nine blocks away was Manhattan's Diamond District, where every other man who looked like him was bustling up and down the streets.

"Mr. Gonnella, this isn't exactly the kind of place I was expecting to have lunch with you. After all, it isn't kosher," the man said in a thick Yiddish accent.

"Hello, Ruben. I actually didn't invite you to eat with us, but please have a seat. Can you at least have a cocktail?" Vic asks.

"I can have a ginger ale. A paper cup please. Better yet...make it a scotch."

Carlo heard the order and quickly goes to the bar.

"This is my partner and my gal Raquel Ruiz," Vic introduces Raquel.

Raquel stuck out her hand.

"Missus, I'm sorry but I can't shake a woman's hand."

"Sorry, I should have known better. Pleasure to meet you, Ruben."

"It's my pleasure, I'm sure."

Raquel looks at Vic and made the slightest movement of her shoulders. It was her subtle way of asking who this strange man was.

"Anyway. To business. As I mentioned, a group of my associates from Rotterdam are interested in purchasing an American detective agency, and you of course are among their top targets," Ruben says.

Raquel sits back in the chair and glares at her partner.

"I'd like to think we are more than a detective agency, Ruben," Vic blurts. Raquel feels her face going scarlet.

"Nu, so we can call it whatever you like," Ruben shoots back.

Raquel clears her throat to stifle a scream.

"Ah...I didn't think we were for sale...honey." Raquel's voice is dripping with sarcasm.

"Missus, everything is for sale for the right number," Ruben fishes.

"So, let's start at 12 billion. Will that work, dearest," Vic asks.

Raquel is floored. Her mouth is agape. Soon, there would be a Puerto Rican hurricane inside Il Tinello.

"Not a bad starting price. Look, perhaps what I have here in my bag will convince you to go forward with us."

Ruben slides open the zipper of his bag and takes out a square velvet box. He places the box on the table and points a crooked finger at it.

"Go ahead. Take a look already," Ruben teases.

Vic looks at Raquel. "What to choose? Hold it...lets flip a coin." Gonnella digs into his pants pocket and comes out with a shiny quarter. "I call heads," Vic blurts. Raquel won. She gives Vic a nasty look. In a second, she would be coming out with a stream of expletives in Spanish.

Raquel picks up the box and brings it in front of her. She opens the box, and her mouth opens again. This time her eyes are as big as espresso cups.

"Holy shit! What the hell is this?" Raquel asks. Her voice has risen to the level where a few diners look over at their table.

Ruben responds. "It's a five-caret marquis diamond in a platinum setting, with two carets of begets surrounding it. The best quality on the street. I believe it's in your size, Raquel."

"How would you know my..."

"Happy anniversary, baby," Vic said. He leans over to see the ring.

Raquel is speechless.

"And this putz is insisting it's not an engagement ring," Ruben says.

"Now, I'm a putz. I wasn't a putz when I paid for it, Deegan," Vic blurts.

Ruben removes his glasses. His baby blue eyes and distinctive smile let Raquel know it is him.

"What the...?"

Raquel jumps from her chair to hug Vic. She turns to Deegan "And you, you won't shake my hand, but you better take a hug you insane bastard."

"I suppose you like it?" Vic asks.

"Nope, I wanted a pear-shaped diamond. Of course, I love it."

"You mean to tell me you were sitting here all this time while I never knew it was you?" Raquel asks Deegan.

"What was I gonna do, march in here with a Brooks Brothers suit and wing-tipped shoes. I'd be arrested in ten minutes. I'm a master of disguise in case you've forgotten."

Deegan continues. "Vic, now you can order me whatever you two are having to go. An Orthodox Jew eating this treif would bring too many suspicious eyes."

"You two maniacs planned this whole thing? Don't you have anything better to do with your time?" Raquel whispers.

"That's another thing I want to talk about." Deegan adds. "The last killing was in Louisiana. I predicted a transgender person to be the next murder, but that was child's play. In a month, he will hit another person. Questioning for Q. I think I've figured out the who and the where for his next victim."

"So, who and where?" Vic asks.

"Ahhh, that, my dear boy, will remain my secret until I call for you two to come with me to capture this guy. After all, me, John Deegan, the most wanted serial killer since Jack the Ripper, can't do it myself and take all the credit. That's for you two."

"Jesus Christ, John," Vic says.

"It's not Jesus, but I think you are pretty warm. Anyway, I gotta go. Forget the lunch. I'll pick up something at the Prime Grill. I feel like a nosh."

Deegan unceremoniously gets up and walks quickly to the door.

"Christ Almighty! There he goes again. He always does this to me," Vic blurts.

CHAPTER 31

The Manhattan FBI office jumps all over the Thursday Boots store on the West Side of Manhattan like they were having a 70% closeout sale. Agent Samuel Cooper oversees a team of agents to follow up on the size 13 Captains, limiting themselves to only these boots which are sold at the store. Salerno's group is keying in on the credit card data from all online sales.

The agents begin to run down the buyers of the seventeen size 13 Captain style boots which are purchased at the store in the past year. Three of the seventeen boot sales are made in cash. Thinking perhaps the killer of Layla Cole either lived in or near or visited New York City a few months ago, the agents are assuming the boots were purchased at this store. Six agents are put on this high-priority case. Salerno and Cis Burns can taste the collar...and the promotions.

Sam Cooper tasks himself the job of reviewing the Thursday Boots store videos, which are available. Luckily, the store has uploaded the daily videos to a server, so Cooper has his work cut out for him. To help with the job, Cooper contacts the bureau's Facial Analysis, Comparison, and Evaluation Unit to help conduct the review of all the retail store's images. Cooper, pulling out all the stops, also contacted NYPD's Facial Recognition Unit to cross-reference with the FBI's system. It may be an overkill, but every tiny bit of information can possibly be the piece of the puzzle that is needed to break this case wide open.

In 1949, George Orwell wrote his masterpiece novel *1984*, introducing the concept of the government being 'Big Brother'. Orwell's idea has become a reality with the use of facial recognition technology and the biometric data, which is used to track any individual, anywhere in the world. Big Brother is indeed watching. The FBI and nearly 600 other government organizations now have advanced technology tools to apprehend criminals who put the public in peril. Sam Cooper and Special Agent Salerno plan on using everything in their bag of tricks to apprehend the serial killer they are hunting. The needle in the haystack is now more like a railroad track spike.

***

In four weeks Paul Vogelbach will kill again. To the physician, it isn't at all like an act of murder. He is simply following the will of God as proven to him and the world, time and again, in Old and New Testament scripture and in the thoughtful sermons of his mentor.

Reverend Stewart has unknowingly fascinated something within the psyche of Vogelbach, transcending him into a dispassionate killer who plans each killing with surgical expertise. Not simply the actual surgical dismembering and the desecration of the victim's flesh, but premeditating, scheming, researching, and scheduling the mission from its inception.

A switch has been turned on within the doctor's brain to commit cold-blooded killings and bodily atrocities without remorse in the name of the Creator of All Things.

Three days after the Reverend Stewart set the wheels in motion to test a relationship between the lovely and devout teacher Rebecca Sipes and the humble and fervent surgeon Paul Vogelbach, the two single parishioners have their second date.

Rebecca all but makes the date herself, telling Paul what a wonderful and romantic place for a picnic Little Muskego Lake will be, and only a thirty-minute drive from Paul's apartment. Rebecca offers to drive. Paul agrees it is a good place for a picnic, and the next thing he knows, on Wednesday, his day off, when most of Paul's colleagues took time off to play golf, or fish, or play tennis, and when he will normally run and listen to his music or lectures, and plan his next despicable trip, Paul will be joining Rebecca at noon.

On the ride to the lake, the couple gets to know more about each other, and all the boxes are checking positive for both Rebecca and Paul.

Little Muskego Lake is a perfect spot for their picnic, as Rebecca promised. The lovely tree-filled park leads up to a small beach at the lakeshore. There are people kayaking and fishing, with some folks just kicking back and enjoying the scenery. In all his years in Milwaukee, Paul has never heard of this sublime oasis.

Paul wears a brown Adidas tracksuit with white and blue Adidas sneakers. Even though he loves the high-quality footwear and clothing that Nike has to offer, Vogelbach has thrown away all his Nike stuff due to the far-left liberal political stance the company has adopted. He views Nike as part of the LGBTQ+-backed woke movement. Rebecca's trendy Chuck Taylor Hi-Top Converse All Stars white sneakers are under an ankle-high blue and green flowerily peasant dress. The dress is conservative, and there is no plunging neckline to hang jewelry on or display her perky breasts. Her date will only be allowed to imagine.

The couple sits on a vintage quilt which Rebecca's mother has made while she was a teenager in the hopes that Rebecca would meet a nice young Christian man who would court her in a traditional manner. The quilt is a maroon color with a simple repeated pattern of small green trees.

Rebecca packed a rectangular woven wicker picnic basket which is a family heirloom passed down from her great-grandmother and brought over from Bavaria just before the Great Depression in America and the Nazi Party coming to power in Germany.

Rebecca lays out a beautiful spread on fine bone white China plates and silverware. Inside the basket are homemade deviled eggs, small triangle-shaped ham, and brie cheese sandwiches on crustless pumpernickel bread, and a fresh shredded cabbage salad with cranberries and walnuts, along with homemade hummus and fresh baked pita bread. Fresh fruit and an apple crisp, her mom's recipe, would finish off the meal. Rebecca noticed, to her delight, that Paul didn't drink alcohol at their dinner on Sunday, so she packed small bottles of flat and sparkling water along with a freshly made mango-pineapple juice in a quart Tupperware container. Two gold-rimmed, long-stemmed crystal glasses awaits the drinks.

"I must say, Rebecca, this is a very special picnic. Surely beats my regular Wednesday ritual," Paul sprouts. He only glances at the food and the old wicker picnic hamper, not caring a wit about either. Rebecca's face is all Paul can think about since their dinner date on Sunday, and her fresh look and sweet perfumed smell is something he had no idea how to deal with. Even her sneakers are making him interested. Paul has never dated before. Not in high school, undergrad school, medical school, or...ever.

Rebecca has told Paul not to bring anything to their picnic, and instead of doing something romantic or original like strawberries dipped in chocolate or some peanut M&Ms in a 250-ml Pyrex beaker, Paul brought nothing. What he lacks in social graces and romanticism he makes up for in drop-dead good looks and a country boy humility.

"I imagine you've done this before, Rebecca," Paul says quietly.

"Had a picnic? Yes, many times," Rebecca replies.

"Did your dates enjoy all the homemade food and all this lovely preparation?"

"My dates? Which dates are you referring to, Paul?"

"Ya know, the guys you brought here for a picnic," Paul asks. He is starting to show an uncharacteristic insecurity but masks it well by grabbing a few grapes from a China bowl and flipping them galanty into his mouth.

"Yeah, all two of my dates, Paul. One to the senior prom, and he threw up all over the place and my dad had to come get me and the second date to a church dance and the guy was so bashful he stayed in the men's room most of the night. I don't date, Paul. Never had time for it and never had the urge to have a boyfriend. My picnic dates were with my mom and dad."

"Me too, Rebecca...I mean...not about the boyfriend or the mom and dad, but..." Vogelbach stammers.

"I understand," Rebecca laughs.

"So how did you keep all the guys away from you with...with your gorgeous face and figure?" Paul asks. He lowers his eyes to his hands when he said figure.

"Well, I'm glad for the compliments, doctor. To be honest, I was an awkward teenager — you know, braces, bad posture, stringy hair, acne, inferiority complex. I was kind of a mess."

"As a scientist, I would need to see proof of that, Rebecca."

"If you call me Becky and finish your lunch like a good boy, I'll show you some pictures of me from tenth grade that I have in my phone. I was what you would term awkward. Or better yet, maybe you shouldn't have lunch, you may get sick."

"Okay, Becky, but you still haven't answered my question."

"About how I kept men away? Sure, I've had lots of offers. I just never felt the...how can I say this...the desire..."

"I see. Maybe you are a..."

"Don't you dare say it. I'm not that. God Forbid. Maybe you should let a girl finish her thought," Rebecca smiles.

"So sorry, Becky. Bad habit of mine," Paul blurts.

"At the risk of chasing you away, I was going to say... until now."

"Until now? I don't understand?"

"I was not interested in dating until now," Becky says softly. She feels her face redden. She is sure to make eye contact with Paul after her comment.

Vogelbach feels a sort of electric shock in his nether region. He is momentarily speechless, staring at Rebecca, who thinks for a second that her words are a bit forward and likely way over the top.

Vogelbach reaches out for Becky's hand. He caresses it in his hand for a moment and gently grabs a hold of it. Becky leans in slowly, and they kiss for the first time. Not a passionate kiss...but a kiss, nonetheless.

Becky feels a tingle go down through her stomach into her private area and down through her legs. Paul Vogelbach, the serial killer, becomes instantly aroused.

CHAPTER 32

The afternoon Paul and Rebecca were starting their romance, Special Agent Salerno called for a lunchtime meeting in the bullpen at the Child Abduction / Serial Murder Investigative Resources Center in Langley, Virginia. Salerno's superiors are suddenly taking a special interest in the case, which they are all now referring to as "The Surgeon". The Director calls him into a 7 a.m. meeting, along with the Assistant Director and three other FBI bigwigs.

Poking around a bit at the bureau's headquarters, Salerno is able to glean the reason or reasons behind the abrupt flurry of interest.

Salerno learns from an inside source that some du Mont family members are pressuring senators and the current resident of 1600 Pennsylvania Avenue for closure on the death of their relative Blake du Mont. Another source come up with the theory that the LGBTQ+ lobby and individuals throughout the country are beginning to make noise with their local congressmen, and the word is being brought up the line.

Pressure runs downhill at the FBI, and Salerno is passing the weight onto his staff.

Cis Burns does her usual machinations to get GG up to the bullpen. Cis noticed something on GG's right hand. GG saw that Burns has glanced at her fingers. GG has become self-conscious of her nicotine fingers and began some home remedies to remove the dark yellow stains. GG began bleaching the fingers on her right hand. She also uses an emery board to scrape away the softened skin, as quitting smoking is not an option. She keeps her hand balled up into a fist after Cis noticed the change.

Cis enters the Operations Center with GG trailing five steps behind, looking down at the floor as if she has lost something.

"We have to redouble our efforts on this case. The director wants a daily update from us," Salerno announces. "Where do we stand with the Thursday Boots lead?"

GG coughs to alert Salerno that she is ready to report.

"Yes, GG?" Salerno asks.

After the usual look at the ceiling and the awkward delay, GG speaks up.

"There are seventy-three sales at the Manhattan store and one hundred and seventy-one online sales in the past two years of the Captain style boots. Analyzing the database information and cross-referencing potential medical professionals by name, I've determined there are nine possibilities. None came out of the New York store. If my theory is correct, and we should not limit our search to only the nine sales, I think we need to immediately focus on the nine as the probable killer." GG glances at Cis Burns and coughs up a phlegm ball into her throat. Cis isn't the only one in the room who almost gags.

"Do you have a list of the nine suspects?" Salerno inquires.

"GG gave me the list just prior to this meeting. She worked on it all night. It's a mixed bag of cities in the States and Canada," Cis blurts.

"Let's not spare the horses. I want to review the list, and I will personally contact the field offices in those cities. The Mounties will do whatever we ask if it comes down to that. Anything else?" Salerno asks.

"Yes, sir. We now have a video camera clip from Nicholls State University in Thibodaux, Louisiana, where the last victim made a speech the day she was killed," Agent Larry Pieroni says. "Facial recognition has come up empty, but the size and shape of the killer matched up with the video in Manhattan on the street where the first victim lived. There is a clear correlation. Take a look."

The overhead monitors in the bullpen blinked on, and the surveillance black and white video showed a man who was walking into the parking lot at Nicholls State. A split screen of the North Moore Street in Manhattan surveillance camera and the University's video are frozen on the monitors.

"Similar-sized man, same erect posture, and walking gait seems to confirm it's the same suspect. We also have a video of the perp in Las Vegas. Even though he is disguised as he was in Manhattan, this is clearly the same man."

"Fabulous work. Let's go find this fucker," Salerno pronounces.

***

"Okay my lovelies, I have the news you both have been waiting on the edge of your seats for," John Deegan declares. He calls Vic and Raquel from his throwaway cell phone to their home number at their East Side townhouse. It is the Deegan witching hour at 10:30 p.m.

"I've been chewing on my nails for the past month," Vic offers sarcastically.

"Don't pay any attention to him John, he's been in a foul mood all day," Raquel counters. She made a face at her man and sticks her tongue out at him.

"Well, I'm more than happy to share where the next murder will be, and who the unwitting victim will be. The only thing is, I can't nail the exact day and time of when the homicide will go down, but my research has it down to a seventy-two-hour window," Deegan brags.

Vic laughs. "I feel a big 'but' coming our way."

"Naturally. Do you think I'm just going to spill my guts and you guys go to the FBI and let them take all the glory away from you?"

"They really do need some help, John. Their favorable ratings are in the toilet," Raquel adds.

"Screw 'em. Okay, so here's my offer. I'll tell you right now what I have, but...there it is Vic, the big 'but' you've been waiting for. I want both your promises that you will both meet me at the location and plan on staying a few days. Now Raquel, it's a short flight from New York, so your pain will be brief. After you nail him, you can always go back home on Amtrak."

"I can deal with it, if it's worth saving lives," Raquel replies.

"Promise? Scouts Honor, hand to God?" Deegan asks.

"Yes." Raquel blurts.

"I'm all in," Vic adds.

"Here goes, kids. Not to brag, but I was the first to figure out the LGBTQ pattern, and we are now up to Q. There are quite a few plus letters after the Q and growing every day. I have a feeling he may stop here as the rest are a bit, let's say, bizarre even for a serial murderer. After we nab this nut there will be no more killing. At least by this guy. A bit of a lesson now. Q stands for queer or questioning. We all know what queer is, and in my day anyone who was gay was a queer. We would call them queers and homos. That's changed a bit. Today, according to the organization GLAAD, which advocates for people with alternative lifestyles, Queer is now a term for anyone who is anything but straight. With me so far?"

"Yes," Raquel answers.

"Now the Deegan train will be taking off a bit faster, so pay attention, please. Q also stands for "questioning" which allows for those who are still unsure of their gender identity or sexual orientation. They are testing the waters, so to speak. Now, in my research the city of Cincinnati is known as "The Queen City," abbreviated from "The Queen of the West" from the early 1800s. Not because all the queens, as we sometimes refer to gay men, are there but because it was a place of culture, civilization, and arts as the West was growing. At least one of you may need proof of this historic fact, so I point you to part of a poem which was written back in the day by Henry Wadsworth Longfellow:

And this Song of the Vine,
This greeting of mine,
The winds and the birds shall deliver
To the Queen of the West,
In her garlands dressed,
On the banks of the Beautiful River.

"Still with me, kids?" Deegan tests.

"John, remember that train you mentioned? I think I missed it at the station," Vic says glibly.

"Okay, thickhead. Stay with me for just a bit longer. Our killer only knows that what's called The Queer City is Cincinnati, and he has only reason to believe it's about LGBTQ+. He did his research on every victim but guess what...I'm smarter than he is. Everything points to our guy having a scientific mind, and he is uninterested in history. So, he needs to find a victim with the letter Q in his first name. Enter the queer and questioning jazz musician Quincy Davies, who got his first name from his parents, who were Quincy Jones fans. And guess what? By his own admission, Quincy Davies is not really sure which way he is swinging these days, so there is the questioning aspect of the Q. Look him up. He says so in every other interview he does. And just guess where Quincy lives?" Deegan asks.

"Cincinnati," Raquel replies.

"Correctamundo, my petty. Vic? Are you back on the train?"

CHAPTER 33

Two days after Salerno's meeting at CASMIRC headquarters in Langley, every agent in the bullpen has been working day and night. Some of the agents went home, rested for four or five hours, took a shower, and then were back at their workstations searching for "The Surgeon."

Cis Burns returns at 4 a.m. after a brief rest at home. She notices that GG's first floor office light is still on. Cis enters the office, seeing GG slumped in her chair asleep, her mouth wide open, with a thin drool of saliva seeping from her mouth running past her chin and onto her blouse. An ashtray filled with Pall Mall butts on her right side; three cans of empty Diet Coke cans and crumpled cigarette packs litters her desk. The remnants of a McDonalds happy meal sat atop the filled waste basket beside the desk.

Burns began to turn and walk out. GG, sensing a presence, awakes.

"I was only resting my eyes for a bit," GG announces.

"Sorry to bother you. Just wanted to check if you needed anything."

“These numbers start to dance on my screen after so many hours crunching them and cross-referencing data.” GG says.

“Maybe you should take a break. Go home and freshen up like I did.”

“I’m glad you are here. Please take a seat,’’ GG utters. She runs her hands quickly through her hair in a feeble attempt to straighten out the mess. Cis moves the chair out a bit and sits.

“I have something I want to say to you.” GG looks up at the LED ceiling lights, her eyes rapidly blinking.”

“Sure.”

“Well… I…I hope that you have noticed that I am trying to change the way I look. You know…dress better, wearing makeup, lipstick. Having my nails and hair done and getting rid of these stains on my hand.”

“Yes, I have notices. Self-improvement is sometimes good for the spirit,” Burns offers. She felt her stomach churn in anticipation of what is coming.

GG looks at her computer screen not to make eye contact with her colleague. An obvious distressed look comes upon her face.

“I’m happy you at least noticed I’m trying to improve myself. You have been very kind to me. Very compassionate and understanding. I see how the others look at me, but you are more considerate, probably more than anyone I’ve encountered in my entire life.”

“Why, thank you, GG.” Burns utters. She squirms a bit in her chair in a nervous reaction. What she really wants to do was get up and run from GG’s office.

Never taking her eyes off the screen, GG reaches for a pack of Pall Malls, removes a cigarette, and lit it with a Bic butane lighter, almost unconsciously.

"I was wondering if we could be friends outside of the office. You see, all these years of working for the FBI the job has...well, I have no friends. I have been making the changes in my life...for you, Cecelia."

Burns's adrenalin surges in a fight-or-flight natural response. She is befuddled by GG's remarks. She searches her brain for a proper response that wouldn't crush GG's spirit. After all, Dean Salerno has asked her to work closely with GG.

"That's very nice, GG. I must tell you that the job has enveloped my life as well. I recently made some changes also. It's personal and a secret, which I will share with only you. I am seeing someone. He's a military man attached to the Pentagon. I don't really have too much free time for friends at this point," Burns lies. "But I really enjoy working with you every day. I have so much to learn from you."

"So, I guess that's a hard no," GG blurts. She is discomfited and looks as if she is about to cry.

"Don't take it like that. Look, we can have lunch together sometimes. Perhaps here in your office. But I have a suggestion if you want to hear it." Burns tries to sooth GG's feelings.

GG looks away from her desktop, her eyes quickly going to the safety of the ceiling.

"Okay." GG lips are quivering.

"Think about going on a dating service or finding an online friend, for starters. A friend of mine did just that, and she has found a group of people who get together regularly. It's not easy finding decent people these days," Burns lies again.

GG focuses back on her computer. "I don't relate well with strangers. I'm sure you noticed that. Everyone does. I was hoping that you...because of your..." GG stops speaking, taking a long drag on her cigarette. The smoke billowed passes through her sloppy mane toward the ceiling. She takes out a legal pad from her top desk drawer and begin jotting down notes as if Burns isn't there.

Burns waits in her chair for what seems like an eternity.

"Well, I have to get upstairs. I have some calls to make." Burns says. GG ignores her comment. Cis left GG's office. Cis realizes her hands are trembling, and her legs feel as if they are made of lead.

***

That same night, the Friday after Paul and Rebecca have their picnic and first kiss, Rebecca calls Paul to invite him to her home. Her father is well enough to visit out-of-town friends for the weekend. Paul accepts and is at Rebecca's within the hour.

Paul arrives wearing a perfectly pressed pair of beige slacks with a fitted blue blazer and a crisp white shirt. Rebecca looks radiant in a pair of jeans and a plain maroon blouse when she opens the door. They kiss hello. Paul arrives empty-handed.

Inside, the Sipes home has a cozy, lived-in look. The front door opens to a small foyer, which leads into the living room. There is a plain light rust-colored cloth sofa with two identical brown and beige matching throw pillows on either side. A wide red and beige checkered armchair is on the right of the sofa. On the left is a smaller upholstered armchair in a green red and beige flowery pattern with a small matching back pillow. A small coffee table on top of a beige throw rug has a bowl of dried flowers and two *National Geographic* magazines which stands in front of the sofa. The neat country style furniture is old but not at all worn. Two windows have identical long brown draperies with beige pulldown shades. Photographs of Rebecca's parents on their wedding day and a portrait of her mom are on the wall behind the sofa. On the opposite wall hangs a stunning portrait of Rebecca, their only child.

"Very nice home, Becky" Vogelbach says.

"Thanks. My mom did all the decorating years ago. She was a neat freak and kept this place spotless. No need to redecorate at this point. If and when Dad passes, and I hope that's years away, the plan is to sell the house, and I'll get a condo apartment or something.

"I made some fresh iced tea. Can I get you a glass, or are you hungry?"

"I'd love some iced tea. I already ate, thanks." Paul replies.

Rebecca goes into the kitchen, pours out two glasses with lemons, and offers Paul a seat on the sofa. She sits on the opposite side.

"I'm so glad you were able to come over tonight. I felt a bit lonesome with Dad away for the weekend."

"And I'm glad you called," Paul replies. He hopes his voice doesn't betray his nervousness.

"Do you think I'm too forward asking you here?" Rebecca asks.

"Not at all. We're two grown adults."

"What I'm about to say will be even more forward, but here goes. Paul, I feel a strong connection with you, and I'm hoping you feel the same."

Paul nods. His eyes are scanning Becky's beauty.

"Paul...at the risk of you walking out angry, I want to tell you something." Rebecca pauses. Paul waits.

"I'm still a virgin. Frankly, I'm tired of waiting."

Paul nearly drowns in his iced tea. The killer feels his face getting red.

"Well...I have to consider that as forward, but I'm not walking out," Paul laughs.

"That's a load off my mind!"

"And let me tell you something, Becky. And this is difficult for a man my age to admit. I'm a virgin, too."

"Liar," Rebecca laughs nervously.

"God's honest truth. I've never been with a woman. Not that I wasn't interested but I was never good around the opposite sex. Shyness, I suppose."

"I'm sure you have had the opportunity."

"I've immersed myself in medicine. I always ignored flirtations. I couldn't ever make the first move, though."

"Thank God for Reverend Stewart for officially introducing us."

"He's a special man."

"And so are you, Paul."

Rebecca places her iced tea on a coaster on the coffee table. She stands and moves to the other side of the couch. She takes Paul's drink from his hand and places it on a coaster.

"I think I'll make the first move," Rebecca coos.

Paul stays the night.

CHAPTER 34

Paul leaves Rebecca's bed very early Sunday morning. As he does every Sunday, Vogelbach's creature-of-habit personality routine cannot change. He has to do his morning run before he showers and dresses for church. Rebecca plans to meet Paul outside the church. He asked her to arrive early so they could sit together quietly and meditate.

The parking lot of the church is empty when Paul arrived. He waits about two minutes before Rebecca pulls up. They smile at one another but he doesn't greet with a kiss. Paul feels a warmth and closeness which he never felt before. He thinks, *'This is what love feels like'*.

When they enter the church, Rebecca and Paul are shocked at what they saw. They turned and looked at one other in disbelief. There at the pulpit stands the Reverend Stewart. His hands folded over his open Bible; Stewart seems almost catatonic. He is dressed in his usual suit and tie, his eyeglasses perched low on his nose. The reverend's lips seemed to be moving as if he is reading scripture. Paul moves Rebecca to his regular back pew, and they sit closely next to each other. For a moment he thought he should approach Revered Stewart to see if he is alright but decides to just watch him instead.

As the parishioners begin to arrive, they too are shocked to see their reverend on the podium. They are expecting him to make the usual late entry, walking down the center isle to begin the service. Instead of the usual quiet Sunday morning greetings and pleasant banter among the assembly, everyone moves quietly to their seats in stunned disbelief. People begin to look to each other, some shrugging their shoulders. Eventually the church filled. One of the deacons closed the rear door, which made a dull thump.

A minute later, Reverend Christian Stewart finally takes off his glasses and gazed over the crowded house of worship. He clears his throat with a gentle cough into his hand. He starts out speaking in a low tone, as is his oratory technique. The assembly is absolutely quiet.

"Since last Wednesday... I have been despondent over some horrific news. When the leader of the largest Christian church in the world begins to succumb to the world of homosexuality and other perversions, I am devastated to my core."

"Yes, my brothers and sisters, news from the Vatican is the Roman Church is beginning to make a sudden turn toward the dark side. Until last week, the Catholic Church's position was same-sex marriage could not be blessed simply because God cannot bless sin. I'm sure we all agree with this, and one point three billion Roman Catholics had followed this teaching."

Stewart begins to raise his voice in anger. "Suddenly, Pope Francis is saying, '*We cannot be judges who only deny, reject, and exclude*.' WHY NOT!" Stewart screams. He pounds his hand on the Bible on the podium.

"The Bible is very clear on homosexuality, as I have preached in the church until I was blue in the face. I have always shown my deepest respect for the Pope, and I have seen quite a few. From Pope Pius the Twelfth to the current pope, I count seven in all. Even though we are not subject to the rules of the Vatican, I absolutely abhor what this Pope is doing. Catholics have a dogma in their religion which states that when it comes to church doctrine the pope is infallible when it comes to matters of faith and morals. This means his words are without error. I am here to testify that this is likely the greatest mistake in the entire history of Christianity. What morals are they teaching their faithful? That it is moral for men to have anal sex with one another? For a woman to have sexual relations with another woman? For the two genders to suddenly morph into ten, or twenty, or God know what is next?"

Rebecca puts her hand on to Paul's. They have promised not to make their budding relationship a secret to the congregation. This is their first display of affection in public.

"Is this old man crazy? I really want an answer to my question. I have prayed and prayed on this, but the Lord has not shown me an answer yet. I'm certain he will enlighten me in His good time. Maybe this Pope isn't crazy at all. Perhaps the evil one has figured out a way to poison Pope Francis' mind. We all know how cunning and sinister Lucifer can be. No one escapes Satin's wrath, not even the Pope."

"Let's look at what Pope Francis is doing. Instead of protecting children and vulnerable people from some of his priests who are pedophiles and covering up their horrible sins and throwing money at the problem, he is now diluting Catholic doctrine and using the pages of the Old Testament to line the bottom of bird cages. Francis, aside from being an avowed socialist, and that goes hand in hand with this gay attack on our nation's core beliefs, he has now sown complete confusion around the world."

Vogelbach is so taken by Stewart's words and angry that the Catholic Church would permit gay people to be more accepted that he squeezes Rebecca's hand to the point that she tugs on his arm to release his grip. He is so enraptured with what the reverend was saying that he never notices what he has done.

Stewart is sweating profusely. He opens the top button on his white shirt and pulls down his necktie. He is screeching like never before, his voice cracking from strain. "So last week, Francis in his demented speech about homosexuality said, *'Everyone, everyone, everyone,'* must be allowed in. The LGBTQ+ sickos are applauding this action. Of course, they are now, in their twisted and sick rapture. With the help of the biased media in our declining nation, drip by drip they will drink an entire ocean until the Lord decides to end us as he did with Sodom and Gomorrah. And deservedly so. My brothers and sisters, I am drawing a line in the sand here at Unified Free Church of Truth in Milwaukee, Wisconsin, to save our children from a future filled with gay marriages and debauchery. These homosexuals and transgender people will soon see the wrath of the Christian movement in the heartland of America. It is beyond the time when civil war must occur to end this afront to the Lord God in Heaven."

Stewart raises his Bible with both hands above his head. He attempts to speak, but no words come out of his mouth. Two of the deacons move quickly to the podium. One lowers the reverend's hands, removing his Bible from his outstretched arms and clenched hands. Both deacons walk a compliant Reverend Stewart slowly away from the pulpit and through the nearby door.

The parishioners raise as one in an ovation wave which is louder than ever. The sound of one of the faithful speaking in tongues in the front of the church can barely be heard.

Paul and Rebecca re clapping until he stops, and Paul whispers in her ear, "I'm the only physician here, Becky. Come with me. I must see if the reverend is okay. I'm concerned with what I saw." He takes Rebecca's hand and leads her down the side isle toward the door. The entire assembly notices the handsome couple, hand in hand. heading after the reverend.

Once inside the office, they find the two deacons attending to the reverend prostate on his sofa. They removed his suit jacket and are trying to give him some water from a glass, but his mouth just remains open. His eyes are fixed toward the ceiling.

Paul examines Stewart quickly. He turns to one of the deacons. "Please call an ambulance. I believe Reverend Stewart has suffered a stroke."

CHAPTER 35

It was Sunday afternoon. John Deegan is comfortable in his Manhattan hotel suite, planning his upcoming jet excursion to Cincinnati. The coming Thursday morning he, Vic, and Raquel will land in the Queen City at 11 a.m. They are pre-booked in a midtown hotel under the same name he booked at the Lowes Regency in Manhattan. Michael O'Connor was an old schoolmate who passed away 10 years ago. Deegan took on his identity with all falsified credit cards and identification in perfect order.

In Deegan's mind the entire scenario in Cincinnati is already set before he makes the trip. The only piece of the equation which is missing is the date and time the killer is to end Quincy Davies's music career. At this point Deegan knows everything there is to know about Paul Vogelbach down to the surgeon's last prostate examination.

Deegan is in a playful mood. Not satisfied with simply figuring out the LGBTQ+ murder sequence, Deegan is not challenged by predicting the next and in his estimation the last killing the surgeon would ever attempt.

When he becomes bored with the mental exercise of figuring out the serial killer's moves, Deegan amuses himself by using the peripheral players in the case as unwitting pawns for his entertainment.

He makes a mental list of who is to be involved in his performance, a sort of baroque comedy.

The first on his short list is the best and brightest in the case. Gail Gain, a.k.a. GG. Deegan considers Gain to be almost on his level. Almost.

GG answers her office phone on the first ring at the CASMIRC offices in Quantico.

A momentary pause comes after she picks up the receiver. Not because of her social issues. It is simply to exhale a huge plume of smoke into the already stale, smelly office air. GG is back to her old slovenly ways since her depressing talk with Cis Burns. Her hopes are dashed, and she fell back into her familiar habits. Her hair hasn't been washed in days, her dress is stained and wrinkled, her nicotine fingers are coming back with a vengeance, and she smells like a three-day old mackerel.

"Gain," She answers.

"Well, I can see you are working seven days a week on this lovely case," the man with the Irish brogue says. GG immediately begins recording the call.

"Hello, Mr. Deegan."

"So, ya figured me out did ya," Deegan says. "Kudos to you. I'm certain Salerno told you I was dead and buried now, didn't he? Have ya narrowed in on that bloody surgeon yet?" Deegan enquires.

"I'm not at liberty to discuss an ongoing case," GG replies.

"I have, Gail." Deegan replies in his normal voice.

"What makes you so sure?" GG asks.

"Like you, I'm pretty damn smart. I'm even smart enough to know you hit that button on your phone to record this conversation. Hello, Special Agent Salerno and Cis Burns," Deegan laughs.

"So where are you predicting the next murder?" GG fishes.

"Hmmm. That tells me something. It tells me that the entire FBI with all their technology and money and personnel are a beat behind me. I feel like it's a sort of game...a race to the finish line between me and the bureau," Deegan declares.

"Tell me why you are so interested in this case."

"Great question, Gail. Just for the fun of it," Deegan is now toying with the best serial killer profiler in FBI history.

"Fun? We are trying to prevent another murder and you are having...fun?"

"It's all in the wonderful game we call life. How about I give you a few hints, Gail."

"Yes."

"Take a map of the United States. I'm sure your department can come up with one."

"Fine."

"Okay, now draw a line from the first murder to the second. Got it?" Deegan toys. He sounds like a nine-year-old boy.

"I did. It's okay if I use a map on my desktop?"

"Okay, yeah...that's good. Now draw a line to the latest killing. Let me know when you have that. Forget the Vegas stop. 'Cause, after all, you have to go through Nevada for California."

"Ready." GG blurts. Her mind was racing trying to figure out where Deegan is taking this.

"Now draw a straight line up to Minnesota. Right to the tippy top of the good ole USA. Okay...okay... for now I will give you only one hint. It's not going to be in any repeated states, and it's not Minnesota, either. But here is a bonus hint. The killer is from a state none of these lines pass through but he's pretty damn close. Now that state is only three states away from where the next homicide will occur. Okay now, Miss Gail Gain, hope you got all that. Talk soon. Buh-bye, Salerno and Burns. See if you can help out GG with this puzzle." Deegan ends the call. He rubs his two hands together like a kid getting a double chocolate cone with sprinkles.

Deegan's next call is to the office of Centurion Security, Vic Gonnella and Raquel Ruiz's company. Being a Sunday, the office is staffed with a skeleton crew and an emergency telephone operator. Deegan calls and asks to speak with Emilio Ramos. The operator said he is not in today, but she connects him to Emilio's mail. While he is waiting for Emilio's message to end, Deegan put his hand over the phone mic and says aloud, "I just fucking love breaking balls."

Deegan leaves a message at the beep. "Of course, you are out of the office or away from your desk, dear Emilio. After all, it's Sunday. While you and your partner Christopher are off doing who knows what, a serial killer is about to pounce on his latest victim. It's a Q, of course. I was going to give you a hint as to where it would happen, but I suppose working on Sundays like the FBI does is not within your pay grade. By the way, I just gave them, not two minutes ago, a juicy lead. Tell that cheapskate

Gonnella he can't afford a bargain. Just think. You guys could have come out first in a three-man race...and written your own tickets. There is no trophy after first place, Emilio. Next time, work every day until you find the killer. Serial killers never take a day off, guys."

CHAPTER 36

The parishioners remain relatively calm after Reverend Stewart is escorted off his lectern. The worshiper who begins speaking in tongues remains in his pew with his arms outstretched toward the ceiling for a few minutes. He was following the words taught by Reverend Stewart from Deuteronomy 32.40 *'I lift my hand to heaven and solemnly swear; as surely as I live forever'*.

As the ambulance's siren drew closer, the assembly becomes more concerned for the reverend. The deacons attempt to calm the congregation, to no avail. The entire gathering calmly moves toward the exits to offer their prayers and support to Stewart. As soon as the EMTs take the reverend, the crowd begins to dissipate toward their vehicles. Rebecca goes home to await a call from Paul.

When the ambulance carrying Reverend Stewart and Dr. Paul Vogelbach arrives at Milwaukee General Hospital, nurses who work closely with the doctor are waiting by the Emergency Room Door. Things move very quickly. Luckily for the reverend, Paul's early diagnosis of a possible stroke put things in motion, saving precious time.

Dr. Ryan Lorenz, Paul's colleague, and the head of neurosurgery, meets them in the emergency room. Paul has called Lorenz from the ambulance explaining the situation.

Stewart is quickly taken for a bevy of tests, including an MRI to establish whether he indeed has a stroke and to determine the kind of stroke it is, and its severity. Vogelbach is at Stewart's side every step of the way. Stewart is conscious, and his catatonic state has subsided. He remembers Vogelbach, calling him by name, which is a positive sign. The reverend's speech is slurred, and he has no recollection of his sermon or being taken to the hospital.

After a short while, it is determined that the reverend has an ischemic stroke, which Dr. Lorenz begins treating immediately with tPA, a tissue plasminogen activator to break down the stroke. Ischemic strokes are typically caused by a blockage of a blood vessel. There is a short window, perhaps three or four hours when this kind of stroke must be treated to experience positive results for the victim. It is ironic that the serial killer has likely saved Reverend Stewart from either permanent paralysis or death.

Vogelbach remains with his spiritual mentor until just after 8 p.m., when Reverend Stewart is stabilized and out of danger.

Paul calls Becky. Her father has just returned from his visit. Paul wants to see Becky but is reluctant to invite her to his apartment. Although he has a two-bedroom condo and keeps his secret room door locked at all times, Paul has a gallbladder removal for one of his patients scheduled at 7 a.m. on Monday. Besides that, he is tired and stressed from the grueling events of the day.

The couple makes plans to meet on Wednesday. Paul tells his newfound love that after their date he will be leaving that evening for some out-of-town business. He will be back for Sunday services, which they agreed will not be the same without the reverend.

***

Salerno and his crew of dedicated FBI agents and profilers are working around the clock in the bullpen on the leads the Thursday Boots sales has generated. So far, to everyone's dismay, the list hasn't exposed the killer. The FBI field offices has yet to identify any suspects from the list, and the going is slow.

Cis Burns is in Salerno's office, Salerno is sitting behind his desk. Burns is in a chair facing him, her back to the door.

"I thought once we got all the names from the boot sales it would be game over," Salerno says.

"It's why our job is so difficult. Only been a couple of days, boss. We are knocking off the names one by one. Let's see how it plays out," Burns replies.

"The director is calling me twice a day. Not a happy camper, Cis."

"He has all the confidence in the world in you. It's part of the pecking order game," Cis adds.

"And let's remember, he's not the only serial killer we're looking for. It seems to me every other month we have another whack job for the list."

"But Washington is focused on this one. Remember what you once told me, '*Your boss*' priority becomes your priority,'" Cis adds.

Salerno looks up. He has a look of shock on his face.

"GG...hi. You ahh, you came up here alone?" Salerno blurts. Cis turns around and stands up. She feels a surge in her stomach. GG ignores her.

Instead of the normal delay and strange stare, GG comes out with what she wants to say quickly. However, she still doesn't make eye contact with Salerno.

"Yes, I walked up the stairs. I'm trying to fight my fears," GG announces. She still looks like a wreck. A lit Pall Mall is nearly burning her fingers.

"That's a good thing," Salerno replies. He is concerned about a messy scene in his office.

"I had another call from Deegan. I want to share it with you...alone," GG states.

Cis has already informed her boss of the bizarre discussion she had with GG.

"Sure, GG. But you know Agent Burns is a key player in this investigation. I think it's appropriate for her to hear what you have to say," Salerno offers.

"No," GG replied.

"Now, GG...we are all adults here. I must insist Agent Burns remains here."

"Then fuck you, Salerno. I was doing this when you were still chasing girls in high school. I'm not FBI. I'll go and pack my stuff and go home. I don't need money. I have plenty of that. After all, I've never really had a life, and I should retire anyway," GG hollers.

Her voice carries out into the bullpen, and everyone working on their phones and computers stops in their tracks. You can hear a pin drop.

Salerno, now standing, is surprised by GG's outburst.

"No need for any of that now, GG. Come in and sit down. Agent Burns has plenty to do in the bullpen." Salerno has to keep his eyes on the prize.

Cis Burns keeps her eyes on GG, who won't look her way. The agent walks out calmly feeling pity on the eccentric colleague. Cis closes the door behind her.

"Okay, GG. What was the nature of the call?" Salerno inquires. GG refuses to sit.

"It's on your e-mail. I sent the entire taped conversation."

Salerno opens his e-mail and turned the sound up. They listen to Deegan's call.

"And you're certain it's John Deegan?" Salerno asks.

"Absolutely."

"Let's listen again so I can take notes."

"Don't bother. I figured out his puzzle. The killer is from Wisconsin, and the next murder will be in Ohio," GG blurts.

"And you're sure about this?"

"Absolutely."

"Okay, I still want to run it past the bullpen. I just can't take the word of an elderly serial killer we have been perusing for over a decade."

"Fine, but not Burns!" GG yells.

"GG...now listen to me. You are the best profiler in the entire world. You have a brilliant mind. You have a genius-level IQ. Put your differences aside. Burns is an important part of this team, and she will eventually have to know what's going on. I can't have her working in the dark, and I know you want to find this son-of-a bitch as much as anyone."

GG glares up at the ceiling over Salerno's head. She takes a Pall Mall out of its crumpled packet, flaming it with a cheap Bic lighter. She inhales it deeply, holding it in a bit too long, then exhales. She watches the smoke rise to the ceiling.

"Fine. But I don't ever want to speak with that woman again. Is that understood?" GG blurted. Tears well in her eyes.

"I get it, and that's fine. Now let's get to work," Salerno orders.

GG responds quickly. "Please have one of your agents walk me back down to my office."

CHAPTER 37

"Chris, come quick. I got a strange voice mail yesterday. You have to hear this! It blew me away," Emilio announces.

It is the first thing Monday morning, before they have their first cup of coffee. Chris listens to the message intently.

"Play that again," Chris asked. Emilio complies.

"What the fuck?" Chris blurts. "Who the hell was that? And on a Sunday afternoon?"

"Whomever it is, I wonder what he means by coming out third in a three-man race. What race? And who are the three in the race?" Emilio queries.

"No idea. Vic and Raquel should be here in an hour. Maybe they have an idea," Chris notes.

"Screw that. Let's call Vic on his cell," Emilio offers. Vic answers on the second ring. He is having his Café Bustello in the kitchen of the townhouse with Raquel.

"Good morning, Vic It's Emilio. Sorry to bother. I'm at the office with Chris. I received a bizarre message on my voicemail stamped yesterday afternoon. We think you two should hear this right away."

"Sure, can you play it for us? I'll put Raquel on speaker."

It takes a few seconds for Chris to get the audio working. He plays the message. Halfway through, Vic looks at Raquel and put his hands on his head. *"What the fuck?"* he mouths.

After it is finished, Vic says, "Okay, what about it?"

"We ahh, we have no idea who this was, and what does he mean by a race?" Chris asks.

Vic points to Raquel.

"I thought you guys were born in New York and had some street smarts," Raquel says.

"Sorry, what do you mean?" Emilio asks.

"Can't you tell a prank call? Someone is breaking your balls. We used to make calls like that when I was in high school. It's either someone inside the office or a nosy news reporter. Jesus, who in the world would be able to give you and the FBI leads on this case? It could even be someone from NYPD who knows we are on the case. After all, you've been in touch with some detectives there, right?"

Silence.

"But how did they just decide to call? And on a Sunday?" Emilio asks.

Vic starts laughing. "That's what makes it a prank, kiddo. Especially when he called me a cheapskate. I'm leaning toward one of our friends at NYPD."

Silence again.

"I feel like such an asshole," Emilio blurts.

"Not at all. Just inexperienced. We'll play this tape at the holiday party," Raquel adds.

"You did the right thing calling us. See you in a bit," Vic says and he ends the call.

"Can you believe that nut? He loves doing this crap," Raquel says.

"Everything Deegan does he does it for a reason. How he comes up with this shit is just part of the game he likes to play with us. That was fast thinking on your part, baby. I had no idea what to say. The part about high school was gold," Vic pronounces.

"Wait until I get my hands on Deegan," Raquel says.

"Don't even mention it. He craves that kind of attention. Make him bust!"

***

What you don't have you don't miss. Paul Vogelbach reached his mid-thirties and was still a virgin until he met Rebecca Sipes, and she made her move on him. School, study, career, and his faith in God through the Bible has replaced many of what Paul's natural instincts would normally crave. Paul never drank nor smoked nor partied with friends, never tried marijuana or anything harder. He once tried to watch porn but found it repugnant. He was considered a nerd in high school, and his college and medical school colleagues found him to be standoffish and somewhat strange. However, his patients find Dr. Vogelbach to be compassionate, patient, and thorough, with a kindly bedside manner.

Now, after a taste of a woman, Paul's testosterone is kicking in. When he thought of Becky, there is a reaction in his loins which he never dreamed could happen to him. He went from not thinking about sex to now needing it.

After the gallbladder surgery which he performed flawlessly, doing his hospital rounds, and seeing a dozen patients in his office, Vogelbach cannot wait until Wednesday to see Becky. Despite him not wanting to invite her, it seems the only way Paul can see her for an assignation is at his apartment. Going to a motel is not the proper way to be with his newfound lover.

Paul calls. Rebecca takes his address and is happy to meet at four o'clock that afternoon. She, too, has stirrings in her body, which she never had before meeting Paul.

Paul hurries from his office to tidy up his place. Never having a housekeeper, he keeps his apartment clean and neat on his own. He dusts the furniture quickly and makes sure his kitchen and bathroom are spotless. Paul unlocks his second bedroom to make sure his medical bag is supplied with the necessary drugs for his upcoming trip to Cincinnati. The room has a desk and a high-back brown leather chair and with a matching ottoman. Unlike his living room, which has several modern Giancarlo Impiglia original prints and antique art deco furniture, the walls in his office are barren.

The medical travel bag rests on a cherry wood table on one side of the room. On the other side is a matching four-foot-high bureau. On the bureau sits a macabre display of items. Layla Cole's copper-colored gris-gris, the Afro-Caribbean amulet, Gary Pose's golden hairbrush and comb set, Blake du Mont's family heirloom wristwatch, and a gold-plated crucifix which he took from Teri Arceneaux's bedroom wall are displayed in no particular order. His family bible and a black and white portrait photograph of Christian Stewart are on either side of the souvenirs. Vogelbach opens his medical kit to double check the required instruments. Syringes, forceps, no. 10 and no. 11 blades, scissors, hemostats, forceps, sutures, aspirating needle, and a bag valve mask, the anesthetics, vecuronium bromide, and ketamine vials are all ready for his trip. Satisfied, all is right, Paul leaves the room, making sure the door is locked behind him.

Rebecca arrives promptly at four. She looks ravishing in a green Italian knit pantsuit. A rose-colored golden cross hangs on a gold chain just above the slightest bit of cleavage. She takes Paul's breath away.

"Welcome," Paul is able to utter. Becky enters the apartment as the door closes behind her.

Becky moves toward Paul, moving her lithe body closely into his. She kisses him passionately. Paul becomes instantaneously aroused. They kiss for a minute or so until Paul feels he may ejaculate. He picks Becky off the floor in his arms, carrying her directly to the bedroom.

After a long, passionate love-making session, Becky nestles her head into Paul's arm.

"I didn't even see your apartment," Becky says. She smiles, showing her dimpled cheeks.

"Plenty of time for that," Paul responds.

"I can't get enough of you. I was hoping to see you before Wednesday, and here we are," Becky coos.

"I couldn't wait."

"So, I guess you like me."

"This is all new to me, Becky, but I think it's more than like," Paul murmurs.

"It's new to me, too, Paul. I'm glad I waited for you. Now I understand what my body was trying to tell me. You are the most wonderful man in the whole world."

"I have my flaws."

"I can't imagine any, but I'll deal with them as they come along."

"Hungry?" Paul asks.

"Starved."

"I made a reservation at eight. Nice Italian spot a few blocks away. Unless you want something else."

"That's fine. So, we have a little time to go again, I imagine," Becky teases.

"I'm ready when you are." Paul looks under the sheet at his pulsing erection.

Becky laughs and holds up her finger. "I have one question. Do you really have to go out of town this week? I'm not sure I can be without you for a few days."

"I have to go. There's one more thing to do. I need to finish up on something I've been working on for a while. After that, I have no travel plans and certainly none without you."

"May I ask where you are going?" Becky enquires. Paul paused. Becky notices a momentary, strange, trancelike look on his face. He quickly snaps out of it.

"Of course, you may. I'm going to assist a colleague of mine at the Cleveland Clinic. We've been working together on a new surgical instrument. Trying to get a patent," Vogelbach lies.

"Oh, okay." Becky pauses. "I'll be right back." Becky excuses herself to use the bathroom.

Suddenly, Paul's erection goes soft. He doesn't want to lie to Becky but realizes his life is a lie. He hears water running from the bathroom and rolls over onto Becky's side of the bed, whiffing the remnants of her perfume on her pillow.

He wonders if he should abandon the Q. After all, there is a lot of attention being paid to the alphabet killer, as the gay community begins referring to the four murders in the LGBTQ world. Perhaps he should stop now. He can feel changes in himself since Becky came along. But if he stops now, what would the Lord think of him abandoning his crusade?

Paul thinks back to Reverend Stewart's talk with him and the reference from Genesis. *'I am God Almighty: be fruitful and multiply. A nation and a company of nations shall come from you, and kings shall come from your own body'.*

The thought of having children never entered Vogelbach's mind. At least not until now.

Becky climbs back into bed, and for the first time in her life, she performs oral sex.

CHAPTER 38

NYPD 5th Precinct Detective James McLaughlin is having a particularly hard time emotionally and mentally months after the Layla Cole murder.

His partner John Miliots is doing all he could do to help McLaughlin through his rough period. Both well-experienced homicide detectives, with hundreds of cases more gruesome than Layla Cole's, the partners tried to talk over Jimmy's distress. They are having a long lunch in a deli near the 5th.

"She comes to me in my dreams nearly every night, John. She's crying all the time. In one dream she was trying to sing, and nothing would come out of her mouth. It's the strangest thing. Of all the murders we've seen, even the little kids, I have never thought about the victims for more than a few weeks. And never dreamt on one of them. She's fucking haunting me," Jimmy admits.

"And you still don't want to see the department shrink?" John asks. He has advised Jimmy to do that a few times.

"Hell, no! How many times do I have to tell you that goes on your permanent record. I don't care what they say that it's confidential. That's total bullshit. Besides, they don't know shit from Shinola about being a cop on the street. And I can't mention it to Bortugno, that soulless Dracula prick."

John wipes a glob of mayonnaise from his chin. "I'm no expert, but I think it's because we somehow dropped the ball on this one. Maybe Dracula is right. There must be something we missed."

"I've gone over everything seventeen times. The perp has gone on to kill three others, and there doesn't seem to be any mistakes on those either."

"Stop beating yourself up pal," John advises.

"Maybe that voodoo gris-gris thing has something to do with it," Jimmy says.

"Like what?"

"I don't mean the evidence. I mean maybe it has some kind of spell on me."

"You don't really believe in that shit, Jimmy. Good Catholic boy like you?"

Jimmy took a swig of his Diet Pepsi. He raises his eyebrows as if to say, *'Ya never know'.*

Unexpectedly, at least for Jimmy, a familiar voice speaks.

"Look who the hell is here. My old pal Jimmy Cartoons," Vic Gonnella declares.

"Holy shit! Vic, what are you slumming down here for?" Jimmy replies.

"I was just in the neighborhood. Thought I'd say hello," Vic says. Everyone shakes hands and do the old friend chest bump.

Vic sits at the table. Jimmy turns and looks at Miliotis with a probing look.

John puts his hands up next to his chest. "Look, Jimmy, don't get all pissed off at me. I know you and Vic go way back, so I called him to talk about this Cole case with us."

"Jimmy, I'm glad John called me. You and I go way back. I'm here to tell you something like this happens all the time. It happened to me with the Deegan case. I was a mess for a while. I'm also going to tell you the perp isn't perfect and there's some new evidence," Gonnella offers.

"You were a mess? Mr. Cool?"

"For the longest time I could hardly sleep."

"Hey pally, If I was lying next to Raquel I would never sleep," Jimmy laughs. So did Vic and John.

"Yeah...yeah...I get it. But seriously, I still blame myself for Deegan getting away. Shit happens in a case. Some cases just have it piled high and deep. You both did everything you could, period, end of subject."

"What new evidence are you talking about, Vic?" Cartoons asks.

"Off the record?"

"Absolutely."

"The FBI kept certain information about the killing in Louisiana off ViCap. I'm told they have a solid lead on the perp's boot prints. Hopefully, it's a matter of time before the case will be over and done with."

"Son of a bitch. He didn't leave a drop of dandruff on our case, never mind a footprint," Jimmy blurts.

"Last time I looked, there was no mud from the Bayou on the streets of Manhattan," Vic spouts.

John adds. "He finally got sloppy."

"Yes. But let's not underestimate these serial killer genius types. I'll be happy when he's collared," Vic adds.

Jimmy sits back in his chair, just looking at his old friend.

"Jimmy, you have been a great homicide guy. You made first grade in a flash. You closed more cases than anyone I know of. You put up with this Greek prick for years, and I'm here to tell you the day put your papers in you have a job in my organization...the very next day," Vic offers.

"Cypriot," Miliotis says.

"What?"

"I'm a Cypriot. Not Greek."

"Same difference," Vic and Jimmy say simultaneously. Everyone cracks up laughing.

"Pally, I am so grateful for you coming down here. You were always a stand-up guy," Jimmy declares.

"I gotta go. Raquel is home in bed waiting for me." They all laugh again.

The three men shake hands and hug. Vic heads for the door.

"Hey Vic, one more thing. I'll need two weeks off before I start," Jimmy hollers.

"No problem, Jimmy Cartoons. Unpaid leave."

CHAPTER 39

"We received a report an hour ago from Sam Cooper, agent in charge of the Manhattan field office," Cis Burns announces. "All seventy-one sales at the Thursday Boot store are accounted for, including the three cash sales. Facial recognition helped track down the cash payers. Thank goodness for technology. All seventy-one had solid alibis, and none fit the profile of our killer, so even though we know the perp had been in New York City, he did not buy his boots at that store. Which leads to the credit card sales." Burns is addressing the bullpen, with all of the agents in rapt attention.

Salerno stands to the right of Burns. GG is slouching in the back of the room. She has been walked up by the hand to the meeting by Salerno himself, to show GG how important she is to his team and to the case. While Burns is speaking, GG holds her head toward the ceiling and her eyes close. A cloud of smoke wafted over and around her in the non-smoking office. All accommodations are made for Gail Gains's emotional comfort.

Burns continues, "Of the one-hundred and seventy-one credit card sales, there are sixty-three still in process. The others have been determined not to be suspects. We expect the remainder to be completed within the next forty-eight hours."

Salerno cuts in. "The next forty-eight to seventy-two hours are crucial. It's the surgeon's witching hour. We have to hustle. According to his pattern he will be on the prowl for the next victim this week or weekend."

Cis burns continues. "One more important thing on the boots, sir. Ms. Gains's analysis indicates that the perp may be living in Wisconsin. Three sets of boots are purchased in that state. Two have been cleared as not suspects, and one, Edward Auffant, was a person of interest until we discovered that Auffant passed away from COVID in 2019. Our killer likely stole his identity and used a faked credit card to make the purchase. The boots were sent to a now-defunct post office box outside Milwaukee. Our field office in Milwaukee is all over this."

A loose cough comes from GG. She pauses and announces, "Correction. The perp does live in Wisconsin, not may be living in Wisconsin."

Cis Burns inhales deeply but doesn't respond. She doesn't want to get into theory versus fact.

Salerno cuts in again. "We are putting as many assets as possible to track this Auffant lead. It's the best we have so far on the case. If the killer used a fraudulent card and post office box, we soon may have our man."

GG coughs again and raises her hand.

"Yes, GG," Salerno asks.

"I want to know more of this Edward Auffant. Was he religious? Was he affiliated with a church? Did he ever live in Wisconsin? Where did he die?" GG asks.

"We can find out. Why is this information germane, GG?"

GG looks over everyone's heads. She takes a long drag on her cigarette and exhales. She scratches her head. Flakes of dandruff coat her blouse. "Look, I had told you the killer was likely a religious zealot on a mission. That's his profile, in my opinion. If we can tie him somehow to our killer, it will be an important piece of this puzzle and can lead us directly to him," GG offers.

Salerno processes what GG said for a few seconds. "Excellent point. Agent Burns, I want to know everything we can get on Auffant. Where he worked, if and where he went to church, his family, his doctors...everything."

"Yes sir," Burns replies.

***

Reverend Stewart is at home recuperating from his ischemic stroke at the clergy house. His neurologist Dr. Lorenz gave him strict orders to rest and prescribed some medication. Stewart lives alone in a three-bedroom Tudor-like home behind the church on a beautifully manicured parcel, replete with a flower and herb garden. The outpouring of love from his parishioners is almost overwhelming for the preacher. There are so many fruit baskets, home baked cakes and pies, and casserole dinners that the housekeeper fills the church vehicle and delivered the food to a veteran's homeless shelter in town.

Stewart is tired from his ordeal and isn't ready to see guests at the parsonage. Only a few members of the church board, his deacons, who are instructed by Stewart to continue services without him for the time being, and Dr. Paul Vogelbach is permitted to visit.

"There is my life saver," Stewart declares when Paul is brought to his bedroom by the housekeeper. Much like his office, the furnishings are neat but sparce. A double bed, two pinewood side tables with matching lamps, a five-drawer pine bureau, and a standing brass lamp which stand next to a cloth covered gray Lazy-Boy chair. A few religious paintings and pen and pencil drawings made by parishioners hang on the walls.

"Good morning, Reverend. You and I know the only saver of life is our Lord. I was just his vessel last Sunday," Paul utters. He is smiling ear to ear seeing his mentor sitting upright in his Lazy Boy.

"Hallelujah. His name be praised. Paul, thank you for what you did. Getting me to the hospital made all the difference. I have no recollection of what occurred prior to this happening to me. I'm told I was giving my sermon, and perhaps my blood pressure rose too quickly," Stewart says.

"Reverend, I'm told by your physician your blood pressure has been an issue for some time. It has fluctuated and has always been on the high side. You've refused to take your doctor's advice and begin taking medication. It was just a matter of time before you experienced an episode like you had. Or worse. Your sermon was...let me say powerful and brilliant, and yes it could have contributed to an enormous rise in your pressure."

"Paul, I will go to my grave preaching against these sinners and what they are doing to our society and to our children. Let me tell you, this LGBTQ plus nonsense..."

Vogelbach interrupts, "Reverend, you are jumping on that train again. This is not the time for you to get excited. As a matter of fact, I hear you have refused to take the medication to help you sleep and calm you down a bit. I must insist you follow medical advice. We don't want you to go to your grave anytime soon. Please calm yourself. There will be plenty of time for us...I mean for you to make our voices heard."

"I will take your advice, my dear friend. So, tell me, have you seen Rebecca Sipes?" Stewart inquires. Her name brings a smile to the reverend's pale face.

"Indeed, we have seen each other several times, and I want to thank you for your introduction. She's a wonderful lady."

"Several times. Praise the Lord. Perhaps my prayers are being answered for you, Paul."

"I can tell you, Reverend, I have never felt the way I do after getting to know Becky. I have a whole different perspective on things."

"Such as?"

Vogelbach ponders his answer for a moment. "Well, let's see, I never thought I would ever care for someone the way I do about Becky. She is constantly on my mind, and I'm...let me just say my feelings about life are different now. I can't even explain it to you."

"Do you think she feels the same toward you?" Reverend Stewart asks.

"Yes, I do. She's pretty much told me so. I believe we were both unfulfilled."

"Has the L word been tossed around?"

"No. At least not yet."

"That's good. Perhaps it's just too soon for that. Can I give you some advice on the matter?"

"Of course, Reverend. I was hoping you would," Paul adds.

"Paul, nice emotions often accompany love, and we naturally have good and strong feelings toward someone we are attracted to. Remember that those new and good feelings bring along with them the natural coursing hormones when we are near the subject of our affections. Now, and this is very important Paul, if that's all there is to falling in love then we're in deep, deep trouble. What happens when the initial infatuation goes away? After the getting to know you phase of a relationship? What about when the hormones subside? Is that the end of love? What I am saying to you is quite simple. Make sure Rebecca is the real one for you and you for her. That takes time and patience. You've both waited so long, and you may both need to wait a bit longer. Once you have done your homework, the relationship will pass the test of time and your life will be joyous. The Lord willing."

Vogelbach is momentarily stunned by the reverend's words.

"I have never heard anything so eloquent when it comes to love, Reverend. I'll make you a deal," Paul offers.

"I'll heed your words if you will heed mine. Take your medication and calm down. The pulpit can wait a bit."

CHAPTER 40

On Wednesday morning Rebecca arrives at Paul's apartment. She brought fresh-cut flowers in a vase. Paul takes the vase and takes it into his bedroom, where he places it on his bureau. Instead of going on a walk or taking a jog or a picnic at the lake, the couple cannot wait to get into Paul's bed. They make love, this time with enthusiastic energy, each of them climaxing numerous times. They both discover their sexuality and are going for the gusto.

"This is my second time here, and I've never really seen your apartment. How about a quick tour?" Becky asks.

"Sure, there isn't much to see. Let me get my robe," Paul replies.

"I'll just wear one of your shirts...like in the movies," Rebecca coos. Paul hands her the plaid button-down shirt he is wearing. Becky puts it on and fastens the top three buttons. She looks sexy as hell, and Paul momentarily thinks about pulling her back to his bed.

"You've already seen the bedroom and the bathroom," Paul laughs.

“So, this must be the living room. Who decorated it for you?”

“I did it myself. I’ve always been an art deco lover. Something about the symmetrical and geometric lines has always appealed to me. I think that’s just how my mind works. Neat, orderly, sharp lines, defined angles very much unlike the avant-garde period, which I don’t care for too much.”

“These prints look very 1920s to me,” Becky notes.

“Precisely. Impiglia uses people in his work who have angular faces and bodies along with bright or dark colors that fit the period. This work of his is considered to be contemporary art deco. These are all are original prints.”

“I’m learning a lot about you, Paul. I will need to catch up to your love of art. Look at this amazing piece on your coffee table. It looks very familiar.”

“That is glass art. It’s a very good copy of Lalique’s Victoire. She is facing into the wind, giving a sensation of speed. See her hair as if it’s frozen behind her? Maybe you remember it from photos of an old-fashioned car ornament way back in the American auto industry.”

“That’s amazing. There is so much for me to learn about art,” Becky says. She feels out of her element.

“I’m happy to be your guide,” Paul says as he kisses the side of Becky’s neck. She responds with a slight moan.

“And what’s in that room?” She points to Paul’s secret locked room.

“Oh...that’s just a room where I keep some medical things. Papers, books, models.”

“Show me,” Becky asks.

“Not now, my love. It’s very messy.”

"C'mon, let me see," Becky insists.

"I said no," Paul snaps. He raises his voice to her for the first time.

"Sorry, I seem to have struck a nerve."

"There are certain things I believe should be kept private, even between people who care for each other."

"Okay, I get it. You need your space." Becky sits down on the sofa. She is embarrassed. Paul sits next to her. She can see that Paul's face has reddened.

"I didn't mean to upset you, Paul. It's just, I want to learn everything there is to know about you," Becky adds.

"Some things just need to be kept secret."

"So, tell me about a secret you've never told anyone before. And I'll tell you one of mine," Becky fishes.

Paul stands and walks around the living room. Becky's eyes follow him. She can see his mind is racing as he becomes pensive.

"Now is a time I wish I drank alcohol to loosen my tongue. Like you said in the movies. The guy walks around with a scotch with no ice in a tumbler."

Becky laughs. Paul sits back down closely next to her again.

"Okay, I have a secret. You may be upset with it, but here goes. I was just in San Francisco a little while ago. The city has become a disaster, all because of liberal politicians who have given up on morals and are pushing the woke agenda. It sickened me. I left the same day I got there because I had a flashback of an unfortunate incident I had there when I was younger. When I was in medical school, it was a great place to be. I even thought about practicing medicine there. That's how much San Francisco appealed to me. Anyway, I went there and stayed with friends of a fellow student. I never had real friends. Still don't. There were several people staying at the apartment. Some were drinking, some were smoking marijuana. I've never done either. Everyone was rambling about politics and which political party was the better one. I went to bed late that night, and one of the guys followed me into my room. At first, he seemed alright. We were talking about school, and I really don't remember too much else about the conversation. He sat down at the bottom of my bed. I felt uncomfortable and sat up. He said he really admired me and my surgical studies, things like that. He ran his hand up my leg toward my privates. I pushed his hand away. He persisted telling me he wanted to have sex with me. I got out of bed and was trying to leave the room when he pulled me toward him and tried to kiss me. He grabbed my crotch. I pushed him away. I told him I wasn't interested in that sort of thing. He came at me again, this time even more aggressively. We started pushing back and forth at each other. That turned into a real fight. The fighting seemed to turn him on. I beat him so badly he had to be taken to the hospital. I immediately packed the few clothes I had and fled. The next day I was back home. No charges were ever filed, but I found out later the guy nearly died and lost sight in one eye. I felt terrible about what happened, but I must admit I was happy I beat him. I never did anything like that before. But I enjoyed it. There was something sadistic about it. Something...I don't know...unholy."

Becky is stunned by Paul's secret. Her mouth is agape hearing such a distressing story. She is going to tell him how she masturbated in the shower using the handheld shower head. Her secret is silly compared to Paul's.

"Oh, God. What a frightening story. No wonder you dislike gays so much," Becky blurts.

"I think I could have handled it differently. I could have made it out of that room, I suppose. I didn't have to beat him so badly. I just couldn't stop. For years I thought perhaps I was secretly gay. There was something about pummeling this guy that I took pleasure in."

"Well, I'm here to bear witness that you are certainly not gay," Becky chuckles.

"I've never verbalized that story before. I keep it buried inside. I'm glad I finally got the story out," Paul utters.

"And I'm happy it was me you told."

"Now then. Let's return to the boudoir for a bit. We can have lunch after, and then I have to get going. I need to do a few things and pack."

"Do you really have to go, Paul?"

"I was thinking about cancelling the trip to be with you, but that would be inappropriate. I am one who finishes a project that I think is important."

CHAPTER 41

Vic and Raquel are packed and ready for the trip to Cincinnati. Deegan's private jet is taking off at 6 p.m. from Teterboro airport in New Jersey. Gabriella is in good hands with her recuperating abuela Olga, who has just returned from the Lenox Hill rehab facility. The abuela can now walk with the help of a cane, and her recovery from her broken hip is nothing less than miraculous. A home health aide is staying at the townhouse 24/7 just in case. Pando is on call if he is needed.

Instead of having Pando take them to the airport for fear that he might somehow see and recognize John Deegan, the couple call an Uber for the ride to New Jersey. Vic and Raquel say their goodbyes to Gabby and Olga at 4:30 that afternoon for the hour and fifteen-minute ride to Teterboro. Normally, the ride is no more than forty minutes from the townhouse, but traffic at rush hour on the dread FDR drive increases the time.

"Baby, they've been fixing this damn highway since I'm eleven years old. Can you imagine the poor guy who needs to drive home in this mess every day? I'd throw myself into the Harlem River," Vic says.

"I'm just glad we can walk to our office," Raquel notes. Vic is holding Raquel's hand in the back seat of the Uber car. He can tell she is getting nervous about the flight, as her hand is clammy and she is fidgeting. She never does well flying.

"Baby, try to relax. It's only a two-hour flight. Probably less on a private jet. These guys know how to save time. The ride is generally smoother, plus we will have our friend to entertain us. We'll be back on the ground before you know it," Vic whispers.

"I'll be fine. I'm sure we have a lot to discuss. That will keep my mind off being in that friggin' tube," Raquel blurts.

An accident on the George Washington Bridge from New York to New Jersey follows the traffic jam on the FDR Drive. Raquel is getting anxious about being late. Vic couldn't care less. He knows Deegan wouldn't leave without them. The Uber arrives a few minutes before six. There is no security delay getting on the private jet, so the couple just walks aboard with their two small, wheeled pieces of luggage. Raquel feels her legs trembling and tries to make the best of the situation. She wants to run screaming down the tarmac, but that would be too embarrassing.

Vic and Raquel walk up the five steps onto the jet. A smiling John Deegan meets Vic and Raquel inside the door. His disguise is unique even for Deegan. Like a throwback hippie artist, he wears a white wig with stringy hair passing his shoulders. A tie-dyed t-shirt with white and black stripped bell-bottomed pants and open toe sandals make him look like a refugee from the Woodstock Music and Arts Festival from 1969.

"Deegan, if you start passing around a joint, I swear I'll kick your old ass," Vic laughs. Raquel is too nervous to notice Vic's glib remark.

"I enjoy this look. I always wanted to look like a Greenwich Village artist or a musician. There's a certain panache that goes along with my disguises. I'm able to live vicariously through my creativity," Deegan announces.

Within a minute they are up in the air. Deegan takes off the wig and sits back facing Vic and Raquel. Raquel is white knuckled until the jet reaches cruising altitude.

Vic has a McCallan 15 on the rocks. Deegan waits patiently for Raquel to calm down. When she seems calmer, Deegan announces, "So, let's go over our plan, shall we?"

***

Paul Vogelbach says his goodbyes to Becky. He isn't practiced at such emotions. He feels awkward and doesn't know how to handle the tears in Becky's eyes. Paul promises he would be home before Sunday's service, even though Reverend Stewart wouldn't be officiating. Through her tears Becky becomes a bit sullen, and she makes Paul promise to call her at least once a day, even though he says he would be back no later than Saturday night.

Rather than fly and risk any issues with security and the facial recognition he has read about, or being somehow discovered by law enforcement, Paul decides to drive his BMW around the tip of Lake Michigan and through Chicago for the six-hour ride to Cincinnati. To be extra cautious not to be tracked by road cameras or while paying tolls or while driving around Cincinnati, Paul purchases Ohio license plates on E-Bay for $25.00. He leaves his Wisconsin plates well hidden in the trunk. Vogelbach has booked a room on Airbnb and would pay cash for his stay, except for a fifty-percent deposit which he has put on his PayPal account, drawing the funds directly from his personal checking account.

Once he arrives in Cincinnati, Vogelbach's plan is relatively simple. Quincy Davies lives his life on social media. The well-known musician has a few million fans who follow him, watching him do everything but take his daily bowel movements. Sometimes twice or three times a day, Quincy posts everything from his music, favorite recipes, his sexuality, including photographs of himself and his latest lovers as well as his performance schedule.

Davies holds Instagram and Tik Toc mini concerts where he plays keyboards, guitar, and some saxophone with his classic jazz quartet, which goes by the name 'Real'. The Queen City has a long and rich history of jazz dating back to the turn of the century, and Quincy loves the vibe. Big-name jazz musicians from all over the country played in the plethora of venues all throughout the city, and Quincy is smack in the middle of the scene.

Quincy has played every jazz spot there is in Cincinnati. Among his favorites was Schwartz's Point Jazz and Acoustic Club on Vine Street in the middle of the Queen

City. On Thursday and Friday night this week, Quincy Davies and his boys will go on at 8 p.m. The cover charge is ten bucks. The joint closed at 11:30.

Quincy even posted his address in the Walnut Hill neighborhood in the near east side of Cincinnati. Vogelbach has everything he needs right on Instagram and Facebook. All he needs is to scope out the venue and his victim's apartment and track Quincy's movements on Thursday and do his thing on Friday night. He will be on the road back to Milwaukee and to Becky, and his one-man crusade against the LGBTQ community will finally be finished.

Man plans, and God laughs.

CHAPTER 42

On Wednesday night, while Paul Vogelbach is well on his way in his BMW to Cincinnati, listening to recordings of Reverend Stewart's anti-LGBTQ+ sermons through his ear buds, and Vic, Raquel, and John Deegan are flying to the Queen City working their plan, Agent Dean Salerno and his crew of serial killer profilers in Langley, Virginia, are about to break the case wide open.

"Listen up, everyone, please. Looks like we are about to hit paydirt and let me say none of this was because of luck," Salerno announces. He is in the bullpen of the Child Abduction / Serial Murder Investigative Resources Center. Even though it is getting late and everyone is spent, Salerno still expects his agents to be committed to the case, neat and buttoned up. GG stands in her usual spot in the rear of the room puffing away on her beloved Pall Mall cigarette. All the agents sit in their cubicles awaiting the latest news on the case. Some of them already know what is going on.

"Agent Burns has the floor," Salerno says.

An exhausted Cis Burns reads from her notes. She momentarily looks up in GG's direction, but there is no eye contact.

"We did a deep dive into the late Edward Auffant. Evidently, he had issues with faith and religion. GG's theory of the killer being a religious fanatic was spot on." Coming from Cis Burns, the only reaction GG has is to inhale her cigarette. She looks up at the ceiling with her eyes tightly closed.

Burns continues. "Born in 1950, Auffant was brought up by extremely strict Roman Catholic Puerto Rican-born parents in the Bronx, New York. He graduated from Catholic grammar school and high school and briefly attended Hunter College in New York. He began his career as a social worker in the South Bronx and later moved on to be a probation officer, also in Bronx County, where he retired, fully vested, in 2015. He seemed to be trying to find himself through a variety of religions and dabbled for a while in Santería. For those of you unfamiliar with this religion, Santería is a religion with African roots. It was brought to the islands of Cuba, Puerto Rico, and the Dominican Republic by African slaves. It is a combination of Roman Catholicism and Yorùbán religious beliefs. Santería involves animal sacrifice, mostly with chickens, and dedication to many saints. Auffant moved on for a while as a Jehovah's Witness and then to the Church of Latter-Day Saints. Finally, he became a born-again Christian in an Evangelical church in the Bronx, where he served as a deacon until his death from COVID in 2019 at New York City Presbyterian Hospital."

"All that being said, we discovered that Auffant was a staunch anti-gay, anti LGBTQ+ proponent. That brought him to follow a few outspoken anti-gay pastors in the South and Midwest. One of the preachers he followed and communicated with was a Reverend Christian Stewart in Milwaukee. We have downloaded numerous e-mails and contributions from Auffant to Stewart on his computer, which we were able to obtain from a girlfriend. Our Milwaukee field office is quietly nosing around until Special Agent Salerno and I can fly to Milwaukee. The director has approved the use of an FBI jet out of Dulles. Again, Kudos to GG, who determined that the killer resides in Wisconsin. The pieces of the puzzle are connecting nicely."

GG seems to be frozen until Cis Burns stops speaking. She holds her cigarette in her right hand, which rests in the palm of her left. The ash from her Pall Mall is bent and longer than the cigarette itself.

Salerno picks up the discussion. "We are leaving in an hour. By early morning we will arrive in Milwaukee and determine if this is real. In the meantime, I'm asking you folks to do an analysis of the members of Stewart's congregation, assuming you can find that information. I trust you will use your intuition and imagination to get this data. We are specifically looking for any number of Stewart's parishioners who are involved with medicine or surgery or have knowledge of operating room procedures. You can communicate with us on our cells or in the company jet. If we follow the killer's pattern, he is due to strike again any day now. Let's get cracking."

Deegan is correct. The case of the surgeon is now a three-way race to his next killing. The United States of America, Vic Gonnella, Raquel Ruiz — backed up by Deegan himself — and the surgeon. The surgeon and Gonnella et al. are heading to Cincinnati. The FBI is heading toward Milwaukee and in last place.

CHAPTER 43

Salerno's team does a fabulous job with the Reverend Christian Stewart's data. By the time Salerno and Burns land in Milwaukee, the team has gathered information on the Unified Free Church of Truth and its congregation. First, they determine that Reverend Stewart did not fly on a commercial airline for the past two years, so it is unlikely that he is a suspect. Further analysis of the crunched data indicated that there are six registered nurses in the parish and one board-certified surgeon, Dr. Paul Vogelbach. They know that Vogelbach is on the surgical staff at Milwaukee General Hospital, with a photo of him on their website. The photo matches the few indicators on the facial recognition software.

Armed with this information, Salerno and Burns, along with three Milwaukee-based FBI agents, head directly to the home of Reverend Stewart.

The team waits until 9 a.m. to knock on the door of the clergy house. They are greeted by the housekeeper. She is shocked when she sees five FBI agents at the door and Salerno and Burns' identifications.

"We would like to have a word with Reverend Stewart, please," Burns says.

"Good Lord, what is this about. The pastor is resting. He had a stroke a few days ago."

"We understand that. It's important that we see Reverend Stewart immediately. I assure you we will not take too much of his time," Burns adds.

"Please come in and wait in the living room. I will tell him you are here."

A few minutes later Revered Stewart comes into the living room, finding the agents all standing. He shuffles wearing a long white terry-cloth robe and slippers.

"Good morning. How may I help you? Please be seated." Salerno and Burns sit on the sofa. The three other agents remain standing, looking around the room for any details they can capture.

Reverend Stewart sits in one of the chairs facing the sofa.

"Reverend, we are on a case which may come as a shock to you, so please try to remain calm," Salerno utters.

"At my age the entire world comes to me as a shock," Stewart blurts.

"We are aware of your stance on the gay and lesbian world. You are of course protected by your First Amendment rights of free speech, and we have no issue with that," Salerno states.

"Thank you. I am happy that our forefathers wrote the amendment."

"Indeed, so are we. Reverend, there have been a series of murders in the LGBTQ+ community over the past several months. While none of the offenses transpired near your parish or in Wisconsin, the homicides occurred in various cities around the country. We have reason to believe one of your parishioners may be a suspect."

"That's impossible. Our flock are all God-fearing, good people. Solid Americans," Stewart replies.

"What do you know of an Edward Auffant?" Salerno asks.

"Hmm. I can tell you he was never a parishioner here. If I recall correctly, he and I traded thoughts on homosexuality for a while. However, I haven't heard from him in years."

"Yes, Reverend, he is deceased."

"I see. May he rest in peace. What are you asking about him?"

"We believe one of your parishioners has stolen his identity. This has brought us to you," Salerno offers.

"Five FBI agents come to my home over stolen identity? That seems odd," Stewart says.

"It's more than that, Reverend," Cis Burns adds.

Stewart looks up at the three standing agents. He seems uncomfortable with their presence.

"What can you tell us about Dr. Paul Vogelbach?" Burns queries.

"If you are asserting Paul had anything to do with stealing this man's identity, I will say, unequivocally, you are incorrect."

"Why do you say that Reverend?" Burns asks.

"Dr. Vogelbach is one of the pillars of our parish and of this community. He is well to do and has no need to take advantage of a dead person's identity or money."

"And you know this because....?" Salerno asks.

"Paul has recently made a sizable donation to our church. He attends services every Sunday and recently saved me from great harm when I had a stroke. He probably saved my life with the help of our Lord and Savior Jesus Christ."

"May I ask how much the donation was?" Burns asks.

"That is privileged information, madam. Paul asked that his donation, along with his more than generous tithe, remain confidential."

"Reverend, we are the FBI. We have our ways of discovering how much he gave, so please, I'm asking for your full cooperation," Salerno states.

"Well, I guess I must tell you then. I don't recall the amount of his tithe, but I can look at that and let you know. The tithe is based on income, and the doctor does very well. His recent donation was a quarter of a million dollars," Stewart replies.

"Is that outside the norm in your parish?" Burns asks.

"I started this church many years ago. There has never been a donation that came anywhere near Paul's generosity."

"Do you know where Dr. Vogelbach is now?" Salerno asks.

"I'm sorry, but I don't. I can tell you he has not missed Sunday services since he became a member of our church, which was years ago. However, I don't recall at the moment exactly when that was."

"Do you know if he has any friends within the parish, Reverend?" Burns probes.

"Paul is a very private person. He is a very busy man at the hospital and in his private practice."

"So would you say he's a loner, Reverend?" Burns asks.

"Why yes but hold on a second. There is a recent development in his Paul's life .A few weeks ago, maybe a month ago, I introduced him to another parishioner. I believe him to be quite smitten by her," Stewart admits.

"And who might she be?" Salerno inquires.

"Again, I must say this is confidential. Rebecca Sipes. She recently rejoined our flock after living out of town for a while. She lives not far from here with her father, whom I may add was saved by Dr. Vogelbach."

"Thank you for your cooperation, Reverend Stewart. We may return should we need further information," Salerno says.

"You don't suspect that Paul has any involvement in these deaths, do you?"

"Our investigation is ongoing. As Special Agent Salerno stated, we may come back to gather more information."

"But you stated one of my parishioners may be a suspect. Is it Paul?" Steward fidgets with the belt on his robe.

"Let's see. We have a lot of work ahead of us," Salerno states.

Stewart looks baffled and concerned. Burns hands him her card.

The agents quickly leave the parish house.

***

Rebecca Sipes has just finished washing the breakfast dishes for her and her father when the doorbell rings. She peers out of the front door window and sees three men and a woman in dark suits. Her dad has gone down to the basement to work on a hobby.

Rebecca opens the door. Cis Burns introduces the crew as FBI.

"My goodness, what's wrong?"

"Ms. Sipes, we have a few questions to ask. May we come in?" Burns inquires.

"Yes, of course. Please come in and have a seat."

Like at the parish house, the three agents stand while Salerno and Burns sit on the sofa. One of the agents picks up a *National Geographic* magazine from the coffee table. The other two are making mental notes of the neat home.

Salerno gets right to business. "Ms. Sipes, what can you tell us about Dr. Paul Vogelbach?"

"Is Paul, okay? Is anything wrong with him?" Rebecca stands up from the chair.

"Please relax. Sit down, Rebecca," Burns says.

"Oh my God. Is he dead?"

"We would like to know some information about Dr. Vogelbach as part of an investigation," Burns offers.

"An investigation about what, may I ask?" Rebecca is trembling.

"How do you know Paul?" Burns asks. She ignores her question.

"Well...we are dating. We met at church."

"Yes, we are aware that Reverend Stewart introduced you. Can you tell us where Paul is today?" Salerno probes.

"Cleveland. He said he was going to Cleveland on business for a few days," Rebecca blurts.

"Do you know what kind of business, Rebecca?" Burns asks.

"Something to do with a medical invention with a colleague is all I know. I believe he said at the Cleveland Clinic."

"When did he go to Cleveland? Did he fly there?"

"He drove."

"Do you know, when is he returning"? Salerno inquires.

"Yes, I do. Sometime Saturday."

"And when did he leave?"

"Last night." Rebecca is on the verge of tears.

FBI agents are trained not to look at one another during an interrogation. Burns has all to do not to look at her boss.

"Have you been to his apartment, Rebecca?" Burns asks.

"Well...yes I have..."

"Anything out of the ordinary, would you say?" Burns counters.

"No. He's an art lover is I all I can recall."

"Is your relationship a serious one," Burns queries. It is easier for a woman to ask this of another woman.

"I would say yes. We are very fond of one another. Has Paul done something wrong?"

"This is an ongoing investigation. We really can't say any more at this moment." Salerno states.

"When was the last time you spoke with Paul?" Burns pushes.

"Just before he left. He promised to call me every day he is out of town."

"Rebecca, I know this may be difficult for you. We would ask that you not take his call. It's important that he doesn't know we were here. Can you do that?" Burns states.

"I want to know what he's done. This is ridiculous." Rebecca stands again.

"Please stay calm, Ms. Sipes. Paul is a suspect in a homicide. It's a matter of life and death you don't speak with him," Salerno says sternly.

Rebecca falls back into the chair.

CHAPTER 44

Salerno and Burns waste no time. They quickly return to the FBI field office with the three agents speeding through, with the black SUV's horn blaring and lights flashing. Salerno calls the FBI director in Washington from his cell phone to alert him they have a bona fide suspect in the four serial murders. As the killings are committed in various cities, it was considered a federal crime. The director immediately phones the federal magistrate in Milwaukee as Salerno and Burns preparing the appropriate paperwork officially asking for the warrant.

Given the written affidavit from Salerno and Burns, the federal magistrate signs the warrant on the spot to search Paul Vogelbach's apartment and office and his personal belongings at Milwaukee General Hospital. Two agents are dispatched to the hospital. Four agents are dispatched to Vogelbach's office to search files and take his computers back for processing. The Cleveland FBI field office has issued Vogelbach's photo and is ordered to go to the massive Cleveland Clinic complex to look for Dr. Vogelbach. Salerno doubts the suspect is at the clinic but is leaving nothing to chance. The Cleveland Police Department is informed of the search by the FBI in

Washington and issues a BOLO, an all-points bulletin to be on the lookout for the suspect.

Salerno and Burns go to Vogelbach's apartment with the three agents assigned to them as well as additional heavily armed uniformed agents in case the suspect returns suddenly.

Salerno bangs on the apartment door, identifying himself as FBI. There is no answer. The team has found the building superintendent, who uses his pass key to open Vogelbach's apartment door. The heavily armed FBI agents enter the apartment first. They scour the apartment in case the suspect is hiding. The lock on the second bedroom door is smashed, and the agents see that no one is there.

Salerno and Burns walk through the apartment.

"For a bachelor, this guy's very neat. I want forensics up here ASAP for fingerprints and DNA samples," Salerno orders. One of the agents makes the call back to the field office.

"Rebecca was right. Vogelbach is an art lover, pretty cool stuff," Burns blurts.

Salerno nosed around and makes his way to the secret room Vogelbach keeps.

"Bingo!" He shouts. Burns is in the room in a flash.

"Jesus Christ." Burns says. Cis gasps when she sees what is on the bureau.

Neatly displayed, the souvenirs Vogelbach has taken from his victims are laid out like a makeshift altar.

"No doubt about it. Dr. Paul Vogelbach is the surgeon killer," Salerno pronounces. Their only problem is that the FBI has no idea at this point where to find the killer.

***

Salerno and Burns are frantically making calls back to the bullpen to report the results of the search warrant. They remain in Vogelbach's apartment while a platoon of FBI forensic personnel and photographers sweep through the apartment. Photos are taken of the four macabre mementos Vogelbach has taken from his victims. The agents sent to Vogelbach's private practice office have returned to the FBI field office with boxes of files and four computers and a laptop. IT specialists comb through the hardware for any evidence what can tie the surgeon to the four homicides. They are specifically looking for any travel arrangements the killer has made as well as Vogelbach's daily itineraries and expenses.

Cis Burns's cell phone rings while she and Salerno are examining papers in the killer's secret room for any bits of information which can determine where Vogelbach's next victim would be.

Burns answers the call.

"Agent Burns." There is no one on the other end of the call. "Hello, this is agent Burns." Salerno stops what he is doing and looks at Burns.

"Cecilia... ahh, this is GG." Burns mouths *'GG'* to her boss. Salerno looks at Burns in disbelief.

"Hello, GG. What's up?" Burns asks.

"I...I want to apologize to you. I behaved very poorly and unprofessionally, and I regret my actions," GG states.

"That's very nice of you, Gail. I appreciate it," Cis mouths *'She's sorry'*. Salerno looks shocked.

"You were always so nice to me, and I took it the wrong way, I suppose. I'm not very good about dealing with people, as you know."

"Let's just leave that in the past, GG. We are all under a lot of pressure," Burns says.

"We are both women in a man's world. There is still a good old boys club at the bureau, and it's not right that I treated you the way I did lately. Women should stick together after all."

Burns can hear GG is taking a drag on a cigarette.

"I want to make it up to you. I have discovered information no one else has of Vogelbach. I know where he is, Cecilia."

"You know where he is?" Burns blurts. Salerno is stunned by Burns's words.

"He is not in Cleveland like everyone is thinking. Hold on a second." GG has a coughing fit. It sounds as if she is gasping for air.

"Gail, are you alright?" Cis asks. She hear more muffled coughing and wheezing. It sounds like more than a smoker's cough to Burns.

"Yes, I'm okay. Vogelbach is in Cincinnati."

"He's in Cincinnati?" Burns repeats more for Salerno's benefit.

"Yes. I knew it would be Ohio, just not exactly where until now."

"How do you know this?"

"He used his PayPal account. I hacked into his account," GG offers.

"Where exactly in Cincinnati?"

"He rented an Air B and B room on 9 Mile Road. 356 Nine Mile Road. I haven't told anyone else, Cecilia," GG blurts.

"Once again, GG, you are the best there is. I'll call you back as soon as I can. I have to move quickly. Thank you so much and thank you for calling me." Cis ends the call.

"Let's get to the airport. He has a room at 356 Nine Mile Road in Cincinnati. GG hacked his PayPal account," Burns says to Salerno.

The pair of agents run out of Vogelbach's apartment, taking the stairs to the street two at a time.

A Milwaukee PD squad car is outside the apartment as backup to the FBI. The officer is standing outside of the vehicle.

Salerno and Burns run up to the officer. Burns halfway in the squad car. "Mitchell Airport...Make noise," Salerno orders.

Salerno calls his boss while on route to the airport. He needs help. He needs his boss's power. Explaining what his team discovered, the director pulls out all the stops. Agents from the Cincinnati FBI office are immediately dispatched, along with the bureau's SWAT team converge on the 9 Mile Road address.

After a fifteen-minute drive, Salerno and Burns board the FBI jet for the fifty-minute flight to Cincinnati.

***

Vogelbach isn't in the Airbnb. He has already left to begin his stalking of Quincy Davies. The killer is wearing the same leather jacket, fake beard, and wraparound sunglasses he has used at the Layla Cole murder. This time Vogelbach doesn't use a surgical mask, thinking it would draw too much attention at Schwartz's Point Jazz and Acoustic Club. After all, this was Cincinnati not Manhattan, where people are still COVID wary.

On his way to the jazz club, Vogelbach calls his Becky from his cell phone as he promised. Her phone rings four times before it goes to Rebecca's voice mail. Paul looks at his phone. He is annoyed that he cannot reach her. He tries again, getting the same result. He tries a third time. This time his call went directly to Rebecca's voice mail. "Damn it!" Vogelbach yells. He is incredulous. "Where can she be? She wanted me to call her. Damn it all," he says aloud.

CHAPTER 45

The Cleveland Police Department is ordered to stand down on the BOLO order for Vogelbach. The Cincinnati PD is asked by the FBI and issued a BOLO. It was now 7:30 p.m. in Cincinnati.

John Deegan, Raquel Ruiz, and Vic Gonnella enter Schwartz's jazz club. Vic pays the cover charge. The trio looks around and takes a table right in front of the stage. Deegan wears the same disguise he has worn on the jet. He looks like he belonged into a jazz club, with the long white hair and '60s hippie look. He added a pair of the rose-colored round glasses, made famous by John Lennon, just for effect. Raquel has on tight denim blue jeans and a plain black t-shirt top with a white linen jacket. Vic wears a pair of black slacks and an Izod terrycloth collared polo shirt. Deegan and Raquel order ginger ale. Vic orders his usual Macallan's 15.

The stage at Schwartz's is small, with six track lights shining down on where the musicians will be playing. There is a long reddish tiled bar with wide, comfortable square bar stools and low black hanging lamps dotted along the ceiling. Behind the musicians hang a beautiful square tapestry with a green and gold pattern. Another smaller tapestry is hanging on the wall to the right with other eclectic artworks. Above are billowing maroon draperies making a sort of tent-like look around the stage.

The trio chats about their musical preferences rather than discussing the case, as the tables are closely set next to each other. Raquel speaks of how much she adores the late Tito Puente and how proud she is of Puente, who is a New York City-born Puerto Rican. Tito Puente composes and performed dance-oriented mambo and Latin jazz music. "At the Bronx clubs, we would dance until our feet ached back in the day," Raquel reminisces. Vic is a Frank Sinatra, Tony Bennett, Vic Damone, and Dean Martin fan.

"You like them only because they are all Italian," Raquel notes.

"Yeah, that's one reason, but their music is the best, in my opinion. They sang great love songs, and what's better than a romantic dance to their melodious ballads," Vic challenges.

"Salsa dancing is way sexier," Raquel insists.

Deegan listens, and finally he turns to chime in.

"I'm Irish and loath Irish music. It always made my skin crawl, especially in those Irish bars on Jerome Avenue in the Bronx. I prefer listening to soothing classical music myself. It transcends time. Oh, yeah...and the Beatles, of course."

"I wanna hold you haaaa-haaaa-hand," Raquel sings. "So corny. We called that white boy popcorn music."

"You have no idea what you're talking about, my dear," Deegan blurts. "I'm going to send you the entire Beatles anthology. Popcorn music my Irish arse."

Vic looks at Deegan and makes a slight nod towards the door. Raquel picks up on the nod.

Paul Vogelbach is paying the cover charge.

The killer walks towards the bar, with his wraparound sunglasses and hoodie. He sits at the end of the bar as other patrons begin to fill the stools. He is carrying a black bag and has a backpack hanging off his right shoulder. The moment he sits on the stool, Vogelbach makes a call. The trio watches him intently as he pressed numbers into his cell phone. The killer is calling Becky for the fourth time. Once again, the call went directly to her voicemail. Vogelbach tosses the phone onto the tiled bar in disgust. It is clear to the trio that he is agitated.

Every table in the place is occupied.

Promptly at 8 p.m., the house lights dim slightly in the already dark room. A woman steps up onto the stage and in a masculine voice announces, "Ladies and gentlemen and all others, welcome to Schwartz's. It is my distinct pleasure and great honor to introduce tonight's performers, Quincy Davies and his band REAL!"

From the side of the stage comes Quincy leading the other musicians. The applause and whistles from the audience are almost deafening in the small club. Vic, his back facing the door, keeps his eyes on the prize.

Quincy is shorter than Raquel has expected. He wears a well-used Panama hat and what looks like Hawaiian swim trunks. Over his well-toned body, Quincy wears a tight white 'wife beater' t-shirt. The rest of the band wears blue jeans or khaki pants with similar blue button-down shirts. They begin tuning their instruments. Quincy starts with an alto saxophone. He looks back at his musicians and says, "Take it from the top."

“Let’s get him now. End this thing once and for all,” Vic whispers slightly above the music.

“Do you have no sense of adventure, man? We planned. Now let’s work the plan,” Deegan says.

“And sacrifice Quincy’s life? You must be insane,” Vic says.

“Yes...I am. We all know that. That’s the fun of it,” Deegan blurts.

***

Salerno and Burns arrived at the 9-mile road address. The house where Vogelbach rents his room is swarming with FBI agents and forensic personnel. Other than an unmade bed, the room is empty. Vogelbach left nothing behind, not even a piece of paper in the tiny trash can.

“Now what, boss?” Burns asks.

“I have no idea. It’s a big city,” Salerno sighs.

***

Paul Vogelbach turns on his barstool to face the stage. He is staring straight ahead, focusing his attention and his hatred towards Quincy Davies. When Quincy plays a riff, the real jazz fans in the audience applauded to show their enjoyment. Vogelbach never changes his murderous look. Davies is everything the killer loathes. The musician’s sexual diversity and his flaunting of it on various social media platforms is intolerable for Vogelbach. He hears the words of Reverend Christian Stewart reverberating in his brain. He recalls his religious mentor’s words verbatim:

'Gay men and lesbian women and the new misled transgenderites have redeveloped the modern-day Sodom and Gomorrah, and the Bible clearly tells us how God's rath dealt with that debauchery so many centuries ago'. In his warped mind, Paul Vogelbach is proud of his crusade against the LGBTQ+ world. He isn't certain Quincy Davies would be the last person punished for their transgressions against the Bible's words. The plus in LGBTQ+ offers more offenders who should be dealt with to thin the heard of these sexually depraved individuals who are pushing their agenda down the throats of good God-fearing people. The plus individuals are some of those who do not identify as either men or women, individuals who find themselves attracted to many genders. As Vogelbach sees it, and as the Bible ordains, there are only two genders that God created: men and women, who are told in scripture to go forth and multiply.

While he watches Quincy Davies play his various instruments and show off his musical talents, Vogelbach sees the various sexually degenerate actions the musician performed in his mind's eye. To the killer, Davies is a degenerate of the worst kind. Vogelbach wonders what he should do to Davies once he gets him back at the musician's apartment. He is planning to make a special example of Quincy. If this is to be the last in his crusade, he is going to make it something the LGBTQ+ world will not soon forget.

Vic, Raquel, and Deegan don't look much at the band. They focus their attention on the serial murderer, trying not to look overly obvious. When the audience applauds after a particularity great improvisation, Deegan will let out a whistle indicating that he is digging the music. Raquel fakes a snuggle on Vic when the musical mood is softer.

'REAL' plays on without a break. It is approaching 11 p.m. Schwartz's closes promptly at 11:30. Vic feels for his nine-millimeter handgun inside his ankle holster out of force of habit. He knows he would use it if need be.

CHAPTER 46

Dean Salerno, the special Agent with the FBI, is feeling the pressure to find Paul Vogelbach, the medical doctor, surgeon, and serial killer. Salerno knows that any career advancement within the bureau will rest on apprehending Vogelbach. The case has become high profile, with continuing pressure from both the White House and politicians looking to return favors to constituents among those in the LGBTQ+ community.

Salerno enjoys the work at CASMIRC, but the constant pressure of chasing child abductors and serial killers is taking its toll on him. Over the years Salerno has become jaded. Meeting the families affected by the perpetrators is depressing at best. Salerno avoids alcohol because he sees so many of his colleagues turn to drinking as self-medication.

Salerno certainly can remain in his position until he comes close to retirement and then takes a cushy job at headquarters, or he can rise through the ranks, as his lieutenant colonel father did in the Army, if all the stars had aligned. However, things are not going well for the FBI in the public opinion polls, and anything could happen to his position if things go sideways on the surgeon case.

Salerno and Burns are hitting the phones hard. Burns is in touch with the bullpen as the agents on staff are brainstorming as to where in Cincinnati Vogelbach can be. Salerno makes arrangements for agents and the SWAT team to stake out Vogelbach's 9 Mile Road room on the outside on a chance that the killer would return to sleep. "If Vogelbach is not aware the room is discovered, he just may show up," Salerno says to his colleagues from the Cincinnati field office. Burns and Salerno join in the stakeout for lack of a better place to go.

Salerno knows the director will be upset with him if Vogelbach isn't captured. And captured soon. The more time elapses, the greater the chance that the killer can elude arrest. Should Vogelbach sense he is discovered as the murderer, it is possible he would not return to Milwaukee and can flee the country. At this point Salerno has no idea if Rebecca Sipes has kept to the promise, she made to him not to speak with her new boyfriend. For all he knew, Rebecca could have called Vogelbach to warn him that the FBI is on to him. Some people do stupid things when they think they are in love.

For the time being, all Salerno can do is pray for a miracle. He knows his career is likely hanging in the balance.

Burns has the bullpen on speaker on her cell phone, with Salerno standing next to her discussing possible scenarios as to where the killer can be, based on his profile. Will his next victim be a woman? A man? A questioning or queer individual? Where will Vogelbach strike in Cincinnati?

Burns's phone clicks with an incoming call. She glances at her phone display and recognizes the number as GG's.

“Gotta go, I’ll call back. Keep grinding,” Cis tells the bullpen. She accepts the incoming call.

“Hello, Gail. The boss is listening in on speaker.”

Then comes the normal GG pause, and a loose cough comes over the speaker. Salerno runs his right hand through his hair in frustration.

“Ya wanna know something strange about what we do?” GG asks.

“Yes, I do,” Burns replies. She cannot show GG any annoyance or frustration in her voice.

“I’m in my office pouring over our massive computer data and cross-referencing with religious affiliations and stuff like that to bring up a lead on Vogelbach,” Gail offers. She lowers the phone and hacks up a phlegm ball. Salerno nearly loses his patience.

“Then I tried something that is so amateurish and basic, I hate to even admit it. But I think I have it. I did a Google search. A plain old Internet search. I typed in the letter Q and Cincinnati. What came up blew my mind. Q is the abbreviation of a jazz musician by the name of Quincy Davies. His friends and fans call him ‘Q’, or ‘The Q’. I did a quick search on Davies. He’s based in Cincinnati and has a lot of followers on social media and is queer as hell,” GG announces.

“Do you have anything else on Davies?”

Another coughing spell. “Yes. He’s appearing tonight at a place called Schwartz’s Point Jazz and Acoustic Club on Vine Street from 7 to 11. I have a feeling that’s where you will find Dr. Paul Vogelbach,” GG states.

“On it!” Cis Burns says. She ends the call.

“All that bullshit when she could have just said...Ahh forget it,” Salerno blurts. He looks at his watch. It was 11:20.

Thinking ahead, Burns tells the agents to find where Quincy lives and stake out his apartment. He is to be brought in for protective custody.

***

At 11:05, Quincy Davies and his quartet have wrapped up the show with Davies giving a riff on his acoustic guitar, which brought the crowd to its feet. Vogelbach sits like a stone facing the stage. As the musicians leave the stage, Deegan tries to get to Quincy to stall him and delay him from leaving the club, but the band moves quickly for the rear door. They aren’t hanging around for autographs or drinks. Raquel and Vic make their way towards the front door as Vogelbach hops off the barstool and is first out the door. Not wanting to blow their cover, Vic and Raquel try pushing their way through the lumbering crowd. Deegan is outside in the rear of the club. He calls out to Davies, who has climbed into the passenger side of a dark Mercedes E350 sedan. The driver speeds away. Deegan memorizes the Ohio license plate. “Fuck me!” Deegan yells.

Vic and Raquel are too late to get to Vogelbach, who pulls out of the parking lot and headed north on Vine Street. The killer is getting away.

“Man, did we fuck that up like a pair of rookie cops. One of us should have gone outside and collared the motherfucker,” Vic bellows.

***

Salerno and Burns hop in one of the Cincinnati FBI agents' black sedans. They speed toward Schwartz's. There is no traffic, and red lights mean nothing to the driver. At 11:35 the sedan screeches to a halt outside the club. The doors are locked.

Burns pounds on the door. The woman who introduces the band comes to the door mouthing, "We're closed," as she points to the hours displayed on the door. Burns slaps her FBI identification against the door.

"FBI. Open the door." The woman complies.

"We are looking for Quincy Davies," Burns states.

"He left right after his set. Anything wrong?"

"Any idea where he went?" Salerno asks.

"I really don't. It's still early. Maybe a late-night club or maybe home."

"Do you happen to have his cell number or any member of the bands?" Burns probes.

"Nope. We deal through his agent."

"We need the agent's number. It's a matter of life and death," Salerno blurts.

The duo followed the woman as she sashays towards the office. She suddenly stops.

"Wait. I have their number on my phone." The woman takes out her cell and finds the number.

"Go ahead and dial it, please," Salerno orders. The woman dials the agent. The call goes straight to voicemail.

"Shit," Salerno says.

Burns asks, "Do you have any internal cameras?"

"Sure do."

"Let's see it, please."

Salerno and Barns follow the woman into the rear office.

On the desk sits a black and white monitor with a four-way split screen.

"Please replay the tape, starting when the doors opened," Burns requests.

The woman is quick and hits a few buttons, and the replay is on the screen. The monitor shows that it was taken at 7 p.m.

"It's very dark," Salerno says.

"Yeah, baby, it's a jazz club."

They see Vic, Raquel, and Deegan enter the club. Neither Salerno nor Burns recognizes the well-known couple.

"Fast forward please. Slowly." Salerno orders.

They watch as the crowd began to enter the club.

"There! There he is. The guy in the sunglasses and wig carrying a bag and knapsack. It has to be Vogelbach. He was here," Burns barks.

"Yup. Looks like him. He wore that same disguise in New York. I remember it from the videos we have. Hopefully for Davies and our sake he went directly to Davies' home."

CHAPTER 47

"Looks like Davies is either going home or going somewhere with the driver of that Benz," Deegan says.

The trio are still standing outside Schwartz's. It was fifteen or twenty minutes before Salerno and Burns pull up to the club.

Vic isn't happy.

"Dammit! We could have collard him when we had the chance like I said. Then we fucked it up even more. We should have posted one of us outside to intercept Vogelbach," Vic offers.

"Shoulda, woulda, coulda. What's past is prologue, as Willy Shakespeare once said. Now we are faced with a problem that we must solve. It's a game of chess, my young friends. Standing here with our fingers up, our arses will do nothing. I have the license plate number from the Benz. Pretty easy to remember. A vanity plate. Equality, in front of a gay rainbow," Deegan announces.

"That's appropriate. I'll get a taxi," Raquel said.

"I'll call NYPD. They can at least give us a name and address," Vic spouts.

"At this time of night?" Raquel says. She stands out in the street and hails a cab.

"Hey, I'm Vic Gonnella, dammit."

"Okay gumby...Go for it," Raquel replies.

***

David Clarke, the bass player for 'REAL', and Quincy Davies decide to go to a late-night club for some drinks, weed, and hookah. After the set, the two musicians are wound up and want to relax a bit. They plan to return to the bass player's apartment not far from the Walnut Hills neighborhood on the east side of Cincinnati. Apart from their musical connection, of late Quincy is spending most of his time at David's place. Monogamy isn't possible for either of them, but they are very fond of one another. From time-to-time Quincy will run off with an interesting new lover of various sexual appetites. David is gay and doesn't swing in the variety of ways his friend and lover Quincy does, but he never judges him.

Clarke has inherited a beautiful old Victorian home, which he is slowly renovating. He rents out a couple of rooms to other musicians to defray the construction costs. Walnut Hills is an up-and-coming diverse area within a ten-minute drive of downtown Cincinnati. Clarke is investment-minded and has sharp business skills, while Quincy Davies is foolish with any money that touches his hands. Davies is basically broke and poor. Without his incredible musical talents, he would no doubt be homeless or dead.

David and Quincy entered the Gypsy Hookah Lounge not far from the Walnut Hills neighborhood where Quincy also has an apartment. The lounge is really their kind of place, and the two musicians are both friends with the owner. The spot stays open until 2 a.m. The crowd is always mixed, with mostly blacks, some whites, and a few Hispanics, and everyone is cool and peaceful. The Q, as everyone calls Quincy, is known in the lounge for always having the best weed and the funniest stories.

Q and David shake hands, with most of the clientele doing the shoulder bump with those to whom they are closer.

Inside the Gypsy are mostly long wooden tables where groups of between four and eight people will line up hookah pipes and smoke their choice of product. Most of those at the Gypsy smoke flavored tobacco, some use hashish or marijuana, and from time to time there will be the hard-core opium users. The cops never bother them.

Quincy and Clarke chose a small table and have their own multi-stemmed pipes, which they keep in a private locker. They lit the hookah using Quincy's good weed and kick back to relax and enjoy their high.

"Look at this dude," Quincy says. "Very cute." Paul Vogelbach enters the Gypsy and stands inside taking the place in. He has followed David Clarke's Benz on the short ride from Schwartz's jazz club.

"I'm usually weary of guys who wear sunglasses at night," Clarke says.

"That's what we are so different, David. That look makes my heart skip beats. Besides, I like them big like that." Quincy declares.

"You like anything with a hole. I guess I'm not tall enough for you?"

"You fit perfectly, honey," Quincy replies.

Vogelbach scans the room, moving his head slowly around the room. Quincy tries to make eye contact. The killer turns on his heals and leaves the lounge.

"I guess I scared the poor guy away," Quincy announces loudly to a chorus of laughs from those who heard him.

Vogelbach returns to his BMW, he parked a bit down the street from the Gypsy. From his spot, he can see the Mercedes and will be able to follow it to finalize his duty. He is originally going to make his move on Friday night but wants to be back in Milwaukee earlier to surprise Becky.

Vogelbach is furious at the lifestyle Quincy Davies lives. He was angry as he followed the Benz with the rainbow flag and EQUALITY in bold letters on the license plate. *"They flaunt their debauchery in the face of our Lord and Savior Jesus Christ,"* Vogelbach said to himself while tailing the Benz at a reasonable distance.

While he waited in his car for his target to leave, Vogelbach tried calling Becky again despite the late hour. Three calls in rapid succession with the same result as earlier. Directly to voicemail.

"Why doesn't she answer? Perhaps she's angry I went out of town. Maybe her phone isn't working. Why did I start this up with her?" Paul keeps saying these things over and over to himself. He has no idea he is on the verge of being captured for being a fanatical serial killer. In his mind he is ordained to protect his Lord, his scripture, and his country from an immoral hoard wanting to destroy everything he thought to be good and holy.

***

"Got it! 1790 McMillan Street, Walnut Hills. Car is registered to David Clarke. No wants or warrants," Vic announces. He is right. Vic has the information Deegan took from the license plate within minutes. His name opens a lots of doors at NYPD.

"Very impressive, if I say so myself," Deegan says.

"John, please! His head is big enough already," Raquel counters.

Vic gives the address to the taxi driver and a crisp hundred-dollar bill for driving them around.

They are taken to the McMillan Street address, which isn't far. On the way, Raquel Googles Quincy Davis and comes up with his address, 91 Park Avenue, also in Walnut Hills. She asks the driver if he knows where that is and how far it is from their destination. It is less than ten blocks away.

The driver drops them off across the street from the old Victorian house on McMillan. The house is dark except for a porch light and the blue light from a television on the basement level.

They stand in the darkness of an older, boarded up house, also Victorian vintage.

"Now we wait, just like any stakeout," Vic states. "If Quincy's brought back to spend the night with his butt buddy, we can bring him in for protective."

"Vic, why are you always so crude?" Raquel demands.

"That's exactly what we don't do, Gonnella. If Quincy comes back here, we wait and see if Vogelbach shows up.

He is very determined and very cunning. If the surgeon shows, we pounce on him."

"What if they go back to Quincy's place?" Raquel asks.

"Maybe one of us should go stake out the address on Park?" Vic states.

"Good, Idea. I guess that makes me that someone. I can do ten blocks even in these damn sandals," Deegan blurts.

"If you see anything...if they show up on Park Avenue, call or text us, okay?"

Deegan takes out his cell and gets the directions to 91 Park Avenue. "And the same goes for you guys. Should they return here, let me know. I'll be back in two shakes of a lamb's tail."

"A what of what?" Raquel asks.

"Old English expression. I'll be here before you know it," Deegan explains.

"No heroics, Deegan. Do not go in alone," Vic orders.

"Fuck no! This is your collar, guys. I can just see the headlines; Serial killer captures serial killer." Deegan begins walking.

CHAPTER 48

Salerno, Cis Burns, nine FBI agents, and eight Cincinnati PD plainclothes and uniformed men wait as quietly as possible near and around 91 Park Avenue. The FBI SWAT team, consisting of eleven heavily armed, well-trained marksmen, wearing the now iconic black Ninja type uniforms and oddly shaped black helmets, wait in a large black panel truck along with two black SUVs around the block. The vehicles roll up at Yale Avenue, moving around five miles an hour without exterior or interior lighting.

It is just after 2 o'clock on Friday morning, so keeping the neighbors from hearing vehicles pulling up and car doors slamming and two-way radios chirping is in the best interest of a clandestine operation. Everyone in the maneuver needs to remain quiet, still, and smokeless and do their best to hold in any nature calls. At this hour of the morning, the slightest click of a car door opening or a puddling urine stream can send a homeowner's canine into a barking fit. Once one dog starts yelping it becomes a domino effect, a barking frenzy, and then the lights start coming on and the stakeout is busted.

Anyone now walking down Park Avenue would have dozens of eyes on them. Unless that person is John Deegan. Deegan is trained in stealth operations in the jungles of Nicaragua long before most of these cops and agents were born. He isn't exactly about to be strolling down Park Avenue toward number 91 whistling 'Hey Jude'. On the contrary, when Deegan gets within five blocks of Quincy Davies' apartment, he stops walking upright altogether. Deegan hunches down using trees and vehicles for cover, moving slowly enough that his leather sandals don't squeak or make any noise whatsoever on the pavement. As he makes his way down Park Avenue, Deegan heeds the call from his sixth sense telling him that something isn't right in the neighborhood.

Up in the distance, closer to Quincy's place, there seems too many late-model sedans dotting the parking spaces outside the homes. Not everyone in Walnut Hills had company on a Thursday night, and Deegan hasn't seen so many Crown Victoria's and Chevy Camaros in his life. This is how Deegan is able to survive so well in the jungle working for the United States government after he fled the priesthood. He always listens to his gut feelings, his survival intuition, and more importantly, Deegan has an uncanny ability to notice something that is just out of place, just not right.

Deegan crawls around on Park Avenue for a bit, spotting the outline of heads silhouetting in the street lighting in some of the cars. He crawls on a flat seventy-five-foot manicured house lawn to make his exit from Park Avenue. Deegan then plans to hold his position around the corner to wait and see if Quincy returns to his apartment with Vogelbach on his heels. While he is crawling on the lawn his right hand, his lead hand, landed into something mushy. *'Fucking dog owners, they should be executed,'* Deegan says to himself. *'Monkey shit was nowhere as nasty as a German Shepard's.'*

There is no sign of Davies, and Vogelbach hasn't shown a hair on his head. For that matter, there is no sign of anything along Park Avenue. Deegan then spots the large square black panel truck, and the matching color SUVs parked on the street in a neighborhood that would likely have a Ford F 110 or an older model Subaru Outback.

Deegan crawls into an alleyway between two rundown homes. There is a twenty-five-yard trash container being used for construction demolition. He goes behind the container, using it as cover so he can call Vic and Raquel.

"Place is crawling with Feds and cops. Even the Swat maniacs came to the party," Deegan says. Vic has turned his phone to vibrate so his cover will be solid.

Vic cannot tell in Deegan's voice if he is distraught or at all nervous. Deegan's blood runs cold in the face of danger.

"They are a step behind us...maybe. Seems to me they have no idea Quincy went somewhere with his partner," Vic says.

"I told you it was a three-man race. Now ya gotta try to save this Quincy kid. If Vogelbach comes your way, you get the collar. If not...it was fun, and the Feds win."

"You sound like you're bailing on us," Vic notes.

"My boy, FBI and I don't really mix well, if you get my meaning. With all these suits around, I can wind up in the Super Max in damn Colorado for the day. Got you guys this far, now just watch your arses. I'm way too old for the crawling around in the gutter routine. Been there, done that. I ruined a good pair of bellbottoms, and I got dog shit in my fingernails. Next time, you or Raquel do the nasty work. Vic, all kidding aside, this Vogelbach prick is a tough character, and he's mean as a junkyard dog, so if you need to take him out, don't hesitate."

"Trust me, I won't," Vic answers.

"Look, Vic, I feel rotten. I'm leaving you without a means of transportation back to New York," Deegan states.

"With all these Feds and cops around, you have no choice. Get the hell outta here. We're fine. May even take the train. Please be safe, John."

CHAPTER 49

Vogelbach has Quincy's address from the Facebook and Instagram sites where the musician exposes his life to his millions of fans, and unwittingly to a serial killer on a deadly mission.

The real jazz lovers would send donations to Davies to keep the struggling artist eating and paying his rent. Quincy makes a decent living from his music albums, podcasts, and personal appearances, but he blows the funds on anything and everything from dope to female, male, and transexual hookers and partners. Money comes and goes in Quincy's life. He never thinks about the future because he thinks he won't live long enough to have to worry about it. If Vogelbach has his way, Quincy's premonition of a short life will soon come to fruition.

A drunk driver will run through a stop sign, a stoned driver will wait for the stop sign to turn green. High on weed, David Clarke drives back slowly to his old Victorian house on McMillan. Quincy begins the ride humming one of his favorite tunes. In a minute, he is zonked out in the passenger seat in a fetal position. The two musicians have no idea they are being stalked.

Clarke misjudges his driveway, hitting the Belgian block lining with his front and rear driver side tires. Quincy is jarred awake, emitting a *'Jesus Christ'*, which sends Clark into hysterics. Quincy also caught a bout of the giggles. They both sit in the Benz for a while, enjoying the high and the laughs. Vogelbach rolls up slowly in his BMW, parking alongside the neighboring house. He waits patiently until finally, Clarke and Quincy open the doors of the Mercedes. They walk toward the house, taking the uneven wood steps leading to the front door. They seem to be moving in slow motion.

Vic and Raquel, standing across the street in the shadows, surveyed the unfolding scene. They watch as the two musicians enter the home and see Vogelbach exit his car. He is still wearing the disguise he had at Schwartz's club. Raquel takes her handgun, a HK 9-millmeter, from its holster under her jacket. Vic pulls his gun from his ankle holster. They hold their firearms down by their legs and stand next to each other.

Suddenly, Vic and Raquel feel a hand on their shoulders. They both freeze.

"Don't shoot, it's me," Deegan whispers.

"Christ Almighty!" Vic says. "I thought you left."

"And miss all the fun?"

"This is fun to you, John?" Raquel says.

"At my age taking a piss without it hurting and not dribbling down my leg is fun," Deegan replies.

"Do you want to be nailed by the FBI, you idiot?" Vic asks.

"Won't happen. I'm too slick and they're too stupid. Like we used to say in the military, leave no man behind.

In this case it's a man and a woman. Now, let's follow this surgeon into that old house."

***

Salerno and Burns are getting antsy. Salerno begins to squirm in his seat. No movement outside of Quincy's Park Avenue pad by this time is an indication that the musician is not returning home.

"No sign of Vogelbach. Not even one car came by since we're here," Burns offers.

"If Vogelbach has a bead on Davies, we will hear about it soon," Salerno replies.

"I wish GG would call. She always has an ace up her sleeve."

"She's probably in the dark like we are. If Vogelbach gets to his target, it's lights out for me," Salerno says almost in a whisper.

"You've done a great job with so many cases. That's got to account for something. Right?"

"It comes down to what have you done for me lately. That's just how it is," Salerno laments.

"Don't give up just yet, boss. It's like Yogi Berra said. *'It ain't over till it's over'*."

"No sense in everyone staying here. I'll leave two agents just in case and tell SWAT to stand down."

"I hate folding the tent like this, sir." Burns states. Salerno just stares ahead as if he doesn't hear her.

"I can't help but think we left that club too soon. We should have looked at the exterior camera tape to see if there was anything."

"Like?"

"Like where Quincy Davies went. Maybe he got into a car... picked up by a cab...who knows," Salerno utters.

"Let's go back. I'm sure no one is still there at this hour, but there must be some emergency contact. What if there was a fire or break-in," Burns offers.

Salerno thinks about what his lead agent said for a few seconds.

"Great thinking. Let's try it. It's a lot better than just sitting here waiting for bad news."

***

David Clarke puts the foyer entrance lights on inside the house. Quincy trips on the saddle of the entrance door and starts laughing again.

"Shush, you'll wake my tenants," Clarke says.

"Fuck 'em. If we're up, they should be up," Quincy quips.

"You hungry?" Clarke asks.

"Starving."

"Let's go and see what's in the fridge. I think I have some Popeyes fried chicken left over."

"Oh, feed the black guy chicken. Racist prick."

The two musicians make their way into the kitchen. The appliances and cabinets are as old as the house. Clarke flips on a flimsy light fixture which barely illuminates the room. The lamp casting shadows in all four corners. Two long green painted cupboards hang above a small white porcelain pedestal sink which has white single-lever porcelain hot and cold faucets. A couple of green cabinets are next to a white cast iron oven stove which has a modern-day hot plate and microwave oven on its top. A long green tiled countertop runs along the other side of the room. Many of the four-inch square tiles are cracked from age, and the yellowish grout is nearly all gone. Quincy goes to the small green refrigerator that is in a side alcove behind a flimsy gray curtain.

"Yes, sir massa, they are some nice fried chicken fo da negro," Quincy announces.

"Get over it, Q. Look behind the chicken, there might be some Chinese takeout from a couple of days ago. I'll pop it in the microwave."

"Got any hot sauce?"

"Yeah, on the right side."

Quincy fills his hand with the tub of Popeyes, Chinese leftovers, and two bottles of Pabst Blue Ribbon beer. He lays everything on the counter while Clarke takes dishes from the cupboard.

Neither of them hears Vogelbach as he lays his surgical bag just outside the kitchen door. The front door is left unlocked.

Quincy takes a bite from a chicken leg.

"This is another thing I love about you, Davey. You are a real gourmand, especially when I have the munchies," Quincy says.

"I think there is some peanut butter in there too," Clarke notes. They both giggle.

Vic and Raquel, their guns up high in their extended arms, enter the foyer of the house. Deegan is behind them. They can hear muffled voices from the kitchen.

Vogelbach takes a syringe, the bag valve mask, and a surgical blade from his bag and waits for the right moment to pounce on his prey.

***

Salerno and Burns get to Schwartz's and can see movement inside the dark club. The chair legs are all pointing towards the ceiling, with the seats on the tables ready for the floors to be cleaned. One light from the bar is on, and the agents can see three people sitting on stools. The masculine-sounding woman is stooping over behind the bar.

Salerno pounds on the front door. Burns stands by the window to be seen. "Shit, FBI again," the woman says. She walks slowly towards the door and unlocks it.

"Sup?"

"We need to see the videos again," Salerno orders.

"Dude, it's like... late."

"Yeah, we know. Let's go," Salerno says. His voice is gruff. He pushes her. He and Burns walk into the club.

"Okay, baby, be cool."

The woman is drunk and high. She keeps touching her nose and sniffling. Two men and what looks to be another woman stand up from their stools. One is blowing powder off the top of the bar.

The two agents follow the staggering woman to the office.

"We need to see whatever your outside cameras have when Quincy left tonight," Burns commands.

The woman can hardly get her fingers working as she lowers her head to within an inch of the video console.

Burns moves her away. “I got it, miss.”

“Well, thank you for calling me miss, honey.”

“We don’t care what your pronouns are, just step aside,” Salerno barks.

Burns runs the tape at 11 p.m. and moves it ahead until they view Quincy and the band leave the stage. Moments later they see Quincy step out in the rear of the club. They watched as he gets into the passenger side of a dark vehicle. The Mercedes backed out of the parking spot getting ready to pull away.

“Freeze it,” Salerno blurts.

“EQULITY. Wherever Quincy is, he’s with the owner of that Benz,” Burns pronounces.

CHAPTER 50

Minutes after Cis Burns calls the bullpen, they have a take on the EQUALITY plate. The FBI database is master of the universe technology. Two agents race Salerno and Burns towards the McMillian Street address owned by David Clark. Salerno calls for backup.

"I want all agents to converge on 1790 McMillan in Walnut Hills. Notify Cincy PD to have all available units at that address. SWAT is to deploy their vehicles at once. Everyone is to go to the house with lights and sirens. This is not a stakeout, repeat, not a stakeout."

"If Vogelbach is there and hears the troops coming, it will scare him away," Burns warns.

"I get that. I'd rather save Davies and the other guy's lives. For all we know, Vogelbach could be butchering them right now."

***

Vic, Raquel, and Deegan move slowly towards the kitchen door. They see the killer's shadow as he enters the darkened kitchen.

Vogelbach enters the kitchen and in one swift move lifts a half-filled tea kettle from the counter, smashing onto the side of Clarke's head. Clarke falls, hitting his head on the porcelain sink, rendering him unconscious. He hits the faded wood floor with a loud thud. Quincy Davies stands by the counter in shock. Vogelbach grabs the much shorter musician by his shoulder twisting him around until he had his victim in a headlock. In a flash, Vogelbach pushes the syringe into Quincy's neck and plunges the dose of vecuronium bromide into his system. Quincy immediately goes limp. Vogelbach holds his fifth victim upright.

"You move one inch and I'll blow your fucking head off," Gonnella hollers. Raquel, her gun points at Vogelbach's head, moves around to the surgeon's left. Deegan stands to Vic's side, to the right of the killer.

Vogelbach is stunned. He holds his left arm tightly around Quincy's neck, pulling the victim higher up against him.

"Let him go. Just let him drop down to the floor," Raquel orders.

"This pig deserves to die. Leave me to do the Lord's work. This is what I have been ordained to do!" Vogelbach screams.

"It's over. Just let him go," Raquel repeats.

Neither Vic nor Raquel have a clean shot at the killer. Due to a lack of oxygen to his body, Quincy is turning purplish from cyanosis. Without help breathing, the sedation is killing him.

"I swear to God, you have five seconds to drop him, motherfucker," Vic yells.

"Now, I'm not playing with you. Just do it!" Raquel screams.

Under his sunglasses, they can see the whites of Vogelbach's enlarged eyes.

The sound of multiple police sirens begin to fill the kitchen.

Vogelbach whimpers like a puppy and looks up to the ceiling as if he is looking for divine assistance. The killer drops his prey. Deegan moves towards the victim.

Paul takes a small step backward. "Tell Becky I'm sorry. Lord, accept your humble servant in paradise," Vogelbach utters. In a millisecond, he flashes a surgical blade and runs it along his carotid artery. Blood squirts in the air and down onto his hoody. Vogelbach stands for a few seconds with a quizzical look on his face before choking on his own blood and falling into a heap on the floor.

Blood has sprayed onto John Deegan's back before the killer fell. He grabs the bag valve mask from beneath the surgeon's body and began squeezing the apparatus to give air to the dying musician.

Three police cruisers arrive at the home, their tires screeching on the pavement. The officers moving with guns drawn are now on the porch of the old Victorian home.

Deegan leaves the mask on Quincy's face and points to Raquel, "take over until EMS gets here." Deegan quickly moves from the kitchen.

Two officers shield themselves on either side of the door, pointing their Glock 9-millimeters at Vic and Raquel. "Drop the weapons, NOW!" Vic drops his gun and raises his arms in the air. Raquel has already dropped her firearm and is busy with the bag valve mask on Quincy.

"Get EMS here. He needs help!" Raquel hollers.

"Stay calm, boys, we're private detectives. I'm Vic Gonnella, she's Raquel Ruiz." Raquel has blood on her jeans and linen jacket.

One of the cops uses his two-way to call in. More police arrive with guns drawn. The first officer on the scene told his colleagues to stand down. More ear-piercing sirens pull up to the house.

A minute later Salerno and Burns burst into the kitchen. Vogelbach is dead on the kitchen floor with blood everywhere.

Salerno surveys the carnage as he holsters his firearm. Burns looks shocked by the scene.

"Don't just stand there. Help a girl out over here," Raquel blurts in her Bronx accent.

Salerno turns to Vic. "What the hell are you doing here, Gonnella?"

"Collaring a bad guy, what does it look like we're doing? We walked in on a possible homicide, and he slit his own throat."

"You do know this is a federal investigation, right?" Salerno says.

"Well, you guys can take over from here. Do your forensics, take photos, bag, and tag. We got here just in the nick of time. By the time you all showed up, that guy over there would be as dead as Kelsey's nuts," Vic declares. His New York style arrogance burst through because of Salerno's tone and attitude.

"This is total bullshit, Gonnella. You don't have jurisdiction here, and you know it."

"What jurisdiction? Didn't you go to law school? We're not law enforcement. Just two private investigators looking for a serial killer. We've done this before, you know," Vic replies.

"It's still our investigation, end of story," Salerno says. He sounds more wimpy than authoritative.

"Don't pull that shit on me. If you were halfway decent, we could have called it a joint collar. Now, as my grandfather used to say, '*vaffanculo*'." Vic looks around the room. "Any of you guys Italian? Translate what I just said to this prick."

EMS arrives and take over administering aid to Quincy Davies. His normal color has already returned. Raquel and Burns move away. Exhausted, Raquel stays seated on the floor. Vic goes to her, crouches down, and hugs his lady.

After making statements to two other FBI agents for about an hour, Vic and Raquel leave the scene and walk a few blocks before Raquel calls an Uber. Four minutes later they are on their way to find a hotel for the night. Their bags are on Deegan's jet.

Vic calls Deegan's cell.

"Hi John, why didn't you stay around?" Vic jokes.

"Those yokels couldn't get laid in a Louisiana whorehouse with a fist full of fifties. I'm at the plane waiting for you two heroes," Deegan offers.

Raquel gives a throaty laugh. “You missed the fireworks, John. My guy over here got into it with that smarmy agent. It was ugly.”

“Good on you, my boy. I guess they want the glory.”

“I think we need to stay in town to do some press before the FBI twists the narrative,” Vic says.

“Call a press conference, you got the juice,” Deegan adds.

“But you have our bags,” Vic utters.

“The sun will be up soon, you dope. Just call the papers and TV stations. Have your office do a press release. Wake those two lazy boys up and get them hopping. Hyatt Regency at 9:30. I’ll be there!”

“Wait...John...hello? He hung up. He always pulls that shit on me,” Vic seethes.

CHAPTER 51

Just after six in the morning, a disguised John Deegan wheels two small pieces of luggage, one in each hand, into the Cincinnati Hyatt Regency Hotel lobby. Deegan immediately notices a pedestal black notice board with magnetic white block letters which read: PRESS CONFERENCE...CENTURION ASSOCIATES... MAIN CONFERENCE ROOM 9:30. *'Good Boy'*, Deegan thinks to himself.

Vic texted Deegan earlier, telling him they took a room to shower and wait for their change of clothes.

Deegan walks up to the reception desk.

"Good morning, young lady."

"Good morning, father. How can I help you?"

Dressed as a Capuchin friar in a plain brown tunic with a hood, a cord fastened around the waist, and sandals, Deegan wears a white beard with trimmed white hair with large, black horn-rimmed eyeglasses. Whenever he travels outside the safety of his estate in Lugano, Switzerland Deegan brings along various disguises to avoid the long arm of the law.

"Please let Mr. Gonnella know that Father Forgione is here," Deegan states.

Vic and Raquel wait at the door to their room in terrycloth robes that the hotel has provided. Deegan walks off the elevator and down the hallway.

"You have got to be kidding," Raquel blurts. Vic is laughing so hard that he needs to bend down to catch his breath.

"I think I look very fetching. I can hear your confessions after the press conference."

"Where did you get the Father Forgione name," Vic says through his laughter.

"It's the little-known surname of Padre Pio, Saint Pio of Pietrelcina, the Italian prelate," just for shits and giggles.

Raquel orders room service breakfast for the trio. They are starving and scarfed down the food with relish.

Promptly at 9:30, Vic and Raquel enter the conference room to a bevy of television cameras, newspaper and radio reporters, some bystanders, and two undercover FBI agents to gather intel on the press conference. Deegan walks into the large room just as the press conference begins.

Gonnella explains how Paul Vogelbach, the LGBTQ+ serial killer, was apprehended in the act of attempting to murder a local musician and how he committed suicide in front of himself and his partner Raquel Ruiz.

The couple is peppered with questions from the local media for the better part of an hour until Raquel finally ends the press conference. Vic and Raquel pose for photographs and signed a few autographs.

The exhausted couple quickly leave the hotel with their wheeled suitcases and take an Uber to the airport. Deegan took a separate car, notifying his pilot that he and two guests will be departing for Teterboro airport within the hour.

The next day, a major press conference is held at the Centurion Associates office in Midtown Manhattan. Calls from the producers of *Good Morning America, The Today Show*, and several other network programs are asking for the power couple to appear to explain their story.

A tired John Deegan, satisfied with his part in capturing the serial killer, doesn't stay for the New York press conference and returns home to Lugano and a happy and relieved Gjuliana.

"Now John, you need to rest for a while. At least until your next bout of boredom sets in. But I must tell you, when you are out at these jaunts of yours, my heart is in my mouth the entire time until you return. It's very difficult for me," Gjuliana states.

"I can only imagine, my love."

"If only you knew how much I loved you from our days as children on Grand Avenue in the Bronx. And all the years I have pined for you and wished we could be together. You owe me the pleasure of us being together. Time is running out for us."

***

Relaxing in their living room in the townhouse, Vic, Raquel, Gabby, and Olga have just finished a Puerto Rican dinner of pernil, the slow roasted marinated pork shoulder, arroz con gandules, fried plantains, and a desert of flan de queso.

"Mama, I can't believe how delicious that meal was," Raquel states.

"And your daughter helped with every dish. She made the flan by herself," Olga said. "She will make a great cook in her own home one day. Olga was beaming. Gabby kissed and hugs her Abuela.

"I wish my mother was alive to teach Gabby some of the Italian dishes I grew up on," Vic adds.

"Abuela, your rehab has done so well for you. You are barely using your cane," Gabby announces.

"I only wish Maria were doing better. Gladys tells me she is still in a lot of pain, and she has complications from the shooting. I pray for her every day. Maria's doctors told her daughter she may never fully recover because of serious internal damage and her age. Gladys said she doesn't look good at all. And Gladys's diabetes is not good. She is carrying too much weight, and she had to go to the hospital herself a couple of times. I suppose I was clinging to my past going back to Tremont. It was a real community. We had so many good times there, so many good friends, my church, the stores. I've learned an important lesson. There is no going back. I have wonderful memories, and that's where the Bronx must remain for me. I look around here and see what you have done for me. I guess I'm very lucky after all," Olga says.

"Mama, when you are fully recovered, I will bring Maria and Gladys to visit you for a few days," Raquel says.

"We will see my daughter."

Trying to change her mother's somber mood, Raquel announces, "I have an idea. Let's listen to that Beatles anthology John sent to us. It's one of his favorite groups. Maybe there is something to this music."

***

A week later, Vic and Raquel have a visit at their office from Agent Samuel Cooper of the FBI New York office. Cooper is on a fishing expedition.

They are in the conference room.

"First of all, I want to congratulate you both on the Vogelbach case. That was amazing detective work," Cooper offers.

"Thank you," Raquel says. She smiles politely. Vic stays quiet. He is wondering why Cooper has shown up unannounced. 'It's no wonder people don't trust the FBI', Vic thinks. They are really a bunch of slime buckets.

"I've been asked to follow up on some loose ends on the case."

"Okay, who specifically asked you to do this? Was it Salerno?" Vic asks. He has a half smile on his face, his words reek in sarcasm.

"Well, Salerno did some poking around, and his findings uncovered some interesting things. That's what brought me here. Agent Salerno has been reassigned. I've been assigned to take over his position in Langley for the time being," Cooper replies.

"Good for you. Congratulations. As far as I'm concerned, Salerno should be reassigned to work the IHOP kitchen in Teaneck, New Jersey," Vic utters. Raquel shoots Vic a hard look.

"Yes, I heard you two had some words. In any event, Salerno reviewed a few things in the case we would like some answers on."

"Shoot," Vic says.

"In his review of the videotapes at Schwartz's jazz club in Cincinnati, the films show you and Ms. Ruiz in the club the night Vogelbach was apprehended."

"Yup, we were there," Vic confirms.

"There was a third party at your table. Can you clarify who that was?" Cooper fishes.

Vic looks at Raquel. She knows he was signaling for her to answer.

Raquel replies. "Yes, I've forgotten his name. No wait, he called himself Jake. We met him coming into the club. We started chatting and asked him to join us. A real character. Like a throwback to the '60s. Like a hippie. Very big jazz fan."

"Did Salerno also notice on the video that Paul Vogelbach was sitting at the bar?" Vic blurts.

"I don't have any information on that, Mr. Gonnella. Back to the man at your table. Did either if you know him before that night?" Cooper queries.

"Agent Cooper, I just told you we met him going into the club. He was an older man who was alone," Raquel responds.

"Did Salerno, in his infinite wisdom, use facial recognition on the guy?" Vic asks.

"I believe that technology was used, yes."

"And?" Vic follows.

"No recognition," Cooper replies.

"What else, Agent?" Vic says. Cooper moves uncomfortably in his chair.

"How did you obtain intel on Vogelbach?"

"Let me ask you a question, Agent Cooper. So, the perp is dead. The intended victim and his friend are both alive, and it seems as if your agency is investigating us. Is this because we were just a half-step ahead of you guys in our investigation? Is it because the FBI is embarrassed?" Vic asks.

Raquel doesn't wait for Cooper's reply. "We used our assets within the company. Emilio Ramos and Chris Papa were at the helm while we were in the field. They've since been promoted. Plus, good old-fashioned detective work."

"I see. Okay then, I think that about wraps things up for now," Cooper says. "Thank you both." Vic's question is about to take a turn in their discussion, and Cooper knows Vic doesn't play games. He isn't above leaking this to the media.

"Agent Cooper, one more thing, if I may. How is Gail Gain? We worked with her in the past. And the woman agent who helped me work on Quincy Davies?" Raquel asks.

"Agent Burns will be assisting me. Ms. Gain has taken medical leave. I'll pass on your regards," Cooper responds.

***

In Milwaukee, a still despondent Rebecca Sipes is at the church house visiting Reverend Christian Stewart. The housekeeper serves tea and homemade white cake in the living room.

"I think I was in love with Paul, Reverend Stewart," Rebecca says. "I waited so long for the right man to come along and…" Rebecca cannot finish what she wants to say. She fights back her tears.

"We all loved him, Rebecca. How was I to know that my words from the pulpit would turn into Paul murdering four people? When I preached against the gay world, I never expected this result. I have regrets, as you do."

"Reverend, we are both unwitting victims of Paul Vogelbach's insanity. Now, I'll forever be known as the girlfriend of the serial killer everyone is now calling The Surgeon."

"I came to see you to say goodbye. I'm returning to Wausau. I need to start my life over."

ACNKOWLEGEMENTS

I was looking for a concept for the seventh book of the Vic Gonnella Series which would be interesting and challenging to write. My friend and now colleague Paul Youngelson hit upon the concept for this book and helped me greatly with brainstorming characters and research along the way.

I wrote the book at my home in New Jersey, my cigar club in Nanuet, New York, Montauk, New York in Rome, Italy and Palermo and Taormina, Sicily where I finished the chapters overlooking the Mediterranean.

Thanks to Mike Sassone for his input on using Cincinnati for some of the action. Retired First Grade NYPD Detective Joe Guerra lent his homicide expertise to this work.

I appreciate my prereaders Linda Longo, who has worked with me for years and my friend Fran Petrillo.

Nick Levy did the cover after one conversation and killed it in one try. His talent amazes me.

Thanks to my editor David Udoff and proofreader

M. Dutchy for her guidance and assistance.

A huge thank you to my friends and fans who keep encouraging me too.

ALSO by LOUIS ROMANO

ON THE SIDE OF THE ROAD

Gino Ranno Mafia Series:
BESA
FISH FARM
GAME OF PAWNS
EXCLUSION

Young Adults:
ZIP CODE

Short Story & Poetry Series
ANXIETY'S NEST ANXIETY'S CURE
BEFORE I DROP DEAD

Heritage Collection Series:
CARUSI: THE SHAME OF SICILY
IN THEIR FOOTSTEPS

True Crime:
BORN IN THE LIFE
JOHN ALITE MAFIA INTERNATIONAL

BEFORE I DROP DEAD: SHORT STORIES

ABOUT THE AUTHORS

LOUIS ROMANO *BIO*

Born in The Bronx in 1950 Romano's writing career began at age 58 with FISH FARM. Then INTERCESSION, a bloody revenge thriller, an Amazon Bestseller, first in a seven-book series which earned him the title of 2014 Foreword Review Top Finalist. BESA, captured six international film awards for its screenplay. BESA has been translated into Albanian... an organized crime novel in the Gino Ranno series. Romano has 21 published books. louisromanoauthor.com

PAUL YOUNGELSON *BIO*

PAUL YOUNGELSON was born at Lenox Hill Hospital Manhattan in 1975. He graduated from St. Thomas Aquinas College with a bachelor's degree in business management. Paul also studied history at Ramapo College. He also having received an associate degree from Rockland Community College in Sociology. He is currently involved in the education field in Nanuet, New York after spending 25 years as a security agent throughout the tri state area. Paul is an avid reader and Philadelphia Eagles fan.

Do you want to help the author get more recognition?
Please review this book!

Review via:
Goodreads.com
Or via your purchase platform!

Preview:

ON THE SIDE OF THE ROAD

John Gojcaj
Louis Romano

"You were born together, and
together you shall be forevermore …
but let there be spaces in your
togetherness. And let the winds of the
heavens dance between you."

- Kahlil Gibran -

CHAPTER ONE

Nearly every day in the Town of Soledad was the same. The sizzling sun beat down mercilessly upon this municipality in the northern Colombian department of Atlántico in the densely populated metropolitan area of Barranquilla. Temperatures rarely snuck under ninety degrees, accompanied by insufferable humidity. Rain was a rarity, if not miraculous.

A young woman stood on the side of a dirt road off the main two-lane Route 25 which ran past the frenetic Aeroporto International Ernesto Cortissoz de Soledad.

Maria Rodriguez-Garcia was carrying two handmade green wicker bassinets each bearing an infant boy.

The handles on the portable cribs had chafed Maria's hands from hauling the babies for miles in the oppressive heat. She wore a worn but clean full-length yellow and green peasant dress. Her straw hat gave Maria some relief from the blazing sun but none from the breathless clamminess of the afternoon atmosphere. Around her thin neck was a small medallion of La Virgin de Chiquinquira, Our Lady of the Rosary, the patron saint of Colombia.

The identical twin boys were soundly sleeping under a straw coverlet that offered shade to their fair skin. Under their cotton baby tee shirts, each child wore a plain miraculous metal to bring special grace from the Virgin Mary.

The thunderous sounds of aircraft soaring and landing at the airport made Maria shutter. She worried that the noises—which came every few minutes—would startle and waken her sleeping babies.

Maria must have said two hundred Hail Marys as she walked from the bus that left her off on Route 25 to the designated meeting place. Now she asked the Blessed Mother for her holy help, her intercession to her son, El Senior, Jesus Christ.

"Holy Mother, please tell me what I am doing is the right thing for my sons. I cannot bear another night, another day of the pain hunger brings to us."

In the sweltering distance, almost like a mirage, Maria squinted at the cloud of rapidly approaching yellowish road dust.

As the vehicle got close enough to fully reveal itself, Maria bit her lower lip so hard she could taste her blood. The twinge of hunger in her stomach turned into a pang of iron butterflies.

A faded two-tone tan 1973 Chevy Suburban truck pulled off the road near where Maria stood, kicking up stones and a plume of compacted hard pan. The dust and the blinding glare from the cracked windshield of the Suburban truck forced Maria to pull her straw hat below her eyes. She clenched the two bassinets together in one hand, turning her slim body away to protect her two sons from the tumult. She felt the acidy bile from her stomach lodge in her throat.

As the dust settled, Maria heard the door of the truck open and slam shut. She turned and tried to focus her eyes through the remaining road dust.

"Hola, mami. Let's get this done as quickly as possible. I have much to do today," came the raspy smoker's voice of Juan-Jose. In his late thirties with a wrinkled and soiled ill-fitting white suit, the unshaven tour guide—as he liked to refer to himself—approached Maria.

"Here, let me take a look," Juan-Jose blurted. His brownish nicotine fingers grabbed hold of the two bassinets as if simply containing some melons.

"Which one to choose? What does it matter anyway? They're paying for a baby boy. I'll pick this one." Juan-Jose lifted the bassinet in his right hand, almost to Maria's eye level.

Through her tears, Maria could hardly see the young American couple who had exited the truck and stood behind their baby broker.

Juan-Jose ignored Maria as he handed the whicker crib to the couple standing behind him.

"Oh, Chad ... he is beautiful. Just what we were told. He doesn't even look Latino!" the twenty-something woman announced.

In high school Spanish, the woman addressed Maria.

"Thank you very much. We will take good care of him and love him forever."

The husband uttered a weak, "Gracias."

Juan-Jose abruptly steered the new foster parents back to the still running Suburban.

Maria clutched the remaining bassinet to her chest. Juan-Carlos took a white envelope from inside his blue striped sear sucker jacket and tossed it toward Maria as if she could catch it with her trembling hand. The payment fell in front of the mother and child. The baby began to wail as if he knew his brother had been taken from him. Or perhaps he felt his mother's anguish. On the other hand, maybe he wet himself.

The Chevy Suburban moved rapidly into a three-point turn, kicking up rocks and pebbles as it retreated into a cloud of dust.

Maria ignored the protesting baby as she fell to her knees, pleading with the Blessed Mother to guard over her lost baby. An Airbus A300 rose low from the airport above the sunbaked mother and child. Maria didn't notice the
sound.

She watched the SUV through her warm, salty tears until it faded away on the dirt road.

CHAPTER TWO

Carlos Torres worked the streets of Soledad and Barranquilla peddling cocaine for the infamous Cali cartel. He had been vying for a bigger job with the cartel for nearly three years. He envisioned himself as more than just a low-level drug dealer selling small bags of the product to friends, college students, and some well-to-do businessmen.

The big money, and the visibility to the Cali leaders, were found in distributing large volumes of kilos out of the port of Barranquilla. Boats and cargo ships to the Caribbean islands, planes flying to and from as far away as Miami and California and New York was where the real drug money was found. Simply put, more risk more reward.

The Cali bosses were testing Carlos in their downstream operations, but Carlos had his own mental timetable. He ran some weight from Cartagena to Barranquilla and Soledad, but it amounted to the proverbial pimple on the ass of the Cali cartel ... and Carlos knew it.

With each trip to Cartagena, Carlos was endearing himself with Cali leadership.

His entire life, Carlos was used to getting his way. At six-feet-three-inches tall, with the build of an American football linebacker and a wicked scar on his usually unshaven face, Carlos was an imposing figure to most, if not all, his clients. If he was owed money, he would get paid on time or he would brutally crack heads and legs with tire irons, baseball bats, or anything within reach. No one, no matter how tough they were, would dare to step in front of Carlos and his career goals. In his early twenties, he'd done his first killing, one of at least a dozen, knifing to death his drug dealer boss in a dark alley of a slum in Soledad.

After the murder of his boss, Carlos became the main drug pusher of the Soledad barrio until he came to the attention of the main players in the Cali cartel. He moved up in the organization, impatiently waiting for the prize he dreamed of. Carlos wanted to be the *el jefe* of the port of Barranquilla for the Cali Cartel. That position would only be a stepping-stone to a seat at the big table in the rugged area, Valle del Cauca in Cali.

"If I want something, it is mine," was Carlos' mantra.

One more thing that Carlos obsessed over—for almost a year—was the affection of Maria Rodriquez-Garcia.

Almost ten years had passed since the painful and horrible event on the dirt road near the airport, and time had not healed Marias's intense heartache. She lived a modest life in a small two-bedroom apartment in Soledad with her pride and joy, her ten-year-old son, Antonio, whom everyone called Tony. Maria kept the apartment spotless, and home cooked every meal for herself and her son, who took his meals on a small, metal table facing their prized portable television.

On a shelf in the tiny kitchen of their apartment, above the stainless-steel sink, Maria had built a system of wooden shelves with votive candles and black and crystal rosaries entwining statues of St. Antonio di Padua and St. Francesco di Assisi. Tony's brother was named and baptized as Francesco.

The shrine was a constant reminder to Maria about what she thought of as her darkest moment, her most sinful act. There were other moments in her life she was not proud of, but selling her baby boy was the worst. Like anyone who's experienced grief of any sort, life was a bit easier now, years later, to forget the desperate, impoverished life she and her twin sons had been living under.

Maria took communion daily, offering her prayers for both her sons, but especially for Francesco, the void in her soul.

Tony was never told by his devoted and often doting mother that he had a brother, never mind an identical twin whom she was forced give up for adoption. Maria had never forgiven herself for what she had done, and she could not live a single day if Tony found out about his twin and, God forbid, refused to forgive her.

As poorly as she was faring emotionally, the years had been kind to Maria physically. With her large, light green, olive-like eyes and her long, silky, pitch-black hair, perfect gleaming white teeth, and a Victoria's Secret's model figure, Maria turned more than a few heads as she moved about her day.

Maria had worked her way up from cashier to the assistant manager of the Olimpica supermarket. Routinely, Marie worked sixty to seventy hours each week to put food on the table for her and her son. In her scant free time, she volunteered at her church where Tony grew up playing with other children in the churchyard and adjoining soccer field.

There seemed to be an underlying sadness in Maria's countenance. She was serious about her job, dedicated as a mother, and fervent to her religion and an ardent supporter of her church. She had never dated or been with a man since she sold her son to scratch her way out of the poverty and starvation.

The frown lines on Maria's pretty, chiseled, high-cheekbone face seemed to relax a bit when Father Jorge Lopez was present. Frankly, Maria's beaming smile would take the place of her normal dour expression when she was near the prelate.

Short, bespeckled, and the almost too thin, Father Lopez was born in Barcelona, Spain. He was educated in his native country and graduated from *Pontifico Seminario Romano Maggiore,* the Pontifical Roman Major Seminary in Rome. The Vatican assigned Father Lopez to Barranquilla for his love of the Holy Family, his caring demeanor, and his ability to teach English to the children in the region.

Tony became the priest's star pupil with the enthusiastic help of Maria, who was also learning to speak and read English. Even more important to the widowed Maria, Father Lopez—who everyone called Padre Jorge—

had become a father figure to Tony, who had been lacking a male figure in his life.

Carlos had admired and stalked Maria for several months after he saw her one day at the supermarket while she was filling in for a cashier who had become ill.

louisromanoauthor.com